Don't Know
What You've Got
Till It's Gone

Gemma Crisp developed her love of books and magazines while growing up on a sheep farm in the middle of Tasmania in the prehistoric days before the internet. It wasn't until she'd hit the bright lights of London some years later that she realised she could get paid to write about mascara, threesomes and celebrities (not necessarily all at once!). After acing her first magazine internship, thanks to being a photocopying and coffee-fetching ninja, Gemma moved to Sydney and has spent more than a decade working for some of Australia's glossiest magazines, including *New Woman*, *Girlfriend*, *OK!*, *Cosmopolitan Bride* and *NW*. She popped her editorship cherry at teen bible DOLLY, then moved to the editor's chair at CLEO, where she spent her days fending off wannabe Eligible Bachelors, wrangling celebrity publicists and attempting to craft the perfect coverline. Gemma is now based in London again, where she's trying not to buy Topshop out of shoes. You can find her on Twitter and Instagram at @theshowpony.

GEMMA CRISP

Don't Know What You've Got Till It's Gone

ALLEN&UNWIN

SYDNEY · MELBOURNE · AUCKLAND · LONDON

First published in 2014

Allen & Unwin
83 Alexander Street
Crows Nest NSW 2065
Australia
Phone: (61 2) 8425 0100
Email: info@allenandunwin.com
Web: www.allenandunwin.com

Cataloguing-in-Publication details are available from the
National Library of Australia
www.trove.nla.gov.au

ISBN 978 1 74331 718 1

Typeset in 12.5/18.5pt Joanna MT Std by Bookhouse, Sydney
Printed in Australia by Griffin Press

10 9 8 7 6 5 4 3

For Dottie and Joan —
wish you were here

one

'I'm sorry, you said *how* much?'

Nina tried not to strangle herself with the phone cord as Sam, a celebrity manager with some of Australia's biggest stars on his books, repeated the eye-wateringly large figure. She knew the fee for the exclusive magazine rights to Lulu Hopkins and Jason Dell's wedding would be sky-high, but even so she was surprised by the amount Sam had just named. There was no denying Lulu was Australia's sweetheart, the girl-next-door best known for her glossy mane and killer body who spruiked everything from lingerie to vitamins, but her long-term boyfriend Jason was pretty much a zero on the celebrity scale, despite his previous attempts to hitch a ride to Showbiz Town on the back of Lulu's popularity train. It wasn't like Sam was brokering the rights for Brangelina's wedding, so why on earth was he racking up the price so much?

'Hmmm, I see,' Nina said coolly, invoking the first rule of negotiating an exclusive celebrity story – never let them get a whiff of how keen you were. 'And would that fee include the exclusive engagement reveal, plus a follow-up honeymoon story?' She crossed her fingers – if she could squeeze three cover stories out of Sam, maybe her finance manager would approve his astronomical asking price.

'Nice try, Nina, but no cigar. We've already negotiated the sale of the engagement story with another magazine which hits the stands next week, but Lulu wants to share the love around – you know she doesn't like to play favourites,' Sam said, somewhat unconvincingly. It was well-known in celebrity magazine circles that the reason Lulu liked to share the love around was because creating a bidding war between *Juice*, the magazine Nina edited, and its rivals meant more money for her already-hefty bank account. And with Sam taking a healthy cut of every deal he brokered on Lulu's behalf, he wasn't going to argue.

Nina decided to play along. 'I'm not going to lie to you, Sam – of course we're absolutely thrilled and flattered that Lulu wants *Juice* to cover her wedding to Jason later this year –' her tone was all sweetness and light '– but if the surprise engagement story has already been sold to one of our rivals and there aren't any added extras like a honeymoon follow-up story, then to be frank, I'm going to struggle to get your asking price signed off by the Big Cheeses. Of course, I'll do everything I can to –'

'Nina, you know full well that Lulu is cover gold,' Sam interrupted her. 'Your readers love her and, let me tell you, this wedding is going to be SPEC. TAC. U. LAR. Plus she'll be inviting all her celeb mates, so it won't just be pictures of random family members looking awkward. It's the celebrity wedding of the year; you'd be crazy to let this go.'

'Oh, Sam, if it was up to me, I would autograph the contract right this minute, but you know what these finance people are like!' Nina squeezed out a fake laugh – blaming the bean counters was one of her many bargaining tools. As the editor of Australia's hottest weekly celebrity magazine, it was essential that she maintained a cosy relationship with the people who repped the variety of media personalities her readers couldn't get enough of. It wouldn't be a particularly good idea to tell Sam the truth: that his asking fee was completely overpriced for a wedding in which only half the couple was famous; better to blame it on the nameless, faceless accounts department and hope he agreed to drop his original asking price to lock in the sale.

'Look, it goes without saying we have interest from the other weekly mags, but Lulu really wants to do this with *Juice*, so have a chat with your finance people and let me know, okay? Call me when you know what's what.'

Nina sighed as Sam hung up – he was obviously pissed that she hadn't fallen all over herself to lock the exclusive in then and there, but the days of magazines blowing that kind of money on one issue were long gone. She'd have to make sure she buttered him up by taking him to Chiswick, his favourite restaurant, the next time they went on one of their power lunches where every course was doused in a heavy layer of schmooze.

Since becoming the boss lady of *Juice*, Nina had worked hard to develop a good rapport with the most important celebrity managers in Australia's entertainment industry. She wasn't stupid – she was fully aware that her first stab as a magazine editor had left her reputation in tatters – so she set about proving to people that she meant business in ways she knew would work: take them out to the best restaurants in town, lay her cards on the table, lock in an exclusive with their client, get her staff to treat the celebrity like the Second Coming during the interview and photo shoot, make sure she put in a personal appearance at the shoot to make the talent and manager feel special, then follow it up with some impressive sales figures.

Staring out her office window at the afternoon storm clouds gathering over Sydney Harbour, Nina rewound the events of the past eighteen months in her crazy life and pressed play. After humiliating herself via a very public meltdown on live TV that had been helped along by the nasty drinking problem she'd developed to cope with the stress of working under her heinous crime of a boss, she'd quit her job as editor of the monthly women's magazine *Candy*. She had assumed her days of editing a magazine were over, with a capital obvious. At that stage, she was past caring – she'd been so miserable at *Candy* she'd decided that being top dog at a magazine wasn't necessarily the prescription for happiness she'd thought it would be. After all, not everyone was cut out to be an editor — surely it was better to acknowledge and accept it rather than trying to hop back on a glossy show pony that didn't want you in the saddle.

But after six months of drying out, clearing all the debris from her head and getting her life back under control, she was surprised to get an email from Kat, a former boss with whom she'd always got on well, asking if she was interested in a short-term stint as deputy editor while Kat's second-in-command was on maternity leave. Although Nina was worried about stepping back into MagLand after it had all gone so horribly wrong, she knew this could be the first and last opportunity she'd ever have to give it another crack. She'd figured as deputy editor, the stress levels wouldn't be as stratospheric, and she knew Kat wasn't a bitch of a boss. Plus the role was on a celebrity weekly title, which would be something completely different. If Nina was honest with herself, she had to admit she missed the buzz, missed being part of a team, missed the satisfaction of seeing people on the train reading a copy of the latest issue of a magazine she had helped to create. What had she got to lose? She was fully aware that all the staff would have heard about the messy end of her time at *Candy*, but she'd just have to deal with the raised eyebrows and surreptitious stares when she got there. So she bit the bullet and said yes — and had been surprised at just how much she loved it and how easily she had slotted into the world of gratuitous gossip, red-carpet rundowns and juicy scandals. So much so that when the editorship of *Juice* came up just as she was about to finish her six-month contract with Kat, she'd decided what the hell, had stuck her hand up and waved it in the air until the HR department couldn't ignore her any longer, then proceeded to own the interview process like a boss. With the help of a glowing reference from Kat, an impressive presentation detailing all the changes she would make to *Juice* to boost its circulation, some searingly honest answers about her demise at *Candy* and an understanding publisher who just happened to have a substance-abuse problem buried in his own past and who knew the importance of not judging people on past mistakes, she'd killed it.

But it hadn't been all rainbows and lollipops – returning to the magazine industry meant she'd also signed the death notice on her relationship with her long-term boyfriend Jeremy, who had been by her side through all the struggles at *Candy*. He couldn't understand why she would want to return to the world that had almost destroyed her and she couldn't really blame him – it had been tough for him to watch her spiral out of control and then have to pick up the pieces afterwards. But he didn't get how much she missed working in that world, the only world where she'd felt like she belonged, before things had taken a wrong turn. The end of their relationship was devastating for both of them, but deep down Nina had known it was the right thing to do. She needed to channel all her energy into *Juice* so she could prove the doubters wrong, and the less distractions the better. If she stuffed this up, she knew there wouldn't be another chance.

A brief knock on the open door of her office interrupted Nina's trawl through her memory bank. Layla, *Juice*'s photo editor, hovered in the doorway looking like she'd just swallowed a twenty-four-karat canary.

'Hey, what's up?' Nina asked. 'Did we score that set of Beyoncé and Blue Ivy that you showed me this morning? I'm thinking it could make a good cover splash seeing nothing else seems to be happening in celeb world this week.' It was one of the many challenges of putting out fifty-two magazines a year based entirely around celebrity gossip – when a scandal broke or it was awards season, deciding on the main item for the cover was dead easy. But when there were tumbleweeds rolling through the celebrity gossip universe, every weekly editor prayed for a big story to break just before their print deadline. Or failing that, the release of an exclusive set of paparazzi photos featuring a brand-spanking-new A-list couple or a brand-spanking-new A-list baby or, better still, a brand-spanking-new A-list couple with a brand-spanking-new baby they'd just adopted on a whim, despite only having dated for a week. The more ridiculous the story, the better – that way, punters who thought it was crazy would buy the magazine so they could hate on the celebrities involved, while those who loved the celebs would buy it so they could soak up all the juicy details. Nina knew it was an absurd, sensationalist world, but if that's what it took to sell truckloads of magazines, who was she to argue?

'Yep, we got that set with no dramas; the high-res images are saved in this week's folder on the server. But something else has just come through from one of the picture agencies that I think you should see.'

'What? What is it? Is it good or bad?' Nina shot past the editorial assistant's desk outside her office, down the path in the middle of the open-plan space, then through the art department to Layla's desk and waited impatiently for her to catch up.

'I don't know – have a look and tell me what you think.' Layla clicked onto their file transfer site, entered her log-in details then scrolled through the endless folders from the paparazzi agencies until she found what she was looking for. Nina held her breath as several images opened up on the computer screen.

'Oh, it's our good friend Lulu Hopkins – funny, I was on the phone to her manager just before. So a pap has caught her having lunch with someone in . . . where does the caption say they are? It doesn't look like one of her usual sceney, look-at-me haunts.'

'It's a random cafe in Cronulla,' Layla confirmed. 'The caption says the other woman is her grandmother, but that's not the interesting bit – check out her hand.'

As Layla zoomed in on the image, Nina felt like giving her the high five to end all high fives. Although the shots were grainy, probably taken with a long lens at least five hundred metres away and through a cafe window to boot, there was no mistaking the whopping great big boulder of a diamond ring weighing down the third finger of Lulu's left hand.

'Layla, this is amazing! What would I do without your eagle eyes? Has bidding started on this set yet?'

'Nope. And the starting price isn't that high either, which makes me wonder if anyone else has noticed the ring – if Lulu and Jason are engaged, surely this is major news?'

'Oh, it's major news alright – and just between you and me, they've sold the exclusive engagement story to one of the other weeklies. It won't be on sale till next week . . . which means we can snap up this set and do a huge spoiler when we go on sale this Friday!' Nina was tempted to punch the air in celebration. 'Quick, get on the phone and get that set off the market before anyone else notices the rock. What an idiot, I can't believe she's wearing it! Surely whoever got the exclusive put a clause in the contract saying she's not allowed to be seen with it in public until the issue is on sale!'

'I guess if the old duck is her grandma, she wanted to show it off to her. But yeah, it's a pretty stupid move on her part.' Layla called out to her assistant, 'Annie, can you call Spook Photos and get the new Lulu set off the market ASAP?' She began saving the watermarked images into the art department's folder so they could start mocking up the page design. 'But don't appear too desperate,' she added, 'otherwise they'll wonder what all the fuss is about. We don't want them to realise they're sitting on a potential goldmine until it's too late.'

Nina hovered behind Annie's desk as she placed the call. She would have given good money to be a fly on the wall when the staff of the other weekly – probably *Bizarre*, she guessed – feasted their eyes on her spoiler cover and realised the sound they could hear was the gurgle of the money they'd spent on the engagement exclusive going down the drain. Nina almost purred with satisfaction at the mental image.

But then . . . there was no denying this was a risk – a BIG risk. Sam would have a coronary when he saw the cover on Friday morning. He'd be screaming down the phone before she'd even peeled open an eyelid. And if she went ahead with it, she could kiss goodbye the offer of the wedding deal, not to mention any other exclusive stories with Lulu for at least the next decade.

'But it's the silly bint's fault for being stupid enough to wear the goddamn ring in public before the news is official,' she rationalised to herself. Then again, was she cutting off her nose to spite her face? This would ruin her relationship with Sam; he wouldn't let her near any of his other celebs, let alone Lulu. Surely there was a way she could use these photos as leverage . . .

As Annie confirmed the sale and hung up, a devious idea popped into Nina's head. She sprinted back to her office as fast as her rose-gold leather pencil skirt would let her, slammed the door closed and dialled Sam's mobile.

'Sam? Hi, it's Nina from *Juice*. No, I haven't made a decision about the wedding exclusive yet, but I thought you might want to know about a set of pictures we just bought. Yes, of

Lulu. In Cronulla. WEARING . . . HER . . . ENGAGEMENT . . . RING. No, I'm not bullshitting you. I can email you one of the photos as proof.' Nina smiled when she heard his sharp intake of breath on the other end of the phone. 'Now, I know that you know she shouldn't be wearing the ring in public before *Bizarre* or whoever goes on sale next week, so it's lucky for you that my picture editor spotted it and took the set off the market before another magazine could get their grubby paws on it.' Nina paused, enjoying herself immensely. 'I have to say, these photos would make a *great* cover for my issue that's out on Friday. But you know what, Sam? I wouldn't want to do that to you. So let's talk turkey – in return for me killing this picture set of Lulu waving her rock around for everyone and their blind granny to see, you drop the price of Lulu and Jason's wedding exclusive by at least twenty per cent. Oh, one more thing – because I'm being so nice to you by sacrificing a cover we both know would go bananas at the newsstand, I think you should throw in a follow-up honeymoon story, too. What do you say?'

Ten minutes later, after much spluttering on Sam's end, the deal was done. Looking out at the rapidly darkening Sydney skyline, Nina smiled. 'Good job, Morey,' she thought, giving herself a figurative pat on the back.

two

Rushing into the restaurant, Nina scanned the room for Heidi's gleaming red hair. Spotting her friend at the bar, she charged over and slid onto the adjacent free stool, just as the barman pushed a lethal-looking pineapple and mint margarita towards Heidi, accompanied by a not-so-subtle wink that was heavy on the innuendo. Nina furtively scrutinised him: on the short side, with slicked-back blond hair pulled into a stubby ponytail and eyes the colour of the infinity pool at the resort where Nina had stayed during a press trip to Fiji the year before. 'Definitely her type,' she thought, ordering a large bottle of sparkling water and ignoring Heidi's disappointed gaze.

'Sorry I'm late. Whaaat? Quit giving me that look of yours, missy – you know I don't drink during the week,' Nina said firmly.

Having finally admitted she had a drinking problem when she'd quit *Candy*, Nina had attended a few Alcoholics Anonymous meetings, but found them to be more irritating than helpful. She'd replaced them with a weekly appointment with a substance-abuse counsellor who had helped her to understand that she'd been using alcohol as a crutch to handle the ridiculous amount of stress she'd been under. To prove to herself that she didn't need alcohol, Nina had decided to stop drinking for a year. Eighteen months later, she now drank only in moderation and only on weekends. She didn't ever want to go back to the days when she used to polish off a bottle of vodka in the office on a Monday afternoon and not think anything of it.

'Sorry, babe, I forgot it's only Tuesday. Plus the margaritas here are so delicious.' Heidi delicately licked the sprinkle of salt from the rim of her glass while the blue-eyed barman watched, hypnotised. 'It just gives us an excuse to come back here on a weekend, right?'

'Right,' Nina snorted, watching Heidi arch one immaculate eyebrow at the barman when she busted him staring. 'Gee, I wonder why else you'd want to come back – surely the margaritas aren't that amazing?' she said, kicking Heidi with the toe of her Zara leopard-print pony-hair ankle boot. The two girls looked at each other and grinned.

Nina had met Heidi through her book club – in the six months she'd been unemployed, trying to make sense of the mess she'd made of her life, she'd realised that she was seriously lacking in the hobbies department. Especially after her cousin Tess, who was also her best friend, had decided Sydney wasn't the place for her and moved back to London, following in the footsteps of Johan, Nina's other closest friend, who had hightailed it home to the UK after finding out he'd contracted HIV from his Australian scene-queen boyfriend. As devastated as Nina had been about being left behind in Sydney, she couldn't hold it against either of them – Tess had had her fair share of problems too, secretly suffering from anxiety and depression while Nina battled her own demons. The good news was that Tess was so much happier now that she was back in London, she'd even come off her medication and had starting dating again, while Johan, inspired by some of the people who had helped him come to terms with his illness, was retraining to become a social worker specialising in HIV sufferers.

Tess's absence in particular had made Nina even more aware of the empty holes in her life, so she'd made like a bulldozer and set about filling them with pastimes that weren't work- or alcohol-related. The tennis lessons hadn't lasted long and neither had the meditation course – she was never going to be Maria Sharapova or Miranda Kerr. But a stint of volunteering at an abandoned dogs' home had made the cut and so had the book club she'd found via her fashion editor friend, Steph. There were around eight girls in the group who met for brunch once a month at The Grounds, a cafe in up-and-coming Alexandria, supposedly to discuss the latest novel they'd all agreed to read, but more often than not they ended up bitching and moaning about their boyfriends, their bosses, their parents and whatever else was doing their heads in, while tucking into Turkish baked eggs and multiple skim flat whites. At first, Nina was worried about slotting in as the new girl, stressing that she wouldn't have anything in common with the others, but after hopping on the merry-go-round of monthly book club catch-ups, endless group emails, raucous girls-only nights out and the avalanche of invites to their birthday celebrations, house-warmings and engagement parties, Nina realised it was much more than just a book club. She was surprised at how close she'd become to the group, especially Heidi, and how much she had come to rely on them. They debated everything from which salon did the best eyelash extensions to the legitimacy of Israel; they borrowed from each other's wardrobes on a regular basis; they tagged each other in inspirational quotes on Instagram whenever one of them was going through a tough time at work or home. Nina really didn't know what she'd do without them now. With the benefit of hindsight, she could see that a group of girlfriends had been one of the things missing from her life since she'd moved to Sydney – maybe if she'd had more friends she wouldn't have become so obsessed with her job at *Candy*. At least she now had the girls to give her a reality check if things at the office went pear-shaped. They were never afraid to remind her that no matter what happened in the crazy world of celebrity gossip, it wasn't as if anyone had died – although they'd backed off on that expression ever since Whitney Houston's sudden tragic death had resulted in the *Juice* team pulling an all-nighter to ensure a special tribute issue hit the stands before any of their competitors could beat them to it.

Nina pulled herself back to the present to find Heidi busily getting her flirt on with the barman, which reminded her of another reason why they'd become so tight – out of all the girls in the group, they were the only two who were single. Evie and Steph were engaged, Lily had just got married in a cloud of confetti, Natalie had made her mother cry by getting hitched on a whim in Las Vegas a year ago then made her father cry by announcing it was a shotgun wedding, while Bec and Daniela were loved-up in long-term relationships. That left Nina and Heidi to wear the single badge, which they happily did along with a liberal application of MAC LadyDanger red lipstick and the obligatory stash of condoms in the inside pocket of their Mimco clutch bags. Luckily, Heidi's taste in men was completely different to Nina's – her friend liked them average height, light hair, major muscles and preferably younger, whereas Nina's ex, Jeremy, was her type down to a T – six-feet-plus, dark hair, broad shoulders tapering down to a fit, streamlined body. Not too big, not too small – as far as Nina was concerned, that Goldilocks was on to something.

With Heidi in full flirting flight, Nina pulled out her iPhone to check her messages, allowing herself a victorious smile as she saw the email from Sam confirming the details of the deal they'd hammered out earlier. She knew she should keep it on the downlow but it wouldn't hurt to tell Heidi if she swore her to secrecy. It wasn't as if her friend worked in the same industry like Steph did – as a primary school teacher, the worst Heidi could do was share it with the staffroom, most of whom probably thought Lulu Hopkins was a character from *Downton Abbey*. Plus, a girl had to celebrate her wins, right?

'Hey, guess what happened today?' Nina began, seizing the moment as the hectic crowd baying for drinks forced the barman to leave the spot he'd been glued to since she'd arrived.

'Oh my God, I know! I can't believe she announced it on Facebook! Can you believe it?' Heidi screeched, taking a huge swig of her margarita. 'You'd think she could have waited and told us in person!'

'Honey, I have no idea what you're referring to, but we are definitely not talking about the same thing,' Nina said. 'I didn't get time to check StalkBook today; what the hell happened?'

'Oh, nothing really – Lily announced she's pregnant. To be expected, I guess, seeing she and Jake got married three months ago. Honeymoon baby, I guess.'

Nina shrugged indifferently. She wasn't the type to gush over anything baby-related, unlike some of the girls. Out of the book club group, Lily was probably the one she was the least close to; although Lily was a perfectly nice girl, she'd been obsessed with her wedding ever since Nina had known her. She had a fascinating job as a forensic psychologist working alongside the police, but all she'd wanted to talk about was bomboniere and seating plans, which Nina had found hard to relate to. Now that the wedding was done and dusted, she wasn't surprised Lily had moved on to a new project. 'Maybe her job is so hardcore, she needs fluffy things to obsess over, like weddings and babies, to even things up,' Nina thought, pouring herself some more sparkling water. 'I mean, there's a reason why most of the best-selling issues of weekly mags either have a wedding or a baby on the cover. People love that stuff.'

'I guess I better comment on the big announcement if she's gone public,' Nina said out loud, tapping the Facebook app on her phone and scrolling through her feed. 'Hang on, I can't see it.'

Heidi grimaced. 'It's a photo, not a status update. Actually, it's three photos in the one frame – a photo of Lily as a baby, a photo of Jake as a baby and then she's kind of morphed both their baby faces together to make a new photo, to represent what their baby might look like. The actual announcement is underneath the pretend image of Lake – seriously, that's what she's calling the foetus until they know what sex it is. Geddit? Lily plus Jake equals Lake.'

Nina stared at her, horrified. 'Please tell me you're joking. I mean, uploading a photo of your sonogram which looks just like every other freaking sonogram is bad enough, but this is beyond. What's wrong with a status update along the lines of "Hey, guys, we're having a baby. Yay!"?'

Heidi rolled her eyes. 'I know, right? Someone should tell her that all babies look the same – she could have morphed one of my baby pictures with one of your baby pictures and I bet you any money you wouldn't be able to tell the difference between that and the "photo" of Lake.'

As they gazed at the mocked-up image of Lily and Jake's baby, Nina thanked her lucky stars that Heidi was on the same parenting page – while some women had known all their lives that they wanted to be mothers and couldn't wait to start a family, neither Nina nor Heidi were particularly interested right now. It wasn't that they hated kids; both of them thought Natalie's little girl Sasha was quite cute, albeit a little boring (though what else could you expect from a six-month-old?). Besides, Nina's career was her baby. She'd only just shimmied her way back up the slippery magazine pole, so she'd be damned if she was going to let a screaming blob pull her back down. At this stage of her life, she wasn't yet ready to swap dancing on tables at The Ivy for dancing around her living room to The Wiggles with a baby on her hip. And if she had to choose between managing a miniscule maternity-leave allowance while stalking her local day-care waiting list or overseeing her magazine's multi-million-dollar budget while stalking the Kardashians' every move, she'd stick her hand up for the latter every single time.

'Oh God, I haven't even processed the combined name thing yet,' Nina whimpered. 'I get why couples nickname their babies while they're still in utero; it must get really boring calling it "It" all the time, but at least choose something funny, like Natalie did! Call it Giblet . . . or Alien . . . or Thing! Even Thing is better than combining your names. I know that's ironic given I work in a world where as soon as celebrities hook up, magazine journalists spend hours brainstorming their couple nickname, but if you ask me, Bennifer has a lot to answer for.'

'Oh Bennifer . . . those were the days,' Heidi reminisced, giving the hovering barman the eye.

'Stop it, Heids, I need to comment on Lily's announcement. Help me! I know what I want to say – "Have you lost your marbles along with your ability to eat soft cheese and sashimi?" – but somehow I don't think that will go down so well. Ummmm . . . what did you write?'

'Oh, something generic like, "Congratulations, can't wait to hear all about it!" Because you know we won't have a choice – Friday night's conversation is going to revolve around the miracle of Lake, I can tell you now.'

'Hang on, let me finish typing,' Nina muttered. 'Okay, generic congratulations message complete. Remind me again, what's happening on Friday night?'

three

'Can we get two bottles of Veuve, please?' Nina asked the waitress who'd materialised at their table overlooking the water at Sailors Club. 'Oh, come on, it's a celebration!' she exclaimed, seeing Daniela and Evie glance at each other with concern. 'I know Lily probably won't have a whole glass, but surely she can have a little bit?'

'Don't worry, Nina, I'll drink Lily's share,' Natalie butted in. 'I've been looking forward to this dinner for weeks! And now that Sasha isn't on the boob anymore, I'm ready to rock and roll. Just plonk one of those bottles down in front of me and I'll take care of it!'

It was early Friday night and the vibe was boisterous. With the air still balmy outside and the last of the sun's rays lighting up the boats in the Rose Bay marina, they couldn't have picked a nicer night to be dining on the harbour.

'Where is Lily, anyway?' Heidi asked. 'She's the unofficial guest of honour!'

'She texted me five minutes ago saying she'd be here soon,' replied Bec. 'Poor thing, I think she's discovering that morning sickness isn't picky about when it strikes.'

Across the table, Natalie snorted. 'Whoever coined the term morning sickness should be shot,' she said. 'Now, Nina, what's happening in that juicy magazine world of yours? Got any scandalous stories to tell me?'

'Given your addiction to celebrity gossip, you probably know more than I do,' Nina retorted, knowing full well that while on maternity leave, Natalie had developed a raging celebrity gossip habit. She'd gone from thinking Channing Tatum was a new breed of potato to being able to pontificate for hours about Lindsay Lohan's numerous rehab stints, not to mention being able to tell which Olsen twin was which in less than half a second.

'You know, given I watched an *Entertainment Tonight* marathon today, that's probably true,' Natalie admitted without a skerrick of shame, making a grab for the glass of French champagne that the waitress had just poured. 'What about the mag hags? Has anyone tried to claim a Hermès diary on their work expenses again?' As well as copious amounts of celebrity gossip, she also loved it when Nina threw her a tasty morsel about the inner workings of the magazine world.

'Not that I'm aware of, but you never know with the girls who work on the high fashion titles.' Nina smiled grimly. 'I still can't believe that her editor thought it was okay to sign off on a six-hundred-dollar diary for one of her staff members! It wasn't until the expense claim landed on the finance analyst's desk that they both got told off about it. I think that's still the craziest expense claim I've heard about. Although there was that time a freelancer tried to claim the cost of a gram of coke on his expenses after interviewing the lead singer of a supposedly devout Christian boy band for us, but I just had to put my foot down. That was an interesting conversation.'

'Stop it . . .' breathed a wide-eyed Natalie, who obviously didn't want her to stop at all.

'Oh, wait – you'll love this one,' Nina began, remembering the newest story on the magazine block. 'We had an editors' meeting the other day; there's this newbie who only started a month or so ago and she inherited her team from the previous editor. She's been having problems with one of her graphic designers – her layouts are all over the place, she takes ages to design even the simplest page, she's more interested in hanging out in the beauty department, things like that. So she eventually pulled this girl in to have a chat with her about her performance and guess what?'

Natalie slugged back some bubbles while gesticulating enthusiastically for Nina to continue.

'Even though she's supposed to be the deputy art director, it turns out this girl has no graphic design experience whatsoever.

None. Nada. Zip. Apparently the previous editor had hired her because . . . wait for it . . . *she had good hair.*'

Natalie's eyes bulged as she tried not to spit the Veuve all over the table. Managing to swallow it just in time, she started laughing hysterically. 'Oh my God, are you serious? No wonder everyone thinks the women who work for magazines are fluffy bunnies who only care about the latest nail polish colour and whether the Beckhams will have another baby. What a classic! I can't wait to tell my mothers' group about that one.'

As Natalie started to hiccup, Heidi elbowed Nina. Turning towards the entrance, she saw Lily making her way to the table with both arms folded protectively over her perfectly flat stomach. 'Let's see how long it takes for the clucking to subside,' Heidi muttered.

They watched as the other girls made a big fuss over Lily, making sure her seat wasn't in a draught, getting a cushion for her back, asking the waitress to tell the chef that there was a pregnant woman on their table who couldn't have any rare meat, raw eggs, shellfish, soft cheese or one of the zillion other things that were on the forbidden foods list. After fifteen minutes of the incessant squawking, Nina poured a miniscule glass of Veuve and carried it over to where Lily was ensconced at the other end of the table.

'Congratulations, Lily! I thought the occasion called for bubbles so we could have a toast.' Nina offered her the glass that was less than an eighth full, then faced the rest of the table and raised her own glass. 'Ladies! Here's to Lily and, um, Lake! Cheers!'

When Nina turned back to give her friend a kiss on the cheek, she caught the horrified look on Lily's face.

'Nina, I couldn't possibly drink this – it's alcohol! I don't want to poison my baby!' Lily pushed the glass as far away from her as possible.

'Oh . . . ummm . . . sorry,' Nina said helplessly. 'I know pregnant women aren't supposed to drink at all in the first three months, but seeing you announced the big news on Facebook, I thought you'd be past the twelve-week mark by now.'

'I am!' Lily responded. 'I'm twelve weeks, three days, five hours and seven minutes, according to all my pregnancy apps. But even if the doctors say pregnant women can have one or two drinks a week after the first three months, that doesn't mean I want to drink poison,' she said accusingly. 'Lake needs the best nourishment I can give him or her, not alcoholic fizzy sugar! Could you ask if they have coconut water? It's full of minerals and electrolytes which are just what Little Lake feels like, don't you, Little Lake?' Nina tried not to roll her eyes as Lily directed the question at her stomach.

'Sure. If that's what you want,' she replied, slinking back to her seat.

'Tell me if I'm wrong, but did you just get shot down in champagne flames?' Heidi whispered.

Nina nodded, feeling humiliated. 'Christ, how was I supposed to know that Lily had sworn off booze during her entire pregnancy? Natalie still had a glass of wine here and there when she was pregnant with Sasha, so I assumed Lily would be the same. So sue me. I was just trying to make an effort.'

'I know, honey. Don't worry about it — you know Lily can be a bit precious. She's probably feeling rat shit from the morning sickness and took it out on you. Here, let me pour you another glass.'

Nina took a sip, trying to enjoy the bubbles as they slid down her throat. She didn't want to admit how much Lily's outburst had annoyed her, but she felt pretty put out. As the rest of the girls asked Lily endless questions about her pregnancy, Nina listened half-heartedly.

'Of course, Jake and I knew straight away,' Lily was saying smugly. 'I can't explain it, but we just knew. It was like an angel had touched us during our lovemaking; it was magical. And for it to happen on our honeymoon makes it so much more special. I can't wait to tell Lake how Mummy and Daddy created him or her during one of the happiest times of our lives,' she sighed.

'How are your boobs?' Natalie asked with a knowing look.

'Oh gosh, they're *so* sore! Jake's not allowed within two metres of them.' Lily giggled coyly. 'I think I've gone up a cup size already, so he's not happy about being banned. But he needs to understand that they're not his anymore — they're for Lake,' she said firmly.

'Wow, that's romantic,' Nina couldn't help muttering in Heidi's direction. Clearing her throat, she grabbed her menu and called down the table. 'So, does everyone know what they're having?'

No one answered her – they were all too preoccupied with Lily.

Nina pushed her chair back and headed to the bathroom. Locking herself in a stall, she closed her eyes and took a deep breath. 'Get over it, Nina. Someone else is getting all the attention, so what?' she told herself off. 'It happens all the time, that's what being in a friendship group is all about. Of course the girls are excited; it's not every day that one of your friends has a baby. Okay, so things are going to change a bit when it comes to the group dynamics, but look at Natalie – she didn't let pregnancy or motherhood cramp her style. She still made an effort to come out for brunch and dinner and drinks, even if she stuck to one or two glasses of wine. Once the novelty of Lily's pregnancy wears off, things will get back to normal. And remember, there are six other girls in the group; it's not like they're all up the duff, so pull your head in, get back out there and play nice.'

Washing her hands, Nina looked at herself critically as she applied some Blistex. 'You're way overdue for a peroxide appointment, young lady,' she thought as the light bounced off the regrowth that Heidi referred to as her 'Vegemite stripe'. Sauntering back to the table, she pasted a smile on her face as she sat back down next to Heidi.

'Oh, there you are, Nina!' Evie looked over at Daniela and nodded. 'Now that everyone's here, I've got an announcement to make. And by happy coincidence, so does Daniela. We didn't want to rain on Lily's parade so we thought we'd let her share her news first, but . . .'

The back of Nina's neck prickled. Her eyes landed on Evie's champagne glass. It was still full. She checked Daniela's. Practically overflowing. In an instant, she knew what was coming.

'. . . it's not only Lily who's having a baby – I am too!' Evie announced.

'Me three!' Daniela added, her face lighting up like a fireworks display.

While the rest of the group gasped and the cacophony of congratulations started all over again, Nina and Heidi exchanged a look. Without a word, they both picked up their champagne glasses and downed the contents in one go.

four

Faced with multiple piles of work that needed her urgent attention, Nina made an executive decision to ignore the lot and instead logged on to Facebook. After being in back-to-back meetings for most of the morning, she figured her to-do list could wait a bit longer. Her brain needed a break before she made a start on looking at the amended contract for Lulu and Jason's wedding which had finally been approved by her legal department. She also had to check all the details for the following week's cover shoot with Tully Black, the hot new singer on the TV talent show block, plus look at the notes from the daily news conference for that afternoon's briefing with the news writers, brainstorm some editorial specials for upcoming issues so the advertising team could present them to clients for potential sponsorship opportunities, approve the fifteen layouts in her tray so the picture department could order the high-res photos, and start work on a PowerPoint presentation for *Juice's* marketing team.

'God, I hate PowerPoint,' she sighed, scrolling through her Facebook feed. 'God, I hate Facebook,' she added, sighing again. She quickly checked the time, picked up her office phone and punched in Heidi's number, hoping she wasn't on playground duty this particular lunchtime. As a teacher, Heidi didn't have the luxury of spending her lunch hours surfing the Daily Mail website like Nina often did – all in the name of celebrity research, obviously.

'What the hell has happened to our friends?' she demanded as soon as Heidi picked up. 'It's like when they went in for their twelve-week scans, the hospitals also performed partial lobotomies while they were there. If I have to see one more Facebook post where Lily laments how she just couldn't choose between a Bugaboo and a McLaren so decided to get both, or gawp at another artistic black and white photo of Evie's bump, I may run off to India and spend the rest of my days at a Facebook-free ashram. And don't get me started on that app that Daniela signed up to that tells all her friends what stage of development her baby is at in utero every single week. To be honest, I don't care that her baby is now the size of a capsicum and has toenails! And have you noticed how Natalie has suddenly become the mothering guru of the year? She's always been so normal about being a mum but now she comments on their posts all the time, giving them advice about what they can and can't eat and the best place to get environmentally-friendly nappies. I would have thought she'd steer well clear seeing she gets baby talk all the time at her mothers' group, but she's obviously been sucked back into the mummy vortex.'

'I know, it's boring and, frankly, it sucks,' Heidi said soothingly when Nina finally ran out of puff. 'But I guess it was always going to happen. Things are going to change whether we like it or not. The girls are either married, engaged or in de facto relationships, so I guess this is the next logical step. Doesn't mean we have to like it, obviously, but there's not much we can do about it. As for Nat, perhaps she felt like the odd one out being the only mother and now she's enjoying bonding with Lily, Daniela and Evie about it. They're allowed to be excited about becoming a parent for the first time, you know.'

'I know, I know,' Nina said reluctantly, hating Heidi for being the voice of reason but knowing she was right, as usual. 'But why do they have to ram it down our throats all the time? Every time we've got together since that dinner at Sailors Club, all we talk about is pregnancy or baby-related stuff – at MoVida, it was whether they're going to find out what the sex is or not; at China Doll, it was what cravings they've been having and what their obstetrician said about how much weight they've put on; at the Carrington, it was when they're starting antenatal classes and whether they're going to cough up for a pain-management course . . . It's like the outside world has ceased to exist. Even when I try to talk about something different, they're not interested. Did I tell you what happened when I was at Nat's house the other day with Evie and Bec before we met the rest of you for lunch? I was in the middle of telling them how Jeremy had called to tell me he's in a new relationship when Nat brought Sasha downstairs after changing her nappy and Evie literally interrupted me mid-sentence to ask whether Sasha's nappy had been wet or dirty, like it was a vital piece of information. I mean, it's not like I was filling them in on celebrity gossip; it was something that was important to me,' Nina said, trying to keep the hurt out of her voice. 'It wasn't like this when Nat was pregnant. Why did they all have to get up the duff together? Couldn't they have spaced it out a bit so it's not so overwhelming? Evie only just got engaged – surely she could have waited till she got married?!'

'Nina, plenty of people get pregnant when they're not married – this is the twenty-first century, not the Dark Ages. Plus, if you ask me, Evie and Matt were never going to get around to walking down the aisle. I think the only reason he proposed was because she was obsessed with Beyoncé's "Single Ladies" and used to play it non-stop – he thought she was sending him a not-so-subtle message that he'd better put a ring on it, otherwise she'd walk.'

'Well, there's a nice story for their grandkids,' Nina said, feeling her bad mood lift slightly. 'Anyway, sorry to interrupt your lunch hour, I just needed to vent to someone who would understand.'

'Believe me, I understand. It's painful, but I guess they just have tunnel vision at the moment. I'm sure Evie didn't mean to upset you at Nat's house, even though her timing was completely off. We just have to grin and bear it. And it could be worse – at least we're not Steph.'

'Huh? What do you mean? What's Steph got to do with it?'

'Between you and me, Steph's desperate to have kids. If it was up to her, she'd have four already. But she has polycystic ovaries and after some tests, they recently found out Chris has a really low sperm count so the chances of them conceiving naturally are pretty much zilch. They're saving up for IVF but there are no guarantees. To be honest, I don't think she's coping with their infertility very well, but every time I try to talk to her about it she brushes me off. So imagine what it's like for her to sit there, listening to the girls go on and on about pregnancy and babies when it's the one thing she desperately wants for herself. It would be horrific,' Heidi pointed out frankly. 'At least our only problem is that we're just two selfish bitches who are more interested in hitting up Marquee rather than hitting up Baby Kingdom. Anyway, I've gotta go prepare for my next lesson; the year fives are giving me hell today. Talk later, okay?'

Nina felt slightly ashamed of herself after hanging up. Here she was moaning about her Facebook feed being hijacked by pregnancy princesses while Steph was struggling to come to terms with the likelihood that she may never have a family. Heidi always had a knack of putting her in her place, probably from years of dealing with bratty children in her classroom. 'That's what I'm acting like, a bratty child,' she thought, as she hit print on the news conference notes, grabbed her water bottle, notebook and pen, then headed for the meeting table in the middle of the office. 'News briefing o'clock, people!' she called out, picking up the notes from the printer on her way.

Five minutes later, everyone was assembled around the table. Layla began passing around the celebrity photo sets that the picture department had bought that morning, while Meg, the news editor, read through the celebrity news and gossip items that the team of writers had found during their trawl of the internet and international gossip magazines, plus tips from any sources they had in New York, Los Angeles and London.

'Not more "happy families" staged shots of Minnie Pearson at LAX looking ridiculously glamorous with her adorable daughter and amazingly handsome Hollywood husband,' sighed Simone, Nina's deputy editor, looking at the photos Layla had just passed to her. 'I can't bear it; it should be illegal for a family to be so good-looking. And who looks that fresh when they've just spent fourteen hours on a flight from Sydney, with a toddler to boot?'

'Maybe she looks so good because the nanny looked after her kid back in economy while Minnie spent the whole fourteen hours in first class reminiscing about her recent hook-ups with Justin Bieber and Leonardo DiCaprio,' Layla said slyly, pulling the pin out of a celebrity gossip grenade and throwing it into the middle of the table. The *Juice* team erupted.

'No way!'

'Are you serious?'

'I don't believe it, they're the perfect family!'

'She would never cheat on Jackson — he's divine!'

'Where did you hear that from, Layla? One of the paps?' Nina raised her voice to be heard above the babble of writers feasting on this scandalous morsel.

'Yep, it came from Bob in LA. He said it's common knowledge in showbiz circles over there that Minnie cheats on Jackson all the time, just for shits and giggles. But only with guys who are A-listers, like Leo and the Biebs — it's like her way of rubbing Jackson's nose in the fact that his career has gone nowhere since marrying her, while hers has gone platinum.'

'Does Bob have anyone who would go on record about this?' Nina could feel a red-hot cover story in the works, but only if *Juice* could get someone who was happy to confirm Bob's version of events. While Minnie liked to take advantage of her 'homegrown Aussie girl' roots when it suited her, she wasn't afraid to bring in the legal big guns if anyone threatened her wholesome image of loving wife and caring mother.

'That's the first thing I asked — he's going to check for us but said it was unlikely. Not because it didn't happen, but because she's so careful about not getting busted. She knows it would destroy her reputation if she was ever found out. And by reputation, I mean all her multi-million-dollar contracts.'

'Dammit,' seethed Nina, although she wasn't really surprised. If the general public had any idea what their favourite celebrities really got up to, they'd be gobsmacked. It wasn't just the sham marriages, rampant cheating, severe drug addictions and crazy eating disorders, but the all-too-common paparazzi deals where the celebrities received a healthy cut of the sales after informing the photographers where they'd be and when; the children who only saw their parents when they dragged them onto the red carpet in order to promote their latest film; the stars who were adored by millions but were so racked with insecurity they couldn't leave the house without their publicist, make-up artist, hairdresser, three assistants, personal astrologer and a Chanel handbag full of prescription meds. Tinseltown certainly wasn't as sparkly as it wanted the public to believe, hence why every celebrity had a team of legal eagles on call just in case their secret shenanigans ever happened to end up plastered all over the internet or gossip weeklies. The lucrative sponsorship deals brokered with cosmetic brands, fashion labels and global soft drink companies which beefed up the A-list's tax-free Swiss bank accounts also had iron-clad good-behaviour clauses written into the contracts, so they literally couldn't afford for anything slightly salacious or negative to blow up in their faces.

'Okay, what's next?' Nina doodled in her notebook, resigned to the fact that it was another slow news week.

Meg piped up. 'A good source of mine in London reckons Hayley Polkadot and Olly Box's marriage is done and dusted after only six months and is happy to go on record about it. They're going to blame it on their work schedules and living in different countries when the announcement goes out, but apparently the real story is that he wanted to start a family and begged her to give it another chance but she'd already gone and found herself a new man before they'd officially decided the marriage was dunzo.'

Nina sighed with relief. Sometimes she hated trading on other people's misery and misfortune, but when those people were celebrities who lived ridiculously privileged lifestyles, she figured they could cry into their Louis Vuitton luggage while counting their millions as they lounged on their private jet sipping magnums of Krug that had been chilled to exactly 7.77 degrees. Not that she had anything against Hayley or Olly – in fact, she quite liked them as a celebrity couple. The kooky Texan singer had come out of nowhere a couple of years ago, making headlines with her crazy outfits and quirky songs. When she'd started dating Olly, Britain's bad boy acting genius, people were at first horrified, then intrigued. When they'd announced they were getting married in Swaziland with a guest list that looked like the lovechild of the Oscars and Grammys, gossip addicts across the globe had salivated.

'Bingo! There's our cover story for this week,' Nina told the team. 'Meg, get as many details and quotes from your source as possible – try to find out when the divorce announcement is due. Also, who is Hayley's new man and does Olly know about him? Layla, when was the last time Hayley and Olly were snapped together? I want a visual timeline of their relationship, so our readers can chart the downfall of their marriage. Let's package this up nice and tight so our lawyers give it the green light. Okay, peeps, let's get busy. Simone and Gracie, can we have a quick chat about Monday's shoot with Tully? Gracie, Simone said her publicists are being difficult?'

Juice's entertainment editor nodded. 'That's one way of putting it. But it's just the usual stuff – they want picture approval, question approval, copy approval, headline approval, caption approval, breathing approval . . . you get the idea. Obviously I've pushed back and reiterated that we're happy to send them a small selection of images that we've pre-approved for the cover and they can state their preference, but the final decision is up to us. And we will send them the copy once it's written up so they can check it for factual errors, but they do not get copy approval. I love how they try it on every time we shoot one of their celebrities, even though our rules never change. Plus this shoot was pitched to us by Tully's record label, not her publicity company, so as long as the record-label people are happy, we're golden.'

Nina nodded. 'Okay, great. And we've booked her preferred hair and make-up team so she'll feel comfortable on the set? Or is she so new she doesn't have a regular team yet?'

'Her PR team didn't seem that bothered by the creative team, just the photographer – they specifically requested Antonio, who we've booked.'

'Antonio? The guy who shot Lulu for us last time when we did the bikini-body special? He's good but he's pretty heavy-handed with the airbrush when he edits the shots, so make sure he doesn't stretch her to make her look taller or shave inches off her curves before he sends us the edit. It wasn't just Tully's voice that won *Aussie Singstar*, it was also because women around the country could relate to her because she's not a stick insect, so we need her to look like the size fourteen she is. She came across as proud of her body during the show, so hopefully she'll own it on the shoot.'

'I've got quite a few body-related questions on my interview list, so fingers crossed her publicists don't shut me down when I get to them,' Gracie said nervously.

'Simone, will you have time to go to the shoot for a bit tomorrow? If you're there, you can distract Tully's publicists during Gracie's interview so they don't kill any of the trickier questions. Charm and distract, Sim, charm and distract.'

'Sure – Gracie, just text me twenty minutes before your chat and I'll hop in a cab,' said Simone excitedly. 'I loved Tully on the show; I can't wait to meet her.' As they headed back to their desks Nina overheard her deputy ask, 'Reckon I'll be able to get a pic with her for my Instagram?'

'Nina, have you had a chance to look at those layouts in your tray yet?' Layla called. 'Annie wants to do the pic order before she leaves for the day.'

'Sorry, I'll do it right now. Give me ten minutes.' Nina hurried into her office, wondering where the hell the day had gone. Picking up the pile of layouts, she started sifting through them, marking up changes and scrawling suggestions in red pen. Sorting them into two piles, she dropped them on the desk just outside her office, instructing Bella, *Juice's* editorial assistant, to give one pile to Annie and the other to Joe, the magazine's art director, so his team could work on her requested changes.

Grabbing a Diet Coke from the vending machine in the kitchen, Nina mentally prepared herself for the PowerPoint pain and legal-contract hell that awaited her. As she waited for her dinosaur computer to boot up PowerPoint, she flicked over to Outlook to check her emails. In among the endless press releases, narky internal emails about whose turn it was to clean the office fridge and a meeting request from her marketing director was an email from Heidi with the subject line *Who needs babies . . .* Cracking open her can of caffeinated bubbles, Nina clicked on it.

To: Nina Morey
From: Heidi Chambers
Subject: Who needs babies . . .

. . . when you've got the Big Apple?????

    N, I know what we need! A girls' trip! Just the two of us, so we can get away from all the Nappy Valley talk. I'm thinking New York – skyscrapers, shopping, cocktails and cute boys. What do you reckon?????

    H

Below the text, Heidi had pasted a montage of shots from *Sex and the City*, just to ram her point home. Nina took a sip of her drink and considered all the reasons why a trip to New York wasn't a good idea. Her credit card was still suffering from the lingering effects of the Mulberry Alexa bag she'd bought herself for Christmas, plus her annual leave balance wasn't looking particularly healthy. She'd half-heartedly been trying to get both in the black so she could go visit Tess and Johan in London, but the idea of hitting up New York with Heidi was more tempting than a naked Ryan Gosling covered in salted caramel gelato . . . Before she could change her mind, Nina quickly tapped out a three-word response.

To: Heidi Chambers

From: Nina Morey

Subject: RE: Who needs babies . . .

BRING. IT. ON!!!!!!!!!!!!!!!!

five

'Oh my God, I almost forgot to tell you guys – I found the best sale the other day!' Daniela squealed, almost knocking her peppermint tea over in excitement. Nina's ears immediately went on high alert at the mention of 'sale' – as the assistant financial controller of a high-end Australian retail chain, Daniela occasionally got wind of amazing sample sales that even Nina and Steph, the two with the most fashion connections, didn't hear about. The last time it had been Gucci, where the girls had snapped up shoes, bags and jackets at prices that would have made the Mona Lisa break out into an ecstatic grin. 'I really shouldn't be spending any money, I'm about to go to New York,' Nina told herself sternly, before leaning over the table so she didn't miss any of the vital details.

'So spill the beans!' demanded Heidi impatiently.

'Wait till Nat and Lily are back from the bathroom – trust me, they won't want to miss this,' Daniela promised, her eyes gleaming with excitement.

Nina was practically drooling. 'Sounds like it might be even better than the Gucci one,' she whispered to Heidi. 'What do you think – Louboutin? Burberry? Or even P . . . R . . . A . . . D . . . A?' Her friend worshipped at the altar of the Italian label, despite her teacher's salary.

'Don't torture me like that!' Heidi whimpered, her eyes glazing over at the thought.

Nina spotted Natalie and Lily making their way through The Bathers' Pavilion where the eight of them had met up for brunch overlooking Balmoral's picturesque beach. Still weeks away from her due date, Lily looked like someone had stuffed a large basketball up her top and injected a gallon of excess fluid into her body. It was her fifth trip to the bathroom since she'd arrived an hour ago.

'I really wish Lake would stop sitting on my bladder,' she sighed as she sat down awkwardly. 'Daniela, how many times are you getting up during the night to pee? Evie, did you say you were averaging three times now? Nat, what was your record when you were pregnant with Sasha?'

As Nina tuned out at the sound of yet another pregnancy-related discussion, she found herself looking past Bec, who seemed to be enthralled by the nightly tally of how often the three pregnant women went to the bathroom, and straight at Steph, who was sitting at the other end of the table. She rolled her eyes in not-so-mock frustration, before remembering too late what Heidi had told her about Steph and Chris's fertility problems and how desperate they were to get pregnant. As Steph returned her eye roll with a small, sad smile while tugging at the sleeves of her digital print Zimmermann blazer, Nina idly wondered why she was wearing a jacket when it was pushing thirty degrees outside.

'Okay, girls, enough talk about bodily functions,' she interrupted to save her own sanity as much as Steph's feelings when the conversation moved on to the scintillating topic of constipation during pregnancy. 'Sorry, Nat, I'm sure the story of your first post-birth bowel movement is absolutely fascinating, but we have more important things to discuss – Daniela is giving us the heads-up about another one of her special sales. Come on, which label is it this time?' Nina demanded.

Daniela smiled smugly. 'So I just happened to be in a meeting with our head fashion buyer the other day; she's the one who's in the know when it comes to these things. We got talking and she happened to mention this amazing sale she'd just been to – let me tell you, I had to sit on my hands to stop myself from grabbing my bag and running out the door then and there! But when I did eventually check it out, it was so worth it. The range is incredible, they have every size and style and even some pieces that I'd never seen before. I went absolutely nuts; Mitch is going to die when he sees the credit card bill! But I figured I'd get plenty of use out of them so it would have been rude not to –'

'Dani, stop!' Nina managed through gritted teeth. 'We get that the sale was totally beyond, but which brand are you talking about?'

'Sorry – baby brain!' Daniela laughed. 'It's Latte Amore.'

Lily, Evie and Natalie gasped and immediately grabbed their phones to take note of the address. Heidi looked at Nina, confused.

'Is that some brand-new diffusion line from Giorgio Armani that I don't know about?'

'I doubt it,' Nina replied, grimly. 'Dani, what the hell is Latte Amore? I've never heard of it.'

'It's a maternity bra label,' Daniela explained. 'They're the best in the business but their bras are soooo expensive. You should see the fabrics and trims they use, they're just divine. It's like the haute couture of maternity lingerie. Evie and Lily, their feeding bras are apparently the bomb so make sure you don't miss out. And, Nat, I know Sasha isn't breastfeeding anymore but I thought you might be interested in stocking up for next time . . .'

Nina sat back in her seat, stunned. She couldn't believe it – they were frothing over a freaking maternity bra sample sale like it was Tom Ford or Balenciaga! Suddenly she was fuming. She didn't know about Heidi or Steph, but she was sick of the pregnant posse dominating every conversation in the group. If they were like this now, she couldn't bear to think how much worse it would be once they'd actually given birth. Then it would be endless stories about failed epidurals, excruciating labour pains, nappies filled with 'poo-namis', sleep routines, projectile vomit, controlled crying, teething problems, to circumcise or not to circumcise . . . enough already! She was tired of feeling like she didn't matter anymore just because she didn't have a bun in the oven. All she wanted was for things to go back to the way they'd been before everyone had decided babies were the new black.

'Really? Maternity bras? How fabulous. I'm really glad you hyped it up so much when you know full well that Bec, Heidi, Steph and myself have no need for anything maternity-related. It's not all about you guys and the contents of your uteruses, you know.' The words poured out of her mouth before Nina could stop them.

The table was silent, as her rudeness sank in.

'Oh my God, what did you just say?' her brain wailed as she looked around at the mix of expressions that ranged from surprised to appalled. 'They're your friends, you can't just have a massive go at them like that. Who the hell do you think you are? Why do you get to dictate what they do and don't talk about? Stop being such a selfish princess. Say sorry. NOW.'

Her mouth was opening to apologise profusely when Bec piped up. 'Um, Nina? I can't speak for Heidi or Steph, but actually, I am interested in maternity bras.' Looking around the table nervously, Bec confessed, 'I wasn't going to tell you guys until I got the results of my scan next week, but it seems that there's something in the water — I'm pregnant too! It wasn't exactly planned, but now that it's happening, Will and I are pretty excited.'

As the girls fell over themselves to congratulate Bec, Nina was reminded of the time she'd tripped over a fence when she was a little girl on her parents' farm in the Northern Territory and had winded herself. She felt the same now — stunned, shocked and breathless. She couldn't believe another one of her friends had bitten the baby dust. Feeling Heidi's eyes boring into her, she smiled weakly in Bec's direction, then started counting the seconds until she could leave. She didn't say another word for the rest of the brunch.

'What the hell were you thinking?' Heidi demanded later that afternoon, when Nina finally answered one of her calls. 'Do you have any idea how rude you were? Especially to poor Bec — you didn't even say congratulations.'

'I know I was rude, but hello? They're being rude by only talking about all that baby shit whenever we see them and it's going to be even worse now that Bec is knocked up,' Nina pointed out obstinately, not wanting to admit she had been in the wrong. 'Someone needed to pull them up on it, otherwise I was going to physically hurt someone.'

Heidi sighed. 'Nina, you did hurt someone — more than one. You hurt Lily, you hurt Daniela, you hurt Natalie, you hurt Evie and you hurt Bec. Look, I get where you're coming from — I've had a gutful of it as well — but sometimes you just have to suck it up and pretend you're in your happy

47

place. They're our friends, we're supposed to be there for them through thick and thin, not just when they're up for knocking back jugs of Pimm's at the Winery.'

Nina glared at her canary-yellow pedicure before turning her attention to the chipped pale grey polish on her fingernails. Scraping the remains off with her thumbnail as Heidi continued to read her the riot act, Nina let her friend's words wash over her. She knew she had been brutal, but there wasn't much she could do about it now. Then again, they were the closest friends she had, even if they were driving her up the nursery wall. And admittedly, she probably shouldn't have brought the other non-pregnant girls into it, but how was she to know Bec had joined the baby brigade?

'Sorry, what was that?' Nina mumbled, realising Heidi was waiting for an answer.

'I said, what are you going to do about it? You can't pretend everything's fine and dandy the next time you see them, not after you sat there sulking and refusing to make conversation with anyone for more than half an hour. The sooner you address it, the better.'

'Yes, Miss Chambers,' Nina said in a singsong voice, mimicking one of Heidi's year five students. 'I'll call each of them and apologise before we go to New York, I promise. And I'll buy all their babies "I heart New York" onesies while I'm there. And tonight I'll say seven Hail Marys and whip myself repeatedly with a cat-o'-nine-tails made from maternity bras.'

When she heard the unmistakeable sound of Heidi's smirk, she knew the lecture was over.

'Very funny,' Heidi allowed. 'But you're not even Catholic so good luck with those Hail Marys. Speaking of New York, how many pairs of shoes are you going to take? Have you seen the weather forecast lately? Do you think we should take our bikinis?'

'Nope, the Standard doesn't have a pool, unless you're planning to take a swim in the bathtub,' Nina replied, glad to be talking about something else. 'Or go on an impromptu trip to the Hamptons.'

'Well I guess it depends on whether I meet a Mr Big or not, doesn't it?' Heidi pointed out. 'Okay, bikinis are off the list. Although it's not like they take up much room. Maybe I'll pack one just in case . . .'

'Don't bother – if for some random reason you do decide you need a bikini to wear while shopping up a storm in SoHo, slurping cocktails in the East Village or browsing the markets in Brooklyn, then you can buy one over there. Clothes are crazy cheap in the States, remember? Plus all the summer stuff will be on sale,' Nina reminded her.

'You're right, you're right . . . Okay, I've got a million maths tests to mark before the end of term on Friday, so I'm going to love you and leave you. Don't forget to call the girls ASAP – especially Bec, seeing you owe her a congratulations at the very least.'

'Okaaaaaaaaaaay,' Nina sighed.

Throwing herself down on the couch, she buried her head in the cushions and groaned. 'Why did I have to open my big mouth?' she asked herself.

49

She started scrolling through her phone's contact list as she paced around her apartment, knowing she should get the apologies over and done with now before the rot started to set in. She was about to call Bec's number when the name below it caught her eye – Charlie. 'Now there's an idea . . .' she thought, not-so-secretly pleased for the distraction.

Charlie had helped her to get over the break-up of her relationship with Jeremy by the time-honoured tradition of getting underneath her – his favourite position was girl on top, preferably reverse cowgirl. Five years younger than Nina, he was a bearded Bondi boy who spent his days dabbling in a bit of art here, a bit of bartending there and a whole lot of not much else, unless the surf was good. Given he was Steph's baby brother, they'd kept their sexual shenanigans on the downlow after hooking up at her engagement party. It was the perfect arrangement – neither of them wanted anything serious but they were happy to blow off some steam in the bedroom now and then. Nina could definitely do with blowing off some steam right now, but she hadn't heard from Charlie in a while. She debated whether to call her old fuck buddy or not. Maybe he'd gone and got himself a girlfriend? There was only one way to find out.

'Hi, it's me,' she purred down the line. 'You want to come over? Nina's been a naughty girl . . .'

six

'Houston, we have a problem.'

Nina felt a flicker of alarm when she looked up from the contract she was reading through to see Simone and Gracie standing in front of her desk, the latter practically vibrating with anxiety. She tried not to let her irritation show – although her bedroom athletics with Charlie on Sunday night had helped clear out the cobwebs, she still felt a bit out of sorts after her outburst at The Bathers' Pavilion. She hadn't got around to calling any of the girls to apologise either – there was always something that took priority – and she knew the longer she left it, the harder it would be. The last thing she was in the mood to deal with right now was an office drama, but it wasn't like she had a choice in the matter. With a staff made up almost exclusively of females, barely a week went by without one of them letting their inner cry-baby loose, whether it was because of relationship problems, a frustrating encounter with a publicist or picture agency, or just plain old PMS. Heidi and the other girls had been horrified when Nina had happened to mention the amount of tears that were shed in her office; they considered it completely unprofessional to cry in front of their boss. But as Nina had pointed out, the world of magazine editorial was different. She wasn't just an editor – whether she liked it or not, she was a confidante, a mentor, a guide, someone to bounce ideas off, a rock to rely on when things got tough. In a way, she was like a parent of sorts to her team, which was ironic given her current aversion to all things relating to children and parents-to-be.

'What's up? Is this about yesterday's shoot? Gracie, are you okay?' Nina asked, reaching for the box of tissues she kept close by. She'd quickly learnt to have a healthy stash of Kleenex in her office due to the frequency of Niagara Falls-style waterworks.

'Yeah, I'm okay . . . more mad than anything,' Gracie replied, sinking down into one of the chairs. 'It's just so goddamn annoying when you put so much effort into planning a photo shoot,' she sniffed, her voice wobbling dangerously. 'You make sure you've crossed every T and dotted every I but that still doesn't stop it from going to shit on the day.'

Nina pushed the box of tissues towards her and raised an eyebrow at Simone.

'Where do we start . . . ?' Simone said, grimacing. 'First of all, Tully's publicist lied about her size, so none of the clothes the fashion team had called in fitted her. Which wasn't just awkward for us, because it made it look like we didn't do our jobs properly, it was embarrassing for Tully to have to come out of the change room wearing a dress that wouldn't do up at the back or a pair of jeans that wouldn't go past her knees. You could tell she was mortified. So things got off on the wrong track from the beginning, but then Antonio didn't exactly help matters.'

'How do you mean?'

'He obviously wasn't very happy about working with someone who wasn't a perfect size eight, and was quite blatant about it. Why her team requested him as the photographer, I do not know. He was rude, he was insulting, he didn't want to make an effort . . . it was torture. And Tully could tell things weren't exactly peachy, so then she got all insecure and started acting like Miss Stroppy 2014.'

'Really? But on *Aussie Singstar* she was as sweet as candy! She never once said or did anything remotely bitchy – that's one of the reasons why she won,' Nina recalled.

'I know, but either it was all an act or since winning it's all been too much for her and she's become a bitch on wheels. After the wardrobe fiasco, when the make-up artist tried to touch up her concealer, she came out with this classic line: "Do you *have* to touch my face?"' Simone threw in a head toss and attitude-laden finger wag for good measure.

'Whaaaaaaaaat?' Nina practically screeched. 'Are you serious? She asked a make-up artist, whose job is to apply make-up, if she *had to touch her face*?! Um, yeah, honey — that's what make-up artists do. Get with the program.'

'Oh, it gets better,' Gracie announced. 'Seeing Tully's team didn't have a preference for make-up artists, I booked Stella — you know, the one who works with Miranda Kerr every time she's in town? She's amazing. So things between them obviously didn't get off to a good start, but when we switched looks halfway through the shoot, the stylist asked Stella to give Tully a bright pink lip to work back with the fluoro pink heels the fashion team had put her in and do you know what Tully said to her? "I don't want that trashy pink lip. Get it off me. *Now*." Gracie mimicked the tone of a petulant teenager.

Nina shook her head in disbelief. 'But she rocked pink lips all the time when she was on TV! Are we talking about the same girl?'

'The one and same,' Simone confirmed. 'Funny what fame does to people, isn't it?'

'Tell me about it. So how was the interview?' Nina was almost too scared to ask.

'Surprisingly, it went well,' Gracie said. 'Simone managed to lure the publicist away so she wasn't breathing down our necks and Tully opened up about a lot of things, like that rumoured romance with Gareth while they were both competing on the show, and how she felt about her body. I actually felt sorry for her at one stage, because she mentioned that the clothes were always too small for her at the photo shoots she'd done since winning – she obviously has no idea that her publicist is telling people the wrong size.'

'At least the interview wasn't a disaster!' Nina said brightly. 'Sounds like the shoot was a pain in the arse but it wouldn't be the first time. Let's get the interview written up ASAP so we can decide on the main cover line. When are the edited shots due?'

'That's the problem. In fact, there are two problems,' Gracie admitted.

'You mean Tully and Antonio acting like divas on the shoot wasn't the problem?' Nina raised an eyebrow.

''Fraid not. One problem is this email I just got from Marnie, Tully's death bitch publicist.'

'"Death bitch"? Is that a technical term, Gracie?' Nina joked. She picked up the email print-out that Gracie handed to her and quickly skimmed it, becoming more peeved by the second.

'Is she on crack? "Despite what you and Tully may have discussed in your interview, there is to be no reference to Tully's body or how she feels about her size in your write-up. Furthermore, there will be no mention of Gareth or their supposed relationship while in the *Singstar* house,"' Nina quoted. 'What a crock. Does she understand what the term "on the record" means? If Tully knew you were recording the interview and willingly spoke about those things, then Marnie can't tell us they're not to be included in the story. And if she didn't want Tully discussing those things, then she shouldn't have been chatting with Simone during the interview! Or better yet, she should have briefed Tully before the interview on what topics were off-limits so Tully knew when to shut the hell up. Sounds like someone's panicking after Tully told her what you two talked about. Just ignore her, Gracie. Write up the interview like you normally would and after we get the photos and design the pages, send a PDF of the layout through to Marnie so she can check it for factual errors like we promised. But stress they are the only changes we will make – she can't start dictating to us about what we can and can't include now, the silly cow,' Nina said.

'The shots are already in,' Simone volunteered. 'But that's the other problem. Tully looks about ten feet tall and she's half the size she was at the shoot. If there was a Photoshop Olympics, Antonio would win gold.'

Nina groaned. 'I had a feeling this would happen. Antonio can never help himself when it comes to stretching and shaving even when he photographs size-six models, so it figures he'd go to town on someone who's four sizes bigger. I love how photographers think they're God and can't resist distorting female bodies into their warped ideal of what they think women should look like. Simone, can you call his agent? Tell her it's unacceptable and we need him to send over the raw files ASAP. And in future, if he keeps going to town with the airbrush, we won't work with him again.'

It wasn't an idle threat – while celebrity weeklies languished way below style bibles such as *Harper's Bazaar* on the 'magazines that photographers would kill to work for' list, *Juice* paid a hell of a lot more than high-class titles and with as many as five celebrity shoots in each issue, it also had a lot of work on offer. Of course, some photographers' egos were so precious that they didn't want it to be known that they shot for anything less than *Harper's*, but that was easily fixed – *Juice's* sub-editors knew not to include a photography credit on the page when it came to certain names. It meant the celebrity who'd requested their favourite photographer was happy, the photographer's agent who collected fifteen per cent of their earnings was happy because they brought in more money, the photographer was happy because his portfolio wasn't blighted by shots from a trashy weekly and the photographer's up-and-coming model girlfriend was happy because it meant he could buy her that new Chanel clutch she had her eye on. Case closed.

'Roger that,' Simone acknowledged, leaving Nina's office to go do battle with Antonio's agent.

'Um, Nina?' Gracie squirmed. 'I wonder if it would be better if you sent Marnie the PDF of the cover story once it's ready instead of me? You're the editor, so it might have more of an effect if it's you who tells her that the only changes she can make are in relation to any factual errors.'

Nina sighed. She loved her staff but sometimes the amount of hand-holding she had to do grated on her nerves. 'Gracie, you're the entertainment editor – there's no reason why you shouldn't be able to reiterate the rules to Marnie when you send through the PDF. You're a senior member of staff, so you have to step up to the plate even if it means doing something you don't particularly want to do. Toughen up, princess – you're not here to make friends, you're here to do a job. I mean, you *did* tell her that they wouldn't get copy approval before the shoot, didn't you?'

'Yes, of course I did,' Gracie said hurriedly. 'It's just that . . . I don't really want to piss Marnie off right now if I can help it. It's different if it's coming from you because you're the boss — and let's face it, she'll just demand to speak to you about it anyway. So in a way, it'll save time . . .'

Nina looked at Gracie, who was doing her best tomato impression, through narrowed eyes.

'What's going on? Why exactly do you not want to piss Marnie off? Come on, Gracie, spit it out.'

'Well, it's personal,' her entertainment editor mumbled, going even redder.

'Gracie, if it's affecting your ability to do your job, I need to know about it,' Nina shot back. 'It will stay between you and me, but spill it.'

'Uhhhh . . . well . . . Marnie and I . . . aeffgywadolblat-loffating . . .' she mumbled.

'Sorry? I didn't quite get that.'

'Marnie and I are dating,' Gracie said clearly, lifting her head and looking at Nina defiantly.

Nina hoped the surprise she felt wasn't plastered all over her face. She'd had no idea her entertainment editor was a lesbian, not that it was any of her business. Although now that she was hooking up with one of Sydney's celebrity publicists, it had suddenly become her business.

'Oh . . . congratulations!' Nina immediately felt like an idiot given it wasn't the most appropriate response — it wasn't like

Gracie had just announced her engagement – but it could have been worse. Plus she didn't remember seeing 'How to react when a staff member reveals they're gay' in the handbook HR had given her when she'd started at *Juice*. Then she remembered one of Gracie's earlier comments. 'Hang on . . . you're dating Tully's quote "death bitch" unquote publicist? That's not a very nice way to talk about your girlfriend!'

Gracie shrugged. 'Yeah, I went a bit overboard trying to throw you off the scent. Plus we had an epic fight last night so things aren't exactly hunky-dory right now, which is why I don't really want to rile her up any more than I have to. Sorry, Nina, I know it's not very professional, but I promise this is the first and last time.' She looked at Nina pleadingly.

Nina chewed on the inside of her cheek as she thought about Gracie's predicament. She knew she should stick to her guns and make her entertainment editor send off the contentious story just like she would with any other publicist, but maybe because Nina's personal life wasn't exactly kittens and Paddlepops either, she let her arm be twisted.

'Okay, here's what we're going to do – you will send the PDF to Marnie once it's written up and designed like I asked,' she announced, and saw Gracie's face fall. 'But in your email, cc me and tell her that I'm the one who says that everything from your chat with Tully is on the record and is therefore fair game. If she has a problem with that, tell her she can call me on my direct line to discuss it personally. Good compromise?'

'Good compromise,' Gracie agreed, looking much happier. 'Thanks,' she added. 'I know I'm being a wuss, but I really like this one and I don't want my job to mess things up.'

Nina almost retorted, 'If Marnie was smart, she would realise you're just doing your job and it's nothing personal,' then decided to leave it alone. Gracie needed to figure that out for herself. 'Right, let's get this show on the road as soon as the raw images have been downloaded. Time to scoot, Gracie – a cover story doesn't write itself. I fly to New York on Friday so I want everything approved by the time I leave for the airport. It has to be ready to rock and roll in case Simone needs to use it next week.' Before going on holiday, Nina always made sure she had a cover prepared for the week she was away, just in case a meteor landed in the middle of Hollywood and wiped every A-lister off the face of the planet while she was lying by the pool with an obscenely large pina colada in hand – or, in this case, lining up for the Century 21 change rooms with a Starbucks frappaccino in hand. For *Juice*'s readers, Tully was big news after blitzing *Aussie Singstar*, but Nina knew that the cover could run any time in the next couple of weeks. If a huge juicy celebrity scandal broke while Nina was away, Tully would be put on hold and she'd have to rely on Simone to pull a new cover together in her absence.

'Oh, before I forget – what's all this about *Juice* and a reality TV show?' Gracie asked on her way out.

'What do you mean?' Nina asked, confused. 'As in a copy of the mag being featured on *Big Brother* or something?'

'No, as in a reality TV show based around the magazine, documenting how it's put together and all that,' Gracie clarified. 'Like American *Vogue*'s *The September Issue* but a TV series. Although less couture, more C-list celebs,' she said dryly.

'I have no idea what you're talking about. The marketing team haven't mentioned anything to me and neither has Eric.' Nina had seen *Juice*'s publisher recently and he hadn't said a word about any TV show. 'Who told you about it?'

'One of the publicists from Channel Eight mentioned it at a program launch last week – I meant to say something earlier but things have been a bit hectic.'

'She probably got the wrong magazine; you know how people always confuse us with *Joy*,' Nina said, pretending to shudder. *Joy* was another weekly magazine, but instead of targeting twenty-somethings who liked to keep their finger on the celebrity pulse, it was aimed squarely at older women in lower socioeconomic households who couldn't get enough of *Joy*'s Aussie battler real-life reads and weekly scratch-and-win cash prizes. The magazine looked like a cheap rag, but it was insanely popular – Nina had heard that when they'd done a giveaway for a sachet of fabric softener one time, they had received more than twenty thousand entries. For a *sachet*, not even a full-size bottle. 'Although I don't know if the *Joy* office would make scintillating viewing,' she added snarkily. 'Besides, I couldn't think of anything worse than having a bunch of cameras in the office all the time, with producers trying to whip up non-existent drama every five minutes.' She cringed at the thought.

Turning back to the legal contract she'd been reading through for what felt like the seven hundredth time before being interrupted by Simone and Gracie, Nina tried her best to concentrate. It was the final version for Lulu and Jason's wedding exclusive and no matter how many times she read it, she couldn't shake the feeling that the lawyers had missed something. The wedding was still a month away but she wanted to put this baby to bed before New York so it wasn't hanging over her head and getting in the way of boys, Bloomingdales and Ben & Jerry's. She almost screamed in frustration when Bella, her assistant, knocked on the door.

'Nina? Sorry to interrupt but I thought I'd let you know that a massive box of cupcakes just arrived in the office. I've put them on the meeting table.'

Nina smiled gratefully. Sugar was exactly what she needed right now.

'Bella?' she called out. 'Are any of them Valium-flavoured?'

seven

Nina was busy thanking the universe that it was finally Friday – aka New York day – when her direct line started to ring. She leant over to shut her office door, took a deep breath and went into battle.

'Juice, Nina speaking . . .'

'Nina, it's Marnie, Tully's publicist. Gracie sent through the PDF of the cover and interview and said I should contact you if there were any problems. And believe me, there are definitely some problems,' she said ominously.

'Oh, hi, Marnie, lovely to hear from you,' Nina said, ignoring the publicist's tone. 'Don't you think Tully looks amazing in the shot we like for the cover? Our readers are going to love it.'

As promised, they'd sent over three potential cover shots, but what Marnie didn't know was that Nina and Joe had purposely selected two of the most unflattering photos for the second and third options so Marnie would have no choice but to agree with their preferred shot. Sometimes you had to load the odds in your favour.

'Nina, can I be blunt? She looks like a heifer. I told Antonio to reduce the size of her arms and legs and stretch her to give her some extra height – what the hell happened?'

Nina didn't know why she felt a flicker of surprise – given Marnie had told her fashion team the wrong clothing size, it made sense that she was behind Antonio's 'creativity' when it came to altering Tully's body shape. Although she was sure the photographer hadn't needed any encouragement.

'Marnie, I don't know if you need to get your eyes checked, but Tully doesn't look like a heifer at all – she looks like a healthy girl who is proud of not being a stick insect, which makes her a great role model. I'm sure I don't have to tell you that one of the reasons she got so many votes on *Aussie Singstar* was because women appreciated the fact that she refused to apologise for not being wafer thin. We want her to look like she did on the show, not like the "after" shot from a Weight Watchers commercial. Our readers would be absolutely outraged if we ran a shot where she'd been digitally slimmed down. It's sending out the wrong message, not only to the public but also to Tully, and I refuse to do it,' Nina declared.

'Oh, come on, Nina! You can't tell me you haven't ever digitally altered the body of a celebrity when they've asked you!' Marnie scoffed. 'We all know that Photoshopping is rampant in this industry – no one expects celebrities to look like normal people! Your readers don't want to see zits and cellulite; God knows they see enough of that every day when they look in the mirror!'

Nina bristled. If there was a sure-fire way to get on her wrong side, it was to insult her readers. 'Excuse me, Marnie, but you have no idea what my readers look like. But I do know what Tully looks like, and it's certainly nothing like the manipulated images that Antonio sent through. Maybe if he'd been a little more subtle, we wouldn't have noticed and you would have got the Photoshopped cover you want, but seeing the instructions given to him were so over the top, it was kind of obvious . . .' Nina trailed off, making sure Marnie knew full well who she was pointing the finger at.

'Well . . . I . . .' Marnie spluttered for a second then quickly moved on. 'It's not just the cover that's the problem, Nina. This cover interview is an abomination! I can't believe your writer took such liberties after I strictly told her that anything to do with body image and relationship rumours were totally off-limits.'

'You mean my writer who's also your girlfriend?' Nina felt like saying, but managed to control herself. 'Gracie was only doing as she was told,' she said out loud.

'By whom? Certainly not by me!' came the belligerent reply.

'By me, Marnie,' Nina said, not bothering to hide her irritation. 'I'm her boss. I don't know about your office, but at *Juice*, when your boss tells you to do something, you tend to do it. And since Tully's weight and her love-life are two things that our readers are particularly interested in, I gave

Gracie explicit instructions to include them. As you have been told several times, the only changes you can make to the cover interview are to correct any factual errors.'

There was silence. Nina checked the time – she needed to leave for the airport in an hour and still had a million things to do before she walked out the door. It was time to wrap up this ridiculous conversation.

Then Marnie's voice trumpeted down the phone, 'Well, in that case, there are quite a few factual errors in this interview. It's a factual error that Tully hooked up with Gareth in the *Aussie Singstar* house and it's a factual error that she's felt a lot of pressure to lose weight since becoming famous. So you'll need to remove those quotes from the story,' Marnie instructed, sounding pleased with herself.

Nina rolled her eyes – there were no prizes for guessing who Tully had been feeling that pressure from. 'I appreciate your efforts, but seeing we have those quotes on record from Tully, I'm not quite sure how they can be factual errors.'

'They are! She made them up on the day! They're factually wrong! You need to take them out!' Marnie shrieked down the phone.

'She made them up just for the hell of it? You seriously expect me to believe that? Listen, Marnie, I don't have time for this. I hardly need to point out that if there were certain topics you didn't want Tully to discuss with Gracie, a good publicist would have briefed her client before the interview, especially a client who is still so new to this media game,' Nina pointed out bluntly, before switching gears. 'Tell me, how badly does Tully want this cover? After all, it is her first magazine cover since winning *Aussie Singstar*.'

'Oh, she wants it badly. She's been talking about it non-stop ever since it was confirmed,' Marnie admitted.

'So you wouldn't want to disappoint her, would you? Or disappoint her record label, who were the ones who originally approached us about the cover?'

'What do you mean? Of course I don't want to disappoint her or the record label!'

'I can quite easily kill this cover, Marnie,' Nina said airily, playing her trump card. 'At the moment, it's scheduled for next week, which I don't need to tell you is perfect timing seeing that's when Tully's new album is released, but if you're going to carry on like a pork chop about a couple of quotes in the interview – quotes which, I will remind you again, were on the record – then Tully can say sayonara to being the cover splash. If I'm feeling generous, I might use her as a small inset or, then again, I might not include the story in the magazine at all. Which I can't imagine the record label will be happy about, especially when I tell them why. How do you feel about those quotes now?'

eight

Leaning back in her window seat, Nina wondered how it would go down if she asked the flight attendant who was offering her a glass of champagne to bring her the whole bottle – and an extra one for Heidi while she was at it. 'Probably not the smartest idea seeing we've only just taken off,' she decided. 'Not to mention the fact that we already put away a bottle between us in the Qantas Club before we even boarded. Oops. Oh well, it's not every day we go to New York.'

In the premium economy seat next to her, Heidi was talking as fast as a ten-year-old who'd been mainlining red cordial. 'I'm going to watch Bradley Cooper's new comedy and then maybe that Mila Kunis film everyone is talking about,' she said excitedly, waving the entertainment guide in Nina's face. 'They've got the third season of *Game of Thrones,* too. Do you want my copy of US ELLE to flick through? I've already tagged the pages that have the things I want to buy, but I'm pretty sure I've got different coloured Post-its in my bag if you want them.'

Nina shook her head and closed her eyes. Now that she was on the plane, where no one could contact her to kick up about on-the-record quotes that were supposedly factual errors, she just wanted to chill for a bit. Marnie had backed down after Nina delivered her ultimatum, just as Nina knew she would – sometimes it paid to remember that celebrities needed magazines just as much as magazines needed them.

'So you've stayed at the Standard before, right?' Heidi was like a girl who had just hooked up with a new guy and couldn't resist bringing him up in conversation at every opportunity, only it was their New York trip she couldn't stop talking about. Not that Nina could blame her, but she'd been so busy at work that she hadn't really had time to get excited. 'Is that the fashion-bunny hotel with the dive bar across the road?' Heidi continued. 'You know, the one you went to last time you were in New York when that alcohol company flew you over for the launch of their new pre-mixed cocktail?'

Nina nodded. 'Yep, that's the one. It's in the Meatpacking District, right next to the High Line; a lot of the fashion pack stay there during the shows. It has its own bar and nightclub, but the marketing manager of the booze company wasn't the swanky type, so we ended up in Hogs and Heifers across the road almost every night. We'll have to go there at least once while we're in town; it's an experience you'll never forget.'

Sipping slowly on her bubbles, Nina remembered the crazy nights during that press junket. Not surprisingly, given his job, the marketing manager had been an enthusiastic drinker, as was Max, the editor of the lads' magazine who'd also been invited on the trip. Nina's 'no drinking during the week' rule had gone straight out the window as soon as they'd arrived – after attending the VIP launch party for the new cocktail, they'd staggered back to the hotel where Max had spied the dingy entrance to Hogs and Heifers, with its blacked-out windows, graffiti-plastered walls and intimidating bouncers, and had made a beeline for it. Nina had tried to wriggle out of joining them, pretending she was jetlagged when she really just wanted to watch the new episode of *Keeping Up With the Kardashians* in the comfort of her hotel room, preferably with a bag of chocolate-covered pretzels, but the guys ignored her protestations. Before she knew it, she was inside the dive bar, a frosty cold can of Pabst Blue Ribbon in her hand, staring at the hundreds of bras hanging from the ceiling while one of the heavily-tattooed barmaids screamed abuse through a loudspeaker at a punter who had vomited down the front of himself. Just as Nina had been wondering how all the lingerie had got there, one of the barmaids rang a bell. Tequila shots lined up on the bar were quickly consumed by the other barmaids, then the music was cranked up as they all clambered onto the bar, wearing nothing but denim cut-offs or mini-skirts, boots and bikini tops. As they'd started a half-hearted bootscoot among the empty shot glasses and crumpled beer cans, Nina was almost flattened by the stampede of women who were determined to have their own *Coyote Ugly*-esque moment. In various states of inebriation and clothing, the bar was soon packed with ladies pulling out their best moves, while the crowd started chanting, 'Take it off! Take it off!' As the song started to wind up, a couple of the girls reached under their tops, removed their bras, then tossed them up to the ceiling, where they snagged on the wire mesh, as the barmaids screamed encouragement through the megaphones and Max and the marketing manager gave each other high fives. What it lacked in class and gender equality, Hogs and Heifers made up for in character by the truckload.

'Okay, Hogs and Heifers is go. What about restaurants?' Heidi said eagerly, looking like she was about to take dictation as she opened up a new note on her iPhone and start making a list.

'Ummmm . . . let me think. There are the usual suspects, like the Spotted Pig, Beatrice Inn, Schiller's, Balthazar, SushiSamba . . . Bar Pitti, an Italian place on Sixth Avenue, is good too; I know Jay-Z and Beyoncé go there sometimes,' Nina said absentmindedly.

'Oh my God!' Heidi squealed. 'I LIVE for Beyoncé! I am her DISCIPLE! I would DIE if I saw her in New York! Imagine if she's there with Gwyneth!'

'Shhhhhh . . . we're on a plane, remember?' Nina clapped her hand over her friend's mouth for good measure. 'How much champagne have you put away?'

'Sorry, sorry.' Heidi hoisted herself up in her seat to apologise to the people sitting around them. 'I'm just so excited!' she whispered to Nina. 'I haven't been to New York for, like, ten years. Back then I was staying in a grubby hostel and living on hotdogs and popcorn because that's all I could afford. This time, we're going to live large, baby! Go hard or go home!' she proclaimed loudly, pouring the rest of the champagne down her throat and pushing the button to call the flight attendant to their seats. 'Could we pretty please have some more . . . oh! Well, that's service for you, isn't it?' she exclaimed when the smiling flight attendant appeared, already holding an open bottle of fizz.

'Let me guess, girls' trip to New York?' she winked, filling their glasses right to the top. 'Left the kids at home and going to shop up a storm, hmmm?'

'Uh, we don't have kids,' Nina muttered.

'Oh, really? That's a shame.' The older woman looked at them sympathetically. 'Well, you'd better get a wriggle on. Young women are leaving it far too late to start families these days, if you ask me. Trust me, you don't know what love is until you have a child; it's just the most wonderful thing you can do. My kids are grown up now, that's why I'm back at work, but they're still my pride and joy. It's such a pity that people have become so selfish; they put their careers first or they don't want to give up their superficial lifestyles to have a family but then they wonder why they're so unhappy. I know it's probably old-fashioned but I truly believe you're not fulfilled as a woman if you're not a mother. After all, it's what we were put on the earth to do, isn't it? Now, is there anything else I can get you, ladies? Lunch will be served in approximately forty-five minutes.'

Nina scowled at the flight attendant as she strode back down the aisle to help another passenger retrieve their hand luggage from the overhead compartment.

'God that annoys me,' she hissed to Heidi, who looked at her with raised eyebrows.

'What annoys you?'

'Didn't you hear her? How she just lectured us about not having children yet? It's like we're being stalked by baby fanatics,' Nina seethed. 'At first she presumed we had kids, then she told us we were leaving it too late and pulled out the "There's nothing like a mother's love" card which drives me insane! Who's to say the love she feels for her kids is more worthy than the love I feel for someone else? Of course it's a different kind of love, but it doesn't make hers better. And how dare she assume that I even want children? I can't stand this expectation that just because I have XX chromosomes, I should pony up and pop out a baby no matter what. And if a woman admits she isn't interested in procreating, either there must be something wrong with her, she gets told she'll "change her mind" or she gets a condescending look of sympathy because she'll be "missing out". Well, newsflash – parents miss out on things too! Sleep, for one. Money, for another. Kids are expensive, you know! It's bad enough that all our friends are procreating, I don't need a lecture from a flight attendant about how "unfulfilled" I am because I'm not a mother. She doesn't even know me!' Nina was just getting warmed up when she realised Heidi was looking at her like

73

she'd just confessed to pulling the tails off kittens and using them to strangle puppies.

'Alright, settle down! Why are you so sensitive about anything related to children? I know it feels like a baby epidemic at the moment but you've still got me — I'm not pregnant or a parent, remember? And won't be for quite some time, the way my love-life is going. So get off your rocking horse and stop obsessing already. I know it was a bit uncalled for but she's just a random flight attendant who you'll never see again. It's not like I'm going to put a breast pump to your head and force you to spend hours in the kids' department of Macy's. We're going to New York, we're going to have a great time and we're not going to talk about children or babies or pregnancy for the whole week we're there, okay?'

'Sorry, Heids, you're right,' Nina said. 'I just can't stand the automatic assumption that every woman wants to have a family and if she doesn't, she must be selfish or career-obsessed. You never hear a guy being called those things when they don't have kids. Anyway, with all the baby stuff going on with our friends, I guess I just really miss how things used to be. You know, when we used to organise girls' nights out and get all tarted up then spend the night quaffing cocktails and dancing on the banquettes at Beach Haus. Remember that time we saw Leonardo DiCaprio there when he was in Sydney filming *The Great Gatsby*? Fun times, huh? Anyway, that flight attendant's comment just rubbed me up the wrong way. It's been a stressful day; I think I might take a quick nap before lunch lands in our laps.' She grabbed her pillow and rested her head against the window.

'Sounds good. Hey, just before you snooze,' Heidi interrupted, 'speaking of the other girls, you did call Bec during the week to apologise for not congratulating her last weekend, didn't you?'

Nina opened one eye and looked at the concerned face of her best friend.

'Sure did,' she lied.

nine

Throwing the shopping bags onto the bed in their hotel room, Nina crashed onto the couch and moaned in ecstasy.

'I can't begin to tell you how good it is to not be tramping around SoHo anymore,' she called out to Heidi, who had dashed straight into the bathroom to pee. 'My feet are killing me.'

'Tell me about it,' Heidi replied. 'I'm too scared to get off the toilet in case my legs fall off.'

'I guess that's our punishment for going on an eight-hour shopping marathon,' Nina said, reaching for her iPad to check her work emails. Even though she was on annual leave, she still needed to be across what was happening back in the office. It was the curse of being an editor — you never got to switch off, unless you'd accidentally booked a holiday on a remote island with no internet access.

'Eight hours?! There's no way we were shopping for that long!' Heidi exclaimed, crawling in on all fours from the bathroom. Nina took one look at her and burst out laughing.

'Get up, you muppet! And yes, we did shop for eight hours. We left the hotel at eleven am and it's now seven pm. You do the maths, Einstein.'

'I guess we did go to a lot of stores,' Heidi admitted, eyeballing the bags from Zara, Marc Jacobs, Barneys, H&M, Sephora, Topshop, Abercrombie & Fitch, Opening Ceremony and a whole lot more. 'But hey, we're here for a good time, not for a long time, right?'

'Correct. Speaking of good times, what do you want to do tonight? You know, when we're able to walk again,' Nina added.

'I'm still suffering from last night's effort at Hogs and Heifers,' Heidi groaned.

Nina sniggered. 'Well, you did insist that we stayed until four am. And it wasn't me who was drinking tequila with the barmaids after taking my bra off and tossing it up to join its new friends.'

'How was I supposed to know it wasn't going to catch on the ceiling with all the others?' Heidi complained. 'It wasn't my fault that it landed on that barmaid's head and I had to do laybacks with her as penance.'

'One layback,' Nina reminded her. 'You only had to do one, not several!'

'Yeah, yeah . . . I was just getting into the spirit of things. Thank God they don't allow photos in that place; I hate to think what would have ended up on Instagram. And don't tell me you didn't have a good time – I saw you pashing that guy in the corner near the pool table while I was bathing in tequila.'

'Which one?' Nina asked coyly.

'You mean there was more than one?! Go, you good thing! Love your work. Next time, remember to share with me, okay? Redheads don't seem to be flavour of the month in the Big Apple,' Heidi said, somewhat morosely. 'I'm blaming Emma Stone – she should have stuck it out as a ranga instead of going back to blonde.'

'Hey, don't take it out on us blondes. We can't help it if gentlemen prefer us,' Nina ribbed, rolling over to pull two Diet Cokes out of the mini-bar.

'Oooh, I just remembered those red velvet cupcakes from Magnolia Bakery are in here somewhere,' Heidi exclaimed, hunting through the pile of shopping like a French truffle pig. 'Please tell me I wasn't stupid enough to put them in the Opening Ceremony bag, I'll die if my new dress has frosting all over it . . . aha! Crisis averted – they were in with the MAC stuff. Speaking of which, can we talk about how cheap MAC is here? Those eyeliners were only seventeen dollars – at home, they're like thirty-nine! I'm so going to stock up at duty-free when we head back. Ugh, I can't believe we only have three days left.'

Nina glanced at her friend, who was busily destroying a cupcake. They'd had such a great time since digging their spike heels into American soil – as well as doing their best to boost the retail economy, they'd also gazed at Jackson Pollock's paint-splattered masterpieces at the Guggenheim, browsed the hipster flea markets in Brooklyn, chatted up some cute locals at a Yankees baseball game in the Bronx and finally got a decent caffeine fix thanks to Ruby's, an Aussie cafe in Nolita which got the memo that coffee shouldn't taste like dishwater. They'd embraced the concrete jungle that was New York with open arms and neither of them felt like going back home to resume their everyday lives just yet.

'I've decided —' announced Nina, then stopped as she quickly skimmed an email from Simone to make sure it wasn't urgent.

'Decided what? What we're going to do tonight?'

'Well, there's that. I'm thinking Mexican at La Esquina — apparently their blood orange margaritas are to die for. Then we can come back here to check out the Boom Boom Room, the bar at the top of the hotel — Leighton Meester was there last week; I remember Layla showing me the photos. And there's Le Bain, the nightclub, if our feet have recovered enough for dancing by then,' Nina suggested. 'But what I've also decided is that seeing we've had such a great time here, the two of us should go on a girls' trip at least once a year. Just you and me, baby. I mean, it's not like any of the others will be able to go seeing I assume Steph is still saving up for IVF and the others will be too busy analysing the contents of their rugrat's nappies. Actually, I have a better idea — maybe we do one local and one international trip each year, like Byron and Barcelona or Melbourne and the Maldives?'

'Ooh, I love that idea! What about Tasmania and Thailand? Or Noosa and the Netherlands?' Heidi chimed in.

'There's no law saying the two places have to start with the same letter, they were just the first places that came to mind,' Nina said, laughing as Heidi pretended to look hurt. 'But sure, we can totally go to Tasmania, Thailand, Noosa and the Netherlands if you want! Sign me up!'

'It's a deal! To our future girls' trips!' Heidi toasted with her soft drink.

'Amen to that, my friend,' Nina replied, draining the last of her bottle with a flourish.

The Boom Boom Room was packed with what looked like a handpicked selection of New York's most beautiful people schmoozing, flirting, drinking and dancing. Nina felt like she was in a Justin Timberlake music video, especially when she clocked the incredible views from the floor-to-ceiling windows that overlooked Manhattan.

'Can you see any celebrities?' Heidi asked hopefully, her head swivelling in all directions as she tried to locate anyone who vaguely looked like they splashed around in the shallows of the fame game. 'After spotting that Victoria's Secret model with that guy from Maroon Five at La Esquina, I'm on a roll, I can tell.' Clutching at Nina's arm, she gestured to the white leather banquettes. 'I really need to sit down, my new shoes are killing me. Why do things that look so good have to hurt so bad? God obviously isn't a woman.'

'You can say that again. If you think you can manage to get to the bar to order some drinks, I'll do a lap to see if

I can spy any spare seats. I'll text you if I manage to pounce otherwise I'll see you back here.'

'Okay,' Heidi agreed. 'What do you want to drink?'

'I don't think I can stomach another margarita – they were delish but my lips are about to fall off from all the lime and salt. What about champagne?'

'Sure, why not? If I'm lucky, maybe I'll find a cute hedge fund manager at the bar who's happy to pay for it.' Heidi gingerly hobbled off towards the bar.

Nina weaved her way through the crowds, keeping her eyes peeled for any spare seats. Just as she was starting to think she'd have to drink her champagne sitting on the floor with Heidi, she spied two model-types at the far side of the room unfurling their outrageously long legs and picking up their Chanel perspex box bags. Doing her best NFL running back impression, she bulldozed her way through the wall of people, slinging the feathered Sass & Bide clutch she'd picked up at a sample sale onto the spare seats just as another crazy-tall clothes horse tried to claim them.

'Sorry, but I think you'll find these seats have my name written all over them,' Nina announced, shooting her rival a 'don't mess with me' look. She copped a glare as she sank down into the leather plushness, then the other girl flounced off.

'That was an impressive throw,' a voice next to her remarked.

Spinning around, Nina checked out her companions. Two guys were sitting at the other end of the table, with a bottle of Grey Goose between them. Both wearing dark suits without ties, they looked like they'd come straight from

Mr Big central casting. Except, Nina realised belatedly, for the distinct Australian accent.

'Don't tell me the only seats available in this place just happen to be next to two Aussie blokes,' she laughed. 'Small world, huh? Hi, I'm Nina.'

'Simon,' the older-looking guy said.

'I'm Nick,' said his drinking buddy. 'Yep, we're from Sydney. Pleasure to meet you, Nina. What brings you to New York?'

'Oh, I'm here for a few days with a girlfriend – we're staying at the hotel so thought we'd check out the bar. Actually, that reminds me – excuse me while I text her to let her know I scored us some seats.'

When Heidi finally arrived at the table, champagne bucket in one hand and her phone in the other, she looked like she was about to self-combust. 'You'll never guess who walked in when I was at the bar!' she announced dramatically as she plonked the bucket down on the table. Nina craned her neck, trying to surreptitiously spot any faces she would recognise from the pages of *Juice*, but the room was too crammed.

'You're right, I won't – who?'

'None other than your recent cover star, Hayley Polkadot! I told you I was on a roll tonight! She's decked out in this crazy dress with 3D goldfish stuck all over it and a matching orange wig. As soon as she came in with her entourage, they were taken straight to a separate area but it was definitely her. She's teeny-weeny! I tried to take some photos on my phone but they're really blurry, dammit. I couldn't see if she was holding hands with any of the guys she was with so I can't corroborate your source who said she's already hooking up with someone new even though she's only just split from Olly. God, imagine if he turned up too! That would make my life,' she declared. Sliding onto the banquette, Heidi became aware of Simon and Nick for the first time. 'Oh, I didn't realise we were sharing a table. Hi, I'm Heidi. Sorry for all the celebrity dribble, but let's face it, it's not every day you get to see famous people in the flesh, is it?' she said unapologetically.

'This is Nick and Simon,' Nina told her. 'They're from Sydney too, but from the look of those suits, I'm guessing you guys are in New York for work, not play?'

''Fraid so. My brother and I are here to talk to potential investors about some business ideas we have,' Simon explained. 'Don't worry, we won't bore you with the details. You look thirsty after all that excitement, allow me to pour your champagne,' he said gallantly. 'And you're more than welcome to have a Grey Goose chaser if you feel like it. We're drinking it on the rocks but the waitress also brought over a variety of mixers.' He gestured to the array of juices, sodas and garnishes at their end of the table.

Nina noticed he hadn't taken his eyes off Heidi since she'd shown up raving about Hayley Polkadot. Not that she could blame him – with her hair in a sleek blow-out and rocking a silver Marc Jacobs dress as well as some expertly-applied false lashes, Heidi looked the business. Pity that he had a hope in hell of getting anywhere with her – with his jet-black hair and slim build, Simon definitely wasn't Heidi's type. Not to mention he was also about a decade too old. 'Three strikes and you're out, buddy,' Nina thought. 'Shame, you seem like a nice guy.' But while chatting with his younger brother Nick, she detected definite flirt-alert signals coming from her friend as she and Simon engaged in animated conversation. 'She's probably just stringing him along for the hell of it,' Nina decided.

An hour later, Nina was ready to call it a night. Nick was a perfectly pleasant guy but she had exhausted all avenues of small talk with him as Heidi and Simon chewed each other's ears off. Now she couldn't stop thinking about the super-comfortable king-size bed in their room just a few floors below.

'Heids?' she said, giving her a nudge. 'Stick a fork in me, I'm done. Are you ready to make a move?'

Heidi laughed at something Simon said then looked at Nina as if she'd only just remembered she was there. 'Sorry, did you say something?'

'It's past my bedtime,' Nina said, fishing in her clutch for her key. 'Are you going to come back to the room with me or stay here?'

'Oh . . . um . . . I . . . I might stay here for a little bit longer. Simon, what are your plans? Don't tell me you have to be up early tomorrow morning or something hideous like that?'

'I don't, actually. One of the meetings we had arranged has been rescheduled so tomorrow is looking pretty cruisey.'

'Great! Well, there's still some bubbles left so it would be rude not to finish them, don't you think?' Heidi said enthusiastically. 'Nina, Nick and Simon are staying here too, so don't worry about me. I'll just take care of the rest of this champagne and then I'll see you back in the room, okay?'

Nina raised an amused eyebrow at her friend, knowing full well that Heidi wasn't staying for the champagne. While Simon wasn't her usual cup of tea, there was nothing wrong with sampling something from a different section of the man buffet. 'Sure, no worries. I'll probably be dead to the world when you get in, so try to keep the crashing around to a minimum. You know what I'm like when I don't get enough beauty sleep. Nice to meet you guys – best of luck with the rest of your meetings.'

'I'll escort you out; I told my wife I'd give her a call tonight to let her know how today's meetings went,' Nick said, getting up from the banquette as well.

It wasn't until they were almost at the exit that Nina realised she was missing her room key.

'Sorry, Nick, you go ahead – idiot here left her key at the table. I'll just go back and grab it. Really nice to meet you, good luck again.' She smiled and turned back the way they'd come. Through a gap in the crowd, she could see the credit card-sized key sitting on the banquette where she must have dropped it. She'd almost reached the table when she pulled up short.

'Well, well, well . . . looks like I'll be getting a new key from the reception desk. Wouldn't want to disturb the two lovebirds,' she thought with a grin as she spied Heidi and Simon pashing like teenagers, completely oblivious to everyone around them.

ten

As soon as she woke up, Nina had the distinct feeling something wasn't quite right. Rolling over, she rubbed her eyes then squinted at the side of the giant bed where Heidi was sleeping. Except she wasn't.

'Heids?' she called out groggily, thinking her friend must be in the bathroom, even as her brain belatedly told her that the sheets hadn't been disturbed. The only noise that answered her was the faint sound of a helicopter coming from somewhere outside the double-glazed windows. Pulling her phone off the iPod dock where it had been charging overnight, she checked to see if Heidi had sent her any messages. Nada. Zilch. Zip.

W R U? she quickly tapped out. *Still with the Aussie boy, I presume? Going to get brunch at the Diner on the corner of W14th and Ninth in half an hour, let me know if I should wait.* :)

After spending too long under the shower, slicking her hair back into a high ponytail and applying her usual slathering of multiple mascaras, Nina pulled on some loose black leather shorts and an oversized chambray shirt. Rolling up the sleeves, she shoved her feet into silver studded sandals before grabbing her Karen Walker cat's-eye sunglasses and her daffodil-yellow Alexander Wang bag. Checking her phone again in case she'd missed a call or message from Heidi, she bit her lip worriedly when the screen showed no love. It was noon already, and Heidi was usually bright-eyed and bushy-tailed by eight-thirty at the latest, badgering Nina to get up and start the day.

'I'm sure she's totally fine,' Nina told herself while zooming down to the ground floor in the pitch-black elevator, ignoring the trippy psychedelic visuals that played on the interior plasma screens. 'She's probably passed out after shagging Simon all night long or her phone is on silent or something. Nothing to stress about.' But as she sat down outside the cafe and ordered a cream cheese bagel and an Oreo Cookie milkshake, she couldn't stop the worst-case scenarios running through her head. Horrific things happened all the time, especially in a big city like New York – just look at how many spin-offs of *Law and Order* they'd had to create to cover them all! Maybe Heidi and Simon had gone somewhere after the Boom Boom Room and they'd been mugged? Or they'd been in a taxi accident and were lying in hospital somewhere? 'Did Heidi get travel insurance?' she wondered. 'I can't remember if she said she'd organised it or not . . . Did I even ask her? That'll be the last thing she needs: a whopping great big medical bill from a

New York hospital to pay off . . . Bugger it, I'm just going to call her to see if she answers. I don't care if she's still asleep or is going for round six with Simon.'

Logging on to the cafe's wifi, she booted up her Skype app. But after more than twenty rings, she had to admit defeat. 'I guess when I get back to the hotel I could ask the reception desk to put me through to Simon's room to see if they're there . . . except I don't know his surname,' she realised. 'And going by the achingly cool hipster vibe of the guy who checked me in, something tells me they're not going to help me by offering to trawl through their guest names to see how many Simons they have staying at the moment.' Sighing anxiously, she texted Heidi again asking her to let her know that she wasn't lying in a gutter – this time there were no smiley faces.

Feeling sick from a combination of too much sugar-laden lactose and worry about her friend, Nina motioned for the bill. As she waited, she stared mindlessly over the road at the traffic lights in front of Dos Caminos, the Mexican restaurant they'd hit up on their first night in New York, when they'd been too jetlagged to go anywhere further. Watching the crowd of people waiting to navigate the Meatpacking District's tricky cobblestones and speed-freak taxi drivers, Nina couldn't help smiling at a couple who were obviously completely loved up. He was standing behind her, head bent down to whisper in her ear as he simultaneously rubbed her shoulders. Her head was tipped back, totally engrossed in what he was saying, with an ecstatic smile plastered across her face. They looked like they should have been in a Tiffany & Co advertising campaign.

'That used to be me and Jeremy back in the day,' Nina thought sadly, feeling a pang for her ex even though she knew their time together was well and truly over. She'd been shaking her single tail feathers since landing in New York, getting her party pash well and truly on with various guys while out and about, but it was just a bit of fun. If she was honest with herself, she wasn't ready for another relationship right now, but that didn't mean she couldn't appreciate a cute couple when she saw them. As the breeze picked up, the guy brushed the girl's hair back off her face in a gesture that was both intimate and innocent; even from across the road, Nina could see her blush as she . . . 'Wait!' Nina's brain suddenly screamed, kicking into gear despite its sugar coma. The girl had red hair. And she was wearing Ray-Ban aviators, just like Heidi's. 'Oh, come on, this is New York! There would be plenty of redheads who rock aviators, it doesn't automatically mean it's her!' Nina chastised herself. Standing up to get a better look as the couple started kissing, Nina noticed that the guy had dark hair, just like Simon. Squinting furiously, she mentally urged the crowd in front of them to move so she could see what the girl was wearing. As if on cue, the traffic lights turned red and the crowd streamed around the couple, who were still locked at the lips, completely oblivious to the fact that the world was still turning, the sun still shining, the birds still chirping. As she copped an eyeful of silver, Nina threw a twenty-dollar note on the table and bolted across the street.

'Heidi! Heidi! Heidiiiiiiiiiiiiiiiiiiiiiii!' she yelped, doing battle with the pedestrians advancing in the opposite direction. Panting slightly as she reached the other side, she paused, thinking for a moment that she'd imagined it all, before spotting the back of Heidi's dress making its way along West 14th Street. Sprinting after the couple, she practically crash-tackled her friend to the ground outside the Alexander McQueen store.

'Oh! Nina! What are you doing here?' Heidi exclaimed.

Gulping in some oxygen, Nina managed to refrain from throwing her arms around her best friend in relief and instead started to babble incoherently. 'Heidi . . . thought you were dead . . . called and texted you . . . massive hospital bill . . . no travel insurance . . .'

'Wait, you have a massive hospital bill and no travel insurance?' Simon stepped forward, looking concerned, while his arm tightened around Heidi's waist.

Nina grinned weakly. 'No, not me,' she panted, sucking in more air and reminding herself to sign up for a personal trainer when she got back to Sydney. 'Heidi. At least, that's what I was afraid of. You know, when I woke up and she wasn't there, and then she didn't reply to my calls or texts. So I convinced myself you'd both been mugged or had been in an accident and were lying in a hospital somewhere which would mean a huge medical bill and then I couldn't remember if Heidi had organised insurance or not . . . So yeah, I think

I overreacted a bit,' she admitted, realising she was well on her way to giving drama queens a bad name.

'My phone battery died so I haven't got your calls or texts,' Heidi explained, blushing as Nina looked pointedly at her, both of them knowing full well that she could easily have charged her phone on the hotel's iPod dock in Simon's room, if she hadn't had other things on her mind. 'Sorry, honey, I didn't mean to worry you. I guess I just didn't think. Anyway, as you can see, I'm fine! Apart from the fact I'm wearing the same clothes as last night,' she laughed. 'Simon took me for brunch at Pastis and we were just having a little wander around before heading back to the hotel.'

'Sure. Okay. Pastis, huh? Nice,' Nina commented as she fell into step with the two of them, trying not to be annoyed at her friend's thoughtlessness. 'So today, I thought we could take a stroll along the High Line seeing we haven't ticked that off the list yet. That will take us up to West 30th and then we could head over to the Empire State building. What do you reckon?'

'Oh . . . um,' Heidi said awkwardly, glancing quickly at Simon. 'Actually, I've kind of already organised to do something with Simon; I didn't think we had any concrete plans for today. Seeing he doesn't have any meetings until tomorrow afternoon, he asked if I wanted to go on an overnight trip to the Hamptons. I'd mentioned to him that I wanted to go there last night. Isn't that sweet? The concierge at the hotel is already organising it,' she explained apologetically.

Nina couldn't believe what she was hearing. If it wasn't bad enough that Heidi hadn't bothered to let her know where she was, she was now ditching her. Less than twenty-four hours before, they'd been planning to make their girls' trips a regular thing and now Heidi was blowing her off for a random hook-up! Although to be fair, it was a hook-up who had taken her for breakfast at Pastis and was now whisking her off for a luxury sleepover in the Hamptons, rather than Heidi's usual brainless, penniless, immature hook-ups who always ended up scabbing money from her — but that wasn't the point. This was supposed to be a girls' trip, dammit! She could catch up with Simon when she got back to Sydney if she really wanted to — it wasn't like they lived on opposite ends of the world and this was the last time they'd ever see each other! Plus he wasn't even her type!

Nina scowled, about to ask for a private word so she could blast Heidi to kingdom come about her lack of loyalty and blatant disregard of the most basic friendship rules, then remembered how happy Heidi had looked at the traffic lights when she'd spotted her and Simon across the road. Maybe she should cut her some slack just this once? It wouldn't kill her to navigate Manhattan by herself for a day or two. She could take the subway out to Long Island to go to PS1, the experiential MoMA offshoot that Heidi hadn't been interested in seeing. And then there were those killer Jimmy Choos she'd seen in Bergdorf's Shoe Salon on their second day which had been calling her name ever since. After all, a girl should spend her annual bonus on something a bit frivolous, right? And there was no denying her Ben & Jerry's levels were dangerously low . . .

'Right. Well, that sounds lovely,' Nina enthused, successfully keeping the hurt out of her voice. 'You two have fun – can't wait to hear all about the Hamptons when you get back! I'll head up to the High Line now and leave you to it. Oh, and Heids? Don't forget to charge your phone this time, okay? And you'd better ask the concierge if they sell bikinis in the gift shop.'

Strolling along the elevated walkway that threaded through the lower west side of Manhattan, Nina tried to shake off the nagging sense that she'd just been dumped by counting her blessings. She was in New York! The sun was shining! She was about to buy an amazing pair of shoes! She loved her job! Her best friend wasn't lying in hospital after having a terrible accident! Life was great! 'So why do I feel like chopped liver?' she wondered, her eyes welling with tears behind her sunglasses despite her best intentions. As she hunted through her bag for a tissue to stop her mascara from running, her phone started to ring. 'It'll be Heidi calling to apologise, for sure,' Nina thought with a watery smile. But it wasn't Heidi – it was a blocked number. Tempted to ignore it, Nina almost hit reject before realising it could be her bank calling to say they'd frozen her credit card due to 'suspicious overseas activity', when in fact it was just her being a shopping ninja in SoHo the day before.

'Hello?' she said brusquely, waiting for the bank's overseas call centre to come on the line. Instead, she heard the panicky voice of Simone, her deputy editor.

'Nina? It's Simone. I'm so sorry to call you on your holiday but I didn't want to wait till you were back in the office next week.'

'Hi, Sim, what's up? It's not that bloody Marnie again, is it? I thought I got all that sorted before I left.' Nina plonked herself down on one of the benches that looked out over the Hudson River.

'No, no, that's fine. The Tully cover is selling well so far actually, according to the sales data I got from the circulation department. Are you okay? You sound a bit wobbly.'

'I'm fine, it's probably just some interference on the line,' Nina sniffed, finally locating the ratty tissue she'd been chasing around the bottom of her bag. 'So, what's so urgent? Hit me.'

'It's not good, I'm afraid. I just had a call from our lawyers. They've received notice of a writ that's been lodged in the Supreme Court. Brace yourself – Hayley Polkadot is suing *Juice* for defamation. She says our cover story about her cheating on Olly before they officially broke up caused emotional distress, humiliation and has damaged her reputation. But that's not all . . .' Nina heard Simone take a deep breath. 'She wants ten million dollars in damages.'

eleven

Striding into the boardroom to meet with *Juice*'s lawyers, Nina prayed to the Touche Éclat gods that she didn't look as hideous as she felt. The flight home had been pure hell, thanks to a couple who had used their frequent flyer points to upgrade themselves and their twin toddlers to premium economy on the fourteen-hour Los Angeles to Sydney leg. The kids had run riot while their parents did their best to completely ignore the carnage as they drank their way through the extensive bar offerings. It hadn't helped Nina's nerves, which were already pulled tighter than Nicole Kidman's face thanks to news of the lawsuit. She also wasn't in the best of moods given Heidi had defected to Simon's room for the remainder of their trip after returning from the Hamptons, only hanging out with Nina when he was busy with meetings. She was well and truly immersed in the love bubble and although Nina was happy for her, she didn't really appreciate being discarded like last season's Louis Vuitton chequerboard print.

'Gentlemen.' Nina nodded at Malcolm and Lewis, the two legal eagles sitting at the table, along with Eric, *Juice*'s publisher. 'Apologies in advance if I'm a bit all over the place, but I've literally just flown in from New York. Where, I might add, in a rather ironic twist I spent some time in the same bar as our friend Hayley Polkadot the night before she decided to sue our arses to high heaven. Now, on a scale of one to ten, with ten being up there with the closure of the UK's *News of the World* due to the phone-hacking scandal, how bad are we talking?'

'Well . . .' Malcolm cleared his throat, obviously stalling for time. 'It's not the best-case scenario due to the amount of monetary compensation they're seeking, but it's also not the worst. It depends on your sources and how watertight they are. As you know, this isn't the first time *Juice* has been hit with a lawsuit from a celebrity and I'm sure it won't be the last. It's the nature of being a celebrity gossip magazine. Usually we can fob them off with an apology, print a retraction in the next issue and it all goes away quietly. That's the way we like it. The problem with this one is that they've gone straight for the jugular. They're not interested in a quiet apology or letting it slide; it seems they've decided to make an example of us, which is why they've gone directly to the Supreme Court rather than broaching it with us first. I suspect it's because the plaintiff has so many lucrative endorsement deals with brands that make a lot of money from being seen as family-friendly. Her team don't want your story to endanger these deals by making the brands think she's a, um, woman of loose morals, shall we say. So they just need to prove that *Juice*'s allegations could have a negative effect on one or two of her business interests to the tune of a few million each, plus throw in a couple of extra million for "emotional distress" and "humiliation", and bingo! You're looking at ten big ones.'

Nina swallowed hard. This was not good. She decided to go on the offensive. 'Can I just point out that we had this story cleared by you guys before we sent it to print? I seem to remember it came back with a "low risk" assessment. I'm sorry, but I don't consider being hit with a multi-million-dollar lawsuit as low risk,' she said, her anger rising. 'And let's not forget the negative effect it could have on the *Juice* brand – I checked the Australian entertainment blogs on the way here from the airport and every single one of them has this lawsuit as their top story. It won't be long until it's splashed all over the international sites. You know what the schadenfreude is like in this industry – our competitors will be loving it something sick! But that's not the worst thing – our readers will think we're just the same as every other gossip rag, making up stories based around absolutely nothing. You know how important accountability is when it comes to our audience.'

'Nina, settle down. I know you're tired and upset, but these guys are here to help,' Eric said mildly. 'They said it was "low risk", not "no risk". They weren't to know that Hayley Polkadot's team would decide to use us as a whipping boy. Now, let's talk about your sources. Where did this story come from?'

'My celebrity news editor, Meg. She had a source in London who was happy to go on the record about it.'

'Would that source be Jimmy Jones?' asked Lewis, while checking his notes.

'I believe so, yes,' Nina confirmed.

'In the affidavit submitted by the plaintiff, she maintains she doesn't know anyone by that name so he couldn't possibly have inside knowledge of the reasons behind her marriage breakdown.'

'Given it came from London, I'm pretty sure Meg's source was from the ex-husband's camp, not Mademoiselle Polkadot's,' Nina pointed out. 'So it's fair to say that while she may not have heard of him, it doesn't mean he doesn't exist. He could be a childhood friend of Olly's who she never met – don't forget they weren't together for all that long, and even when they were, they didn't spend a huge amount of time in the same country. Or perhaps Mr Jones is a random who Olly met in a pub one night when he'd decided to drown his sorrows and, in his inebriated state, he confessed all those details to him?'

'Both of these scenarios may well be valid, but what's important is that this Jimmy Jones does actually exist and can prove that he has this intimate knowledge of Miss Polkadot's relationship with Mr Box and the details of her alleged affair before they'd officially agreed to end the marriage,' Malcolm explained.

'Right. So shall I get Meg up here then?' Nina asked, reaching for the phone on the table.

'Please,' Lewis nodded.

Two minutes later, Meg appeared at the door, her face turning a whiter shade of polar bear when she saw all the corporate suits in the room.

'Come in, Meg, it's okay. Here, sit down – there's nothing to worry about,' Nina assured her, picking up on the distinct smell of eau de petrified wafting from her news editor. 'It's just that we're having some trouble with the Hayley Polkadot cover story we ran the other week so our legal team are trying to get their heads around how we got our hands on the story. This "Jimmy Jones" – is that the name of your source?'

Meg looked around the table then down at her hands. 'No, not really,' she whispered.

'What do you mean, not really? Is it a pseudonym? Or –' Nina paused, not wanting to go down that road but knowing she had to '– did you make the story up?'

'Of course I didn't make it up!' Meg said indignantly. 'I would never do that! We don't make stuff up at *Juice*, that's why I like working here. If I wanted to work in celebrity make-believe, I'd go back to *Fierce*. That's all they do there – sit around and make up stories about celebrities based solely on paparazzi photos. They don't care if it's true or not, as long as it sells magazines,' she said disparagingly.

'Okay, so you didn't make it up. So who is this Jimmy Jones then?' Nina probed. 'Because you said your source was happy to go on the record but Hayley Polkadot swears she's never heard of him, and she's insisting we've fabricated the whole story. Given you said your source was in London, I'm guessing he knows Olly?'

'Yes, he knows Olly. But Jimmy Jones isn't his real name. I changed it in the story because she . . . I mean he . . . asked me to after I'd pitched the story. Sorry — I meant to tell you but I forgot.'

'Well, it's not ideal but as far as I'm aware, that's not a crime, is it?' Nina asked the lawyers, resisting the urge to throttle her staff member. Of all the times for Meg to forget to tell her that a source had changed their mind about going on the record, it had to be when they were up shit creek without a paddle.

'We can work around it,' Malcolm said tentatively, 'especially if you can give us their actual name. Obviously it will remain confidential, but we need it to prove that we didn't fabricate the story.'

'I . . . I . . . I can't,' Meg stuttered. 'I promised them I wouldn't tell.' She looked at Nina for help, but found nothing. 'Do I have to?' she whined like a five-year-old.

Nina's patience evaporated. 'Meg, for Christ's sake! It's not like your source is giving Julian Assange a run for his money and has been leaking international security secrets that put people's lives in danger! If we're going to fight this lawsuit, we need the goddamn name otherwise we're going to get sued for ten million dollars. That's right — ten . . . million . . . dollars . . .' she repeated slowly as Meg's eyes widened. 'I'm sure you don't need me to tell you that we don't exactly have that kind of money lying around in spare change! This isn't some salacious gossip story you're writing about for the magazine – this is actually happening to us and we need to stop it. It is bigger than you, it is bigger than Jimmy Jones – whoever he or she really is – and it is bigger than whatever promise you made, so I suggest you stop covering for your source and spill.'

'Okay, okay . . . I'm sorry,' Meg apologised. 'I was just trying to do the right thing,' she explained. Taking a deep breath, she looked at the lawyers. 'Jimmy Jones is a pseudonym for my friend Josie Gibbs. I met her a few years ago when I worked in London. She's a celebrity publicist –' she hesitated, then finished in a rush '– and one of her clients is Olly Box.'

Nina's mouth dropped open as the lawyers hurriedly scrawled notes. 'Let me get this straight – Olly Box's publicist not only leaked the news that he and Hayley were about to announce their divorce but she also planted the story that her client's wife had already hooked up with someone else while he was begging her to have a baby? Why would she do that when it makes Olly look like a bit of an idiot?'

'I guess because Olly told her to,' Meg shrugged. 'Maybe he wanted to take control of the situation before Hayley's camp started spreading some rumours of their own? Maybe he was pissed off at her for not wanting to settle down and have a family? Maybe he wanted the public's sympathy on his side? Stuff like this happens all the time – although it's usually the publicist planting stories about their own client rather than their soon-to-be ex-partner. But you know, it's Hollywood – it doesn't have to make sense.'

'You're right, you're right,' Nina admitted wearily. 'Okay, where to from here?' she asked, looking at the suits across the table.

'Leave it with us – we'll submit a response in the next day or so. There are no guarantees, but once we let them know that the source came from her estranged husband's camp and therefore we believed in good faith that the story was true, I suspect Miss Polkadot's legal team will stop pointing the finger at us and go to war on him, albeit in a much more private way. I'd say their divorce lawyers are going to have one hell of a fight on their hands.'

Nina stood and shook hands with Malcolm and Lewis as they left the room. She breathed a sigh of relief. They weren't out of the defamation woods yet but it was looking a damn sight better than it had half an hour earlier. She was following Meg out the door, already thinking about the cover for next week's issue, when Eric asked if she had a minute.

'Sure. Meg, I'll see you back in the office. What's up?' she said, mentally crossing her fingers and hoping she wasn't in for a lecture about making sure her staff were on top of the finer points of the law when it came to celebrity journalism. To be fair, it wasn't really Eric's style to stick his nose into the day-to-day management of her staff – as her publisher, he approved the covers each week, attended the monthly management meetings and made sure she kept a tight rein on her budgets, but unless she needed him in a crisis or wanted to spend big bickies on a celebrity exclusive, he pretty much left her to it so he could concentrate on his problem child titles, which needed more of his attention.

'First, how was New York?' he enquired.

'Oh, it was . . . good,' Nina replied, trying not to think how it would have been better if her best friend hadn't been sucked into the Simon vortex. At least she could console herself with the pairs of sex-on-a-stick heels she'd bought in an effort to cheer herself up, even if her credit card was now once again straining at the seams. She might have gone a little overboard in Bergdorf's, but at least Jimmy Choo, Christian Louboutin and Manolo Blahnik wanted to hang out with her, even if Heidi hadn't.

'Great, I'm glad you had a bit of a break, because we have a busy few months ahead of us!'

'Oh God, don't tell me it's time for business plans again,' Nina moaned, grimacing. There was a whole business back-end to every magazine which meant that each year the marketing, advertising and editorial departments had to brainstorm new ideas and, most importantly, new business opportunities to keep moving the brands forward. They then had to present these ideas to the publisher, sales director and finance controller. It was the kind of admin Nina hated, not only because it usually involved PowerPoint, but also because her best editorial ideas usually came to her at random times when she was in the shower or waiting in line for her morning skim flat white – not when she had the big cheeses breathing down her neck.

'Not quite, but you should start thinking about it,' Eric warned. 'I was actually referring to something else which we're all really excited about – a brand extension, if you like. I think it's going to be great for the magazine and it's a testament to how well the title is regarded that they approached us rather than another magazine. It may involve a little pain in the short term, but I think the long-term gain will be more than worth it. And you never know, it could lead to bigger things for you and your team.'

Nina looked at her publisher warily. 'Excuse my ignorance, Eric, but what exactly are you talking about?'

'Sorry, I'm getting ahead of myself, aren't I? A couple of months ago, a TV production company approached us about filming a fly-on-the-wall series about *Juice* – how the magazine is made, the personalities behind it, the glamour of the celebrity photo shoots contrasted with the blood, sweat and tears you guys put in week in, week out . . . that sort of thing,' he explained. 'They showed us some mock footage and said they already had a few sponsors interested, so I spoke to the managing director and after some backwards and forwards, it got the green light just last week. *Freshly Squeezed Juice* will be a prime-time show on Channel Eight, starting in a couple of months. Ms Morey, you're going to be a TV star!'

'Tell me you're kidding,' Nina said bluntly. 'It's not April Fool's Day, is it?' Then she remembered the conversation she'd had with Gracie just before her New York trip. Dread seeped through every bone of her body. She was an editor, not an actor! Her team were writers and designers, not reality TV stars! She was okay with going on TV to talk about celebrity trends or Oscars gossip if it was one of the vacuous morning programs – seeing as most of their viewers were still half asleep – but a prime-time reality TV show? 'Kill me now,' she thought.

'No, I'm not kidding. Trust me, it's going to be great!' Eric enthused, ignoring Nina's death stare. 'Think of the exposure – not only will our current readers be able to see what goes on behind the scenes, making them feel part of the brand, but we'll be sure to attract new readers who may not have picked up *Juice* or reel in lapsed readers who no longer buy it. It's a brilliant opportunity that any editor would kill for!'

'Not this editor,' Nina thought grimly. Aloud she said, 'Eric, how are we going to get the magazine to the printers on time each week when there'll be a camera crew traipsing in and out of the office, breathing down our necks, wanting us to reshoot scenes or create completely new content to increase the drama?' she demanded. 'We both know how these reality shows work – most of the scenes are completely fabricated and there's always a villain lurking somewhere so the viewers have someone to hate. Who's going to be that villain – me? I get that it's a good marketing opportunity, but as the editor, my main priority is the magazine and making it the best it can be every week, not faffing around in front of cameras while pretending to scream at my staff. I'm not Miranda Priestly and I refuse to pretend I am!'

'You did a pretty good impression just before when you were breathing fire at your news editor,' Eric pointed out.

'That was different! That wasn't for entertainment purposes – that was because we had our balls on the line to the tune of ten million dollars and she needed to realise what a serious situation it was!' Nina protested.

'Settle down, I was only joking. Look, we've raised these concerns with Channel Eight and the production company and they've assured us that it won't be artificial drama – they really want to show how the magazine comes together. Obviously they're not going to turn the cameras off if something creates a bit of tension while they're filming, but you're not expected to morph into a raving bitch or fire your assistant on film because she turns up to work wearing the same dress as you. Just be yourself. Don't worry – the people of Australia are going to love you.'

'So I don't get a choice in the matter? You've gone ahead and signed the deal without even consulting me or my team, even though we're the ones who will have to deal with the camera crew, the producers and the TV critics – not to mention copping abuse from the public if they hate it and being humiliated when no one watches the show because it's boring and Channel Eight kills it after one week? Thanks for getting our buy-in, Eric, it's much appreciated.'

Her publisher at least had the grace to look embarrassed. 'Well, we're hoping it will last more than a week, Nina,' he said reproachfully. 'It starts off as a ten-part series with the option to extend and keep filming another ten episodes if the ratings are good; the episodes will be half an hour long. The marketing team are already working on a social media campaign to create some buzz around it and an official press release will be sent out tomorrow.'

Nina sighed. She knew plenty of people would kill to be on a reality TV show, but she wasn't one of them. Even though she was convinced it was a bad idea, she was just going to have to suck it up.

'So when does filming start?' she asked in a defeated tone.

'In a few weeks – I'll arrange for the producers to come in and meet the team beforehand and you can give them a rundown of how everything works so they can look at ways to minimise interruptions to the workflow. If you could also prepare a list of what shoots and exclusives your team are working on so they can plan some of the episodes in advance, that would really help.'

'Fine. Let me know when it's locked in. I guess I'll go and break the news to my team that they'll soon be moonlighting as reality TV stars. Instead of covering the Logies, they might actually win a Logie,' she tried to joke.

'Exactly! I have every confidence that *Freshly Squeezed Juice* will be a raging success. How could it not when you're leading the charge?! Come on, Nina, you don't have to like it but you need to get behind it. Okay?'

'Okay,' she agreed with a fake smile.

'Great, I'll see you later,' he said, hurrying out before she could change her mind.

When the boardroom door closed behind him, Nina slumped against the table and, without warning, burst into tears.

twelve

'Would anyone like some more pink lemonade? How about a glass of prosecco? We're about to start the games, so get excited!'

Nina grabbed a plastic champagne flute and shoved it in front of Natalie as she made her way around the combined baby shower for Lily, Daniela and Evie. There was no way in hell she'd be able to get through any games without the lubrication of alcohol. 'Please don't let them play the one where you have to guess what's in the dirty nappy,' she begged the universe.

'Okay, ladies, let's get this baby shower on the road!' Natalie announced gleefully once she'd filled up all the glasses. 'Everyone move inside and grab a seat, please!'

'Do you get the impression she's enjoying this a bit too much?' Nina whispered to Heidi as she watched Natalie produce necklaces made of multiple dummies and, with the gravitas of someone presenting the Nobel Peace Prize, hung them around the necks of the three pregnant women who were sitting in pride of place in the living room.

'Sorry, say that again?' Heidi whispered, lingering on the outside deck with Nina as she busily texted.

'You'd better put that away before we go inside in case the Baby Shower Bandit confiscates it,' Nina warned.

'I know, I just need to let Simon know what time to pick me up. After this finishes, he's taking me to Wolgan Valley for the weekend.'

'Wolgan Valley? That plush resort near the Blue Mountains where Mischa Barton stayed when she was in Australia for the Melbourne Cup? Nice work!' Nina said enviously.

'I know, right? He's been in Dubai for the past week and said he missed me so much, he wants me all to himself,' Heidi said dreamily.

'Oh bless . . . excuse me while I choke on my own vomit,' Nina muttered sarkily. She looked down at the limited-edition Missoni-patterned Havaianas that had been delivered to her office that week, then took a deep breath and blurted out, 'So this thing with you and Simon – it's not just a New York fling then? It's actually for real?'

'Why wouldn't it be for real?' Heidi asked, looking surprised.

'Uhhh . . . I don't know . . . I guess I hadn't really thought about it as being . . . you know . . . a proper thing,' Nina tried to explain, avoiding Heidi's gaze. 'I know it's been full-on-dot-com ever since that night at the Boom Boom Room, but

I wasn't sure if it would continue once you were both back in the real world. Don't take this the wrong way, but he's not exactly your usual type, so I figured it might not translate back home.' She shrugged.

'Well, we've been together for a month now and it's translated just fine so far,' Heidi said tightly.

'Heids, settle down – I'm not having a go; I just don't want to see you get hurt,' Nina said, hurriedly repeating one of the biggest clichés in the friendship book as she recognised the pissed-off look on her friend's face. 'If things are great, that's great! I'm happy if you're happy!'

Heidi rolled her eyes. 'Look, I get what you're saying, but does it really matter if Simon isn't my usual type? Maybe that's a good thing! Pretty boys with big muscles and empty wallets aren't exactly the most eligible contenders when it comes to the husband hunt, are they?'

'Is that what this is? A husband hunt?' Nina looked at Heidi incredulously.

'No! I didn't mean it like that! It's not like I want to get married tomorrow or anything, I'm just saying that we're getting to the age where we need to start thinking about stuff like that. I mean, look around you – Nat's already hitched with a kid, Lily's married and about to become a mum any minute, Evie and Daniela are due to join her in Nappy Valley soon afterwards, and Bec will be there too before you know it. It's not like we're in high school anymore, you know?'

'It's not a race, Heids! Just because everyone else is doing it doesn't mean we have to,' Nina pointed out. 'There's no rule saying this has to happen at this time and that has to happen at that time. If everyone's life moved at the same pace, it would be boring. It's bad enough now with everyone deciding to pop out babies at the same time! And if you settle down with Simon and become a Stepford wife, who's going to go out on the lash with me?' she joked, trying to ignore the fear that was snaking its way around her heart.

'Nina, for God's sake! It's not always all about you and what you want!' Heidi snapped. 'We can't keep pretending we're twenty-one forever. Like it or not, some things have to change. We don't all have amazing jobs that involve hanging out in a VIP box at the ARIAs or going to movie premieres and swanky bar openings! I think it's great that you absolutely love your job and I know you've got your fuck buddy on speed dial and aren't interested in settling down after being with Jeremy for so long, but not everyone is in your shoes. The way you've been acting towards Lily, Bec, Evie and Daniela has been pretty pathetic, to be honest. I mean, seriously – someone needs to call you a waaaahbulance. It's the first time you've seen them since your dummy spit at The Bathers' Pavilion and you've barely spoken to them. And Bec says you didn't apologise to her like you said you did, which is unacceptable. If you don't want to pull your head out of the sand and accept that people are moving on with their lives, that's your problem, but you can't expect things to stay the same just because you want them to!'

Nina stared at Heidi, stunned by the venom in her tone. Her eyes started to sting and her throat closed up; she knew she had to escape before she lost it entirely. 'I thought you were on my side?' she managed to choke out, before bolting inside. 'Back in a sec,' she mouthed to Natalie, who was shooting her a stink-eyed glare after realising Nina hadn't been partaking in the baby shower fun. As she headed for the bathroom, she caught a glimpse of the girls handing around disposable nappies filled with different brown-coloured substances and laughing hysterically as they took turns smelling them. She shuddered.

Waiting outside the closed door of the bathroom, Nina dabbed at her watery eyes, being careful not to ruin the subtle flick of liquid eyeliner she'd applied earlier that morning. She had no idea what was up with Heidi, but she was seriously coming up short in the friendship stakes right now. It was bad enough that she'd abandoned Nina for the last part of their New York trip, but now she was having a go at her for being selfish! Of course, if Nina was brutally honest with herself, she knew she hadn't been behaving in the most mature manner, but it was only because she was scared of losing her friends so soon after she'd found them. The girls were the only proper friends she had in Sydney; they had forced her to make room in her life for other things besides work and provided her with an opportunity to vent rather than bottling everything up inside – although admittedly these days her rants were mostly to Heidi about how all the others had become obsessed with procreating and weren't much fun anymore. After all, no one liked change unless they were the ones instigating it. But why was Heidi suddenly turning on her when she'd been right there with her, rolling her eyes at all the baby talk they'd had to put up with every time they saw the other girls?

Wishing she'd thought to grab her bag from the living room so she could check for any eyeliner damage, Nina listened for the toilet to flush. 'God, why do some women take so long to pee?' she wondered as still no sound had eventuated after a good ten minutes. The last thing she needed was for Heidi to decide she had to use the bathroom too – talk about awkward. 'Maybe it's actually empty – that would be just my luck,' she thought, knocking gently on the door.

'Just a minute!' Steph called out. Nina had never been so glad to hear her voice – at least there was one other person at the baby shower who would be happy to steer clear of talking about anything baby-related and who wouldn't give her a lecture about not wanting to accept that the others were moving on with their lives.

'No problem, just wasn't sure if anyone was actually in there,' Nina replied, hearing the water running as Steph finished up.

'Hey, lovebug, how are you?' her friend asked as she emerged from the bathroom, adjusting the cuffs of the pristine white shirt she'd tucked into Ksubi denim cut-offs, secured with a skinny neon yellow leather belt. With her long brunette hair that was partially shaved on one side, Rihanna-style, Steph always looked effortlessly cool, no matter what she was wearing – it was a side effect of being a freelance fashion editor who spent her days shooting lucrative advertising campaigns for brands as diverse as Rebel Sport and Romance Was Born.

'All good with me, honeybunch,' Nina lied. 'I might need your help soon actually – you've done a bit of TV styling, right?'

'Oh God, not for a long time, but yeah, I've done a bit – why? Do you have a few appearances coming up?'

'You could say that,' Nina said grimly. 'Let me go to the loo and then I'll tell you all about the reality TV career that I've been signed up for without any say in the matter.'

'Oh wow, are you serious? This sounds like it needs to be washed down with a couple of glasses of prosecco!' Steph winked.

'You can say that again – give me two minutes, I'll see you out there. Hopefully they've finished with the dirty nappy game and moved on to something a little less revolting,' Nina sniped, closing the bathroom behind her.

Checking her make-up in the mirror, she snaffled a cotton bud from the jar on the windowsill next to the his'n'hers razors and quickly mopped up some stray mascara that had bled underneath her eyes. 'Don't let Heidi get to you,' she told her reflection silently. 'She's just retaliating after I dared to question the state of affairs with the guy she barely knows but who apparently has "husband material" plastered on his forehead. Go back out there, have a chat to Steph, get her advice on what not to wear on TV, then get the hell out of here as soon as possible. That's the plan.'

She chucked the cotton bud towards the bin but missed by a mile. Sticking her hand underneath the bathroom cabinet to retrieve it, she pulled out a wad of tissues as well as the runaway cotton bud. 'Someone else has a crappy aim as well, it seems,' she muttered. About to throw it all in the bin, Nina was surprised to see the tissues were smeared with quite a lot of blood – fresh, bright red blood that hadn't had a chance to dry yet.

'That's weird,' she thought, getting rid of it all and washing her hands thoroughly.

Making her way back to the living room, she was relieved to see Steph standing outside of the baby-crazy circle, holding two glasses of bubbles. Heidi was now seated with the others, making a note of the presents Lily was opening so she knew who to send thank-you cards to afterwards.

'So tell me all about this TV thing!' Steph demanded. 'Who, what, why, when?'

'It's a reality TV show about the magazine,' Nina explained, raising her voice to be heard over the cacophony of 'ooohs' and 'aaahs' and high-pitched squeals of 'Isn't that just adorable?!' every time Lily, Daniela or Evie opened a parcel to reveal yet another mini-sized outfit from Bonds or Seed. 'There's a camera crew moving into the office on Monday to start filming, which is going to be hell, but seeing I have no choice in the matter, I can at least make sure I look good, right?'

'That's super-exciting! Okay, so what you need to remember is that TV doesn't like stripes – they strobe on screen. Thick ones are okay if you really want to go there but steer totally clear of thin. Actually, small patterns in general aren't great; it's best to stick with block colours if possible. And while black helps with the extra kilos the cameras so kindly pack on, it's boring for the viewer. Repeat after me: bright, block colours are your new best friend.'

'Bright, block colours are my new best friend,' Nina dutifully repeated, washing the words down with a mouthful of prosecco.

'Also, they'll probably put a microphone on you so you can roam around the office without the sound guy having to follow you around, so separates are also good because they can clip the mike pack to the back of your skirt or trousers. If you wear a dress, it'll have to clip onto the back of your bra or underwear, which can get annoying because it's quite heavy. Or, if you're not wearing a bra, they'll give you one of those Velcro straps that wrap around your upper thigh – it's like a sort of microphone garter. They're not particularly comfortable and they can ruin the line of a dress if it's fitted, so try to avoid at all costs.'

'Okay, separates are good, braless is bad,' Nina summed up. 'Maybe I should ask the executive producer if there's any room in the budget to pay you to be my stylist,' she mused.

As the rest of the group started discussing what to do for Bec's baby shower, Nina caught a faint glimpse of hopelessness in her friend's eyes. She hurriedly tried to think of something that would help take Steph's mind off being surrounded by four friends who had the one thing she desperately wanted. 'Oh my God, I haven't told you about my New York shoe haul yet, have I?' Nina exclaimed. 'You'll die when you see the Louboutins I brought home; I want to lick them every time I look at them!' She squeezed her friend's forearm in excitement, absently wondering why Steph was yet again wearing long sleeves when it was unbearably humid outside. 'Oh, sorry, did I hurt you?' she asked, as Steph flinched and clapped her hand over the area where Nina had grabbed her.

'No, no, it's fine,' Steph said through gritted teeth. 'Tell me about the Loubs . . .'

Halfway through her description of the neon red pointy studded Pigalle heels that were currently the love of her life, Nina was cut off by an ear-splitting shriek.

'My waters! My waters! I think my waters just broke!' Lily cried, looking shell-shocked. 'Someone call Jake and tell him Little Lake is on the way! Girls, I think I'm about to become a mum! Oh God, oh God, oh God,' she hyperventilated.

As the room erupted into pandemonium while Natalie did her best to take charge, Nina found herself smiling at the chaos. 'Isn't this just typical?' she commented to Steph, who nodded distractedly then turned away – but not before Nina caught sight of the fresh blood that was seeping through the sleeve of her white shirt in long, thin lines.

thirteen

Walking into work, Nina almost spilled her coffee down the front of her aqua Ginger & Smart blazer when she saw the hive of activity that was transforming *Juice* HQ into what looked scarily like the *Big Brother* set. She lost count of the number of cameras being set up by burly technicians as she headed towards her office.

'Where did all these people come from?' she demanded when Bella looked up from her computer screen to say good morning. She was in a filthy mood after barely getting any sleep over the weekend – her brain had gone around in circles worrying about her growing rift with Heidi and wondering whether she should call Steph to check up on her after seeing the strange blood stains on her shirt, only to be interrupted by a text from Lily at three am, just as she was drifting off, to announce the arrival of her daughter Luna, so named *because she was born on the night of a full moon and is the light of our lives.* Nina hadn't bothered to text back; instead she'd thrown the phone across the room in a fit of sleep-deprived frustration.

'They're from the *Freshly Squeezed Juice* production crew — isn't it exciting?!' the editorial assistant said breathlessly. 'The executive producer has just gone to a meeting with Eric, but he said he'd be back soon to check the set-up and then you guys can sit down to discuss the plan for today's filming. Everyone has been asking if they're going to be in the show or not; some of the girls are freaking out because they forgot that filming started today and they're not happy with their outfits . . .' She trailed off once she saw Nina's face.

'Someone needs to remind them that they have better things to worry about, like planning our exclusive coverage of Lulu Hopkins' wedding this weekend,' she said grimly. This was exactly what she'd been afraid of — her staff being more concerned with being on TV than getting their jobs done. 'Who the hell are you and what the hell are you doing?' she asked rudely, walking into her office to find a tall, balayaged caramel blonde wearing black-framed geek-chic glasses giving instructions to a technician who was fixing a camera to Nina's office window.

'Oh, hi, you must be Nina. I'm Scarlett, one of the senior producers for *Freshly Squeezed Juice.* Lovely to meet you,' the cool girl smiled, sticking out her hand.

'That doesn't explain what you're doing in my office,' Nina

pointed out, shaking Scarlett's hand firmly while surreptitiously admiring the producer's neon camouflage nail art.

'It's part of the camera set-up,' Scarlett explained, unperturbed by the distinct chill in Nina's tone. 'Andy, the exec producer, specifically asked for a fixed camera to be installed here to record your comings and goings. He reckons this is where a lot of the action goes on, so he doesn't want the film crew to miss a minute.'

'Wait . . . you're saying this camera will be rolling all the time, filming me non-stop?'

'Yep,' Scarlett replied. 'Can you sit down at your desk so we can check that you're in the camera's line of sight?'

Nina did as she was told, too gobsmacked to argue. When she'd met with Andy on Friday, there had been no mention that her every move, every word, every expression would be recorded for the show's editors to then splice and dice into something that would bear little resemblance to reality. Despite his and Eric's protests to the contrary, she knew full well that they'd be using a whole lot of creative licence in the editing suites to amp up the drama. After all, drama made good TV. Sighing, Nina stuck her tongue out at the camera's unblinking eye.

'That's what we like to see!' Scarlett laughed. 'The camera loves a bit of attitude, so don't be afraid to be yourself, okay? Soon, you won't even notice this baby is here.' She patted the silver bracket that fixed the camera to the window frame.

'That's what I'm afraid of,' Nina replied. 'Your editors are going to get sick of trawling through endless footage of me picking my nose, plucking my eyebrows and getting food in my hair.'

'Nah, don't worry about them, they're used to it. Most of the crew have just finished working on that reality housewives show, so we're glad to be doing something that's a little more interesting than watching grown women have scrag fights with each other over stupid things like who has the better Brazilian waxer.'

Nina smiled despite herself. 'Don't speak too soon,' she warned. 'We have some pretty epic scrag fights in the *Juice* office – only ours are more about whether you're Team Gosling or Team Tatum. Yep, we really drill down into the important matters in life here.'

'How is that even a contest? Have Team Gosling not seen *Magic Mike*?' Scarlett asked incredulously. 'Channing Tatum is an absolute fox.'

'You're welcome to him, honey,' Nina replied, finishing her coffee. 'I'm more Team Gosling myself.'

'Who's what now?' Andy strolled into her office, looking like he owned the place. 'Hey, Nina, great to see you again! You've already met Scarlett, I see – you two are going to be spending a lot of time together over the next few months, so play nice, okay? So, the guys are just finishing setting up the equipment; sorry for the intrusion but it'll be part of the furniture before you know it. Okay, what's first up on the agenda?' he asked, looking at the notes Nina had given him in their previous meeting, detailing how the magazine's schedule worked.

'The picture desk should be finished sorting through all the pap pics that have come in over the weekend,' she explained. 'Once they've turfed the sets of celebs who aren't right for our demographic, Layla and I go through them to see what we want to start bidding on.'

'Great! So Layla prints out all of the photos and brings them into your office for you to go through?'

'No, I usually just sit by her desk and we scroll through them together on her computer,' Nina clarified. 'She usually prints out the ones I like for the news meeting, but that's just a small selection.'

Andy shook his head, tapping his fingers against the sheet of paper. 'Hmmm, I don't think that'll work,' he muttered. 'Not visual enough. Can Layla not print out the pics? That way we can shoot the two of you going through them all, zooming in on the sets you like, capturing you throwing the ones you don't like in the bin . . . We need to create a bit of theatre about it rather than just the two of you staring at a computer screen.'

'Andy, Monday is the biggest day for photos, there are literally hundreds of them. It'll be a waste of trees and time if Layla prints them all. We can't wait around for the printer to spew them out and then for you to film us going through them – other magazines will get the bidding process started while your cameraman is faffing around trying to get the right camera angle of me pretending to throw out a set of Justin Bieber with his arse hanging out of his jeans,' Nina said in frustration. So much for Eric promising that the film crew wouldn't interrupt their schedule and would fit in when and where they could.

'If you're worried about time, why don't you and Layla go through the photos now like you usually do so the picture team can start bidding,' suggested Scarlett, 'and then we can print off the ones you like and a selection of the ones you've ditched and recreate it in your office afterwards?'

'Problem solved!' Andy said jovially.

'But . . . but that's not the way it works,' Nina pushed back. 'It seems a bit excessive to change something as minor as this just because it's not visual enough. Plus I'm sure you're aware that doing it twice, once for real and once for show, means it will take twice as long. Layla and I have got other things to do besides recreate scenes just for the TV show — we do have a magazine to send to print, you know,' she said, not bothering to hide her annoyance.

'Of course you do!' Andy smiled at her ingratiatingly. 'And we don't want to come in and change everything, that's not our intention at all. We want to show the people at home how a great magazine like *Juice* gets made, but we don't want it to be boring, do we?'

Nina took a deep breath, trying to control her temper. 'I hate to break it to you, Andy, but a lot of what we do here is boring. Some of it involves glamorous people, some of it happens at exotic locations and some of it is full of drama, but a lot of it is computer-based stuff that needs to get done ASAP thanks to that pesky thing called a weekly print deadline which doesn't wait for anyone. We don't have time to change the way we do things to make them more TV-friendly; we do things the way we do because it works best for us that way. And if we change this one thing for you now, what else will you ask us to change down the track?' Nina challenged.

'Now, Nina, don't be like that!' the executive producer said, somewhat condescendingly. 'You want this show to work, don't you? I mean, as the editor, you're going to be one of its stars, so it's in your best interests to make it as great as possible. And it will be great! We're not going to come in and railroad you into doing something you don't want to do, we just want to make the best TV we can, and if that means tweaking a few things here and there, then I'm sure Eric will give us the go-ahead . . .'

Nina sighed, remembering her publisher making it crystal clear that while she didn't have to like the idea of the TV show, she had to get behind it. She knew when she was beaten. 'Fine,' she relented. 'Excuse me while I break the news to my picture editor that her workload is going to double now that we have to do everything twice for the sake of a goddamn reality TV show.'

Waiting for the Excel spreadsheet to open so she could keep tabs on how much the picture desk had blown in this week's budget, Nina rubbed her eyes wearily. It was already eight pm and she still had thirty or so unread emails to attend to after she'd sussed out whether the editorial spend was under control. She was running at least two hours behind schedule, thanks to the *Freshly Squeezed Juice* film crew and their constant tweaking of the magazine's daily routine to 'liven things up'. After just one day of filming, Nina had learnt that 'we'll just be a few minutes' was code for 'this could take anywhere from half an hour to half a day'. The highlight had been when they'd spent more than an hour filming her and Layla pretending to go through the photos they'd already edited for real at her computer, only for the sound guy to belatedly realise that the battery in Layla's microphone pack was dead so they'd had to do it all over again from scratch. Needless to say, Nina had almost throttled him. Thankfully Bella had stuck her head in to remind her she had a meeting with *Juice*'s marketing team to discuss the promotion for the TV show, so she'd put her Manolo Blahnik-clad foot down and told the crew in no uncertain terms that seeing there'd be a fresh batch of celebrity picture porn tomorrow and the next day, not to mention every weekday after that, they could just hold their horses and wait to re-record it, seeing it had been their stuff-up.

Feeling satisfied that the budget hadn't been raped and pillaged too early in the week, leaving them a decent amount to play with in case a red-hot exclusive picture set of, say, Brad Pitt having a threesome with Jennifer Aniston and Gwyneth Paltrow was conjured up by the celebrity gossip gods on the day they went to print, Nina grabbed her phone and scrolled through her contacts to find Steph's number.

'Hey, Nina! How did your first day of filming go? More importantly, what did you wear?'

'Everything you told me to and nothing you didn't, Ms Style Guru,' Nina replied. 'Thanks again for the advice. So, how are you?' she asked in what she hoped was a nonchalant tone.

'Me? Oh, you know, same same. Busy with showroom appointments to pull pieces for the General Pants campaign and I've just been asked to style the Alex Perry show for fashion week, so that will keep me out of mischief.'

Nina paused, wondering how to broach the subject she was really calling about without Steph cottoning on to the fact that Nina knew about the problems she and Chris were having conceiving. 'That's great! I loved his last collection. So, I guess I just wanted to call and make sure everything was alright . . . you know, after yesterday,' she said hesitantly.

Steph was silent for a second, then said warily, 'Yesterday? What do you mean?'

'Well, it was all kinds of hectic but just as Lily's waters broke, I noticed your shirt sleeves had blood on them, then I remembered that when I was in the bathroom just after you, I found some bloodstained tissues randomly under the basin, so . . . I just wanted to check that . . . um, you know . . . you're okay . . .' Nina trailed off, hoping Steph would see where she was trying to go with her clumsy attempt to reach out to her without having to spell it out.

'Oh, that! Hah, hah!' Steph laughed – a bark that sounded a bit too forced to Nina's pricked ears. 'It's so silly. I had a nosebleed in the bathroom and I guess I didn't get rid of the tissues properly, sorry. Ugh, so gross that you found them! Anyway, I get them all the time – I must have smeared some blood on my shirt and not noticed. I'm such a grub, you can't take me anywhere! That reminds me, I really should soak it in Napi-San before it's too late – it's McQueen, you know. Anyway, Chris has just walked in the door, so I'd better go,' she announced hurriedly. 'Good luck with the filming; let's catch up soon, okay?'

Nina stared at her phone in surprise after her friend hung up on her. Something about Steph's explanation didn't quite add up but she didn't really feel it was her place to dig any further. Sighing, she switched over to her inbox.

'This is going to hurt,' she murmured, spying an email from her bank announcing the arrival of her credit card statement. Holding her breath, she opened up the PDF and grimaced when she caught sight of the eye-wateringly large balance that was due in two weeks. She knew she'd gone a bit overboard in New York, but she hadn't quite realised her spending had crossed the line into stonkingly-rich heiress territory. Unfortunately, there was no stonkingly-rich daddy to help pay for it. Quickly checking her bank account, Nina grabbed her calculator and did some sums, but no matter how many different ways she adjusted them, her finances remained stubbornly in the red and looked like they'd remain that way for quite some time – she'd still be paying off her credit card bill when she was blowing out the candles on her Adriano Zumbo fiftieth-birthday macaron tower, by the look of it. Nina stared at the list of monthly debits listed on her everyday account, searching for something that could be decreased in order to help pay for her New York shopathon, then eventually admitted defeat.

'Suck it up, princess,' she told herself sternly. 'It's time to get a flatmate to help pay the rent and bills.'

Since Tess had moved back to London, Nina had been shacked up in their two-bedroom Potts Point apartment by herself, with the inner-city suburb's plethora of buzzy bars, cafes and restaurants right on her doorstep. There was temptation lurking on every corner – why would you go to the supermarket when you could eat out every night? She'd had every intention of moving into a one-bedroom place to cut costs but had never quite got around to it – not that anyone would really blame her, given the cut-throat Sydney rental market. She could have got a new flatmate as soon as Tess had jetted off, but after living with her cousin for years, both in London and Sydney, the thought of sharing with a stranger kind of freaked her out. Someone else's food going mouldy in the fridge, someone else's books cluttering up the shelves, someone else's bad taste in art hanging on the walls . . . Not if she could help it, thanks very much. Until now, she'd managed to pay the rent and bills by herself, but there was no denying it had swallowed up a huge chunk of her savings; so much so that she barely had any left. Now her New York credit card bill had pushed her straight over the fiscal cliff without so much as a 'thanks for coming, hope you enjoyed your stay'.

'It's all your fault,' she sternly told the pair of metallic purple Manolos that were strapped onto her feet. 'If you,

Christian and Jimmy hadn't been so disgustingly good-looking, then this wouldn't be happening.'

'What wouldn't be happening?'

Nina jumped what felt like five metres in the air as Scarlett suddenly appeared in the doorway.

'Oh, you scared the bejesus out of me! I didn't realise anyone else was still here,' she said, slightly embarrassed to get busted talking to her shoes.

'Sorry, I didn't mean to startle you,' Scarlett assured her. 'I just finished in the production office across the hallway and saw that your office lights were still on, so I thought I'd stick my head in to say goodnight.'

'You only just finished? I thought I was the only one stupid enough to be working back this late.'

'Yeah, I wanted to have a look at some of the footage we shot today, try to identify who's good on camera and who we should maybe not bother with.'

Nina looked at the beast fixed to her office window, its beady eye silently recording her every move. 'Please tell me I'm not good on camera and I don't have to do this anymore. It would make my job a lot easier.'

'Nice try, sweetheart,' Scarlett grinned. 'But as you know, you're the editor extraordinaire so you don't score a get-out-of-jail-free card, even if you did happen to be atrocious on camera. The good news is, you're not – it loves you.'

'Good to know at least someone loves me,' Nina said under her breath.

'So I get the impression that, unlike some of your staff who are practically throwing themselves in front of the film crew, you're not that interested in being a reality TV star?' Scarlett enquired.

'You've got that right; I thank God every day that my last name isn't Kardashian,' Nina said. 'I'm quite happy dealing with celebrities every day from the relative safety of the *Juice* office, but I have absolutely no desire to become one myself. Not that I think this show is going to make me the next Nicole Richie, but I don't really relish the idea of losing my anonymity.'

'But you could argue that you already have – you've edited two national magazines, both of which feature your headshot on your editor's letter, and I'm sure you get photographed at some of the work functions you go to,' Scarlett pointed out.

'True, but somehow it's different,' Nina tried to explain. 'Having my photo in the mag or appearing in the Sunday social pages when they're scraping the bottom of the barrel to fill them is one thing, but being beamed into people's living rooms on their sixty-inch plasma screens is another. I guess it's because a photo is static, whereas on TV, I'm a living, breathing person. It's not like I'm an actress, playing a fictional character who has nothing to do with who I actually am – I'm putting myself out there even though I don't want to and I know I'm going to get judged, no matter what I do.'

'Yeah, people can be pretty vitriolic when they take a dislike to someone on TV,' Scarlett admitted. 'And with social media like Twitter, things can get quite ugly – just look at that judge from *Australia's Next Top Model* who got told to kill herself. It's nasty. But I don't think you have anything to worry about – besides your reservations about losing your anonymity, of course. There's also an upside to fame, remember. I don't know about you, but I wouldn't mind getting invited to the hottest parties and being sent loads of freebies. I'd love to get papped, just once in my life, so I knew what it was like – but only if I wasn't having a bad hair day, obviously. Anyway, take it from me: this show is going to be great exposure for the mag and great exposure for you.'

'Only if people watch it!' Nina reminded her. 'I'm still not sure if it's going to be the success Eric and Andy think it will be – no offence,' she added quickly, realising that Scarlett might think she was questioning her professional abilities too.

'Don't worry about me, no offence taken,' the other girl laughed. 'Trust me, I've worked on some dogs during my time in TV and I'm pretty sure this isn't going to be one of them. Think about it – it's got celebrities, which people love; it's got magazines, which people love; and it's got drama, which people love. Why wouldn't it work?'

Nina sighed. 'It's the drama I'm worried about. I really don't want to be put in a position where we're getting told to make stuff up from scratch just because an episode needs more "theatre". It's supposed to be reality, not reality that's not really real.'

Scarlett studied her intently, then abruptly changed the subject. 'Hey, what are you doing now? Don't suppose you want to go for a drink? I could murder a mojito. Or three.'

Nina glanced at the unread emails in her inbox, then at the clock. She didn't usually drink on Monday nights but she wasn't in the mood to explain why to this girl with the cool hair and the on-trend glasses who she'd only met twelve hours earlier. And besides, it was nice to talk to someone who wasn't obsessed with babies or boyfriends. She could always insist on ordering the drinks at the bar by herself so she could ask for a virgin mojito on the sly.

'Sure,' she said, pushing her chair back and grabbing her new Saint Laurent handbag – yet another designer treat from her New York trip. 'Why the hell not?'

fourteen

Nina picked up the ringing phone, and almost immediately wished she hadn't – especially given her slightly delicate state after indulging in one too many fully-charged marmalade mojitos with Scarlett's encouragement the night before. Nina had told herself off good and proper that morning when she'd woken up feeling dusty and remembered her original plan to order virgin cocktails had gone AWOL – although she no longer had a toxic relationship with alcohol, she knew she still had to be careful. But she'd had a great time – her new friend was funny and clever, with good taste in cocktails.

'Hello, Tony, how are you?' she said, making a face at the ubiquitous camera that was trained on her. Once upon a time, any weekly magazine editor would have been delighted to get a phone call from Tony – he was an old-school celebrity manager who had made his name in the eighties while steering the careers of the first major breakout stars from Australia's most famous prime-time soap. When most of those stars defected to England to become even more famous pop stars, he'd retired to the Gold Coast and lived off the killing he'd made, before getting bored. Ten years ago, he'd decided to hunt down some fresh meat and work his magic all over again. This time, he seized on Dakota, a rough-as-guts former Miss Indy 500 who had no legitimate talent besides marinating herself in fake tan, falling out of clubs and surgically increasing her breast size to comical proportions. Suddenly Dakota was everywhere, thanks to Tony – spilling out of her dress on the Brownlow Medal red carpet when she dated the Collingwood Magpies captain; flashing her vagina as she got out of the car at the Dally Ms when she dated the Parramatta Eels' star fullback; getting knocked up after a one-night-stand with a visiting LA rock star then revealing to the highest magazine bidder that she was going to keep the baby despite him offering her a million dollars to have an abortion. Although it was obvious Dakota barely had two brain cells to rub together, the Australian public were fascinated. Which meant the weekly magazines fell over themselves to put her on the cover. Tony made sure there was always fresh dirt on Dakota, whether it was grainy-yet-unmistakeable pics of her getting a lap dance while heavily pregnant, or giving inflammatory quotes about other female celebrities. Week in, week out, you could guarantee Dakota would appear in at least one of the weekly trash mags, if not all of them. And because she'd proved so insanely popular, Tony had no hesitation in making it clear that if the mags wanted Dakota, they'd have to cough up some serious cash. The editors weren't happy, but given she moved magazines like no one else, there wasn't much they could do about it. After all, their job was to sell as many copies as possible. There were whispers that Tony engineered every aspect of Dakota's life for maximum column inches, from the multiple pregnancies and the multiple marriages to the multiple surgeries and the multiple breakdowns, but for a few years, Australia couldn't get enough. Until one day, the public collectively decided they were bored with watching this particular car crash, no matter what Tony did to stir up interest. It was as if the country had suddenly woken up, looked at his star client and finally realised she was a vacuous puppet who was playing them all for fools while rolling around naked in a giant haystack of hundred-dollar bills. Dakota was now what magazine editors called 'cover poison', but no one had bothered to tell Dakota. She still got paid to turn up to events here and there, but these days it was the opening of a bathroom tile shop in a random suburban shopping centre rather than strutting down the VIP carpet of the ARIAs. Having Tony on the phone could only mean one thing – he was still trying to resurrect Dakota's 'career' and wanted to pitch Nina a story that no one would care about.

'Nina! I'm great, just great!' Tony boomed down the phone line. 'What's happening there at *Juice*? I hear there's a TV show in the works, is that true?'

'You heard right, Tony. They just started filming this week and it's all systems go. So, to what do I owe the pleasure?' Nina got straight to the point, but made sure she didn't come across as too narky – the thing with fossils like Tony was that you could never be sure if they'd get a second (or in Tony's case a third) wind when it came to clients. Nina couldn't afford to be outright rude, just in case a future hot new kid on the block who everyone wanted a piece of decided to sign with the grizzled old hack because of his decades of experience, only for Nina to find her title had been blacklisted because of some offhand negative remark she'd once made. Celebrity managers were like elephants – they never forgot.

'Have I got a story for you!' Tony bellowed. 'Trust me, this one is a corker! Now, I know she's had her ups and downs, but the Australian public will always have a soft spot for her, especially when it comes to her love-life . . .'

'I take it you're talking about Dakota?' Nina interrupted, trying to hurry him along.

'Yes! The one and same! Now, this is super-duper secret-squirrel, okay, my love? But we want to do an exclusive reveal with your magazine – in fact, it's a double reveal! Your readers won't be able to resist parting with their hard-earned pennies to read about every single juicy detail!'

'That's a big promise, Tony,' Nina said. 'To be honest, we already have a couple of exclusives lined up over the next few weeks, so I don't know if *Juice* is the best title for Dakota's big story right now. I'm presuming you're looking at going to press soon?'

'Oh, we can wait until you're ready; yes we can! Don't you worry about that, we'll just fit in with whatever works best for you,' he reassured her.

Nina closed her eyes and took a deep breath – of course Tony was bending over backwards; he was obviously desperate to find a home for this story anywhere he could. She knew she wouldn't have been his first port of call – he'd probably already hit up *Bizarre*, plus the other weeklies that were aimed at a slightly older demographic.

'Can you give me any idea what the two reveals are?' she asked, playing along even though she knew there was no way in hell she'd be spending a cent of her editorial budget on the story, no matter what it was. Dakota was ancient history and it would make *Juice* look like old news if they ran a big story on her – she couldn't risk looking out of touch with her readers, even if Tony offered her the story for free. People just didn't care about Dakota anymore.

'This is for your ears only – I'm thrilled to tell you that Dakota just got married in a secret ceremony in Bali!' he proclaimed grandly, as if he was announcing it was Prince Harry who had snuck off and got married without anyone knowing about it.

'Again?' Nina blurted out before she could stop herself. Last time she'd bothered to take note, Dakota had just divorced her fourth husband and had immediately got engaged to a Hells Angel.

'Isn't it wonderful?' Tony said, conveniently ignoring Nina's comment. 'I'm sure your readers will be thrilled to read all about it, especially seeing Dakota and Shane have only known each other for five weeks. It's a classic tale of true love sweeping them off their feet when they least expected it.'

'Oh, so it's not the bikie, then? How did Dakota and her new husband meet?'

'At a strip club,' Tony said nonchalantly. 'Shane is a stripper. I'm sure you'll agree it's a fantastic story as is, but the good news is there's another bombshell Dakota wants to reveal to your readers . . .'

'Which is?'

'She's pregnant!'

Nina had to physically cover her mouth to stop herself from repeating 'Again?' Since having the rock star's baby against his wishes then taking him to court in a very public battle for child support, Dakota had gone on to have a child with each of her four husbands. She seemed to pop out kids like she collected marriage certificates – with no thought about what a lifelong commitment both were supposed to be.

'Well, that's, um, wonderful news for Dakota. Please pass on my congratulations to her and Shane, but unfortunately I don't think this story is quite right for *Juice*'s readers,' Nina said, trying to sound regretful.

'Nina, come on now!' Tony said with a note of desperation in his voice. 'We both know it's a fabulous story. And it'll be just perfect for the TV show. We can do a beautiful photo shoot with Dakota and Shane and the TV cameras can be there to capture all the behind-the-scenes shenanigans!'

Nina suddenly realised what this was all about – of course he was offering it to *Juice*, because he was hoping Dakota would feature on the TV show, and he could then use her appearance to reignite her 'career'. 'Not going to happen, buster,' she thought to herself.

'I'm sorry, Tony, but I just don't feel comfortable with splashing Dakota's news all over the magazine when she's so early in her pregnancy. If she's only a few weeks along, she really should keep it on the downlow until the twelve-week mark, right? What if something should happen and she miscarries? I'd feel awful for her,' Nina explained, relieved to have found an exit strategy that didn't make her look like the bad guy.

'But . . . but . . .' Tony stuttered, then rallied. 'You know, I don't mean this the wrong way but that could actually work out well for everyone! If Dakota loses the baby, then we can package that up as another story for *Juice*! I can see the cover line now – *My baby tragedy: How Shane's love is helping me through the heartbreak*,' Tony suggested enthusiastically.

Nina felt a wave of disgust wash over her; she couldn't believe he'd just spruiked his client's potential miscarriage as a tabloid story.

'I'm sorry, Tony, but I don't think so,' she said firmly. 'Good luck with finding a home for this story elsewhere.'

'Promise me you'll at least think about it!' he begged. 'I'll give you a price you won't be able to refuse!'

'Tony, I really have to go; it was nice talking to you. Goodbye.' Nina hung up, half expecting him to call back straight away to say he'd throw in a competition for one of Juice's readers to name Dakota's baby as an added bonus. 'This industry can be really twisted sometimes,' she thought, swigging from the can of Diet Coke on her desk and almost gagging when she realised it was warm. She didn't really want to consider the part she herself played in the very same industry.

Heading to the kitchen to get a replacement drink, Nina stopped at Meg's desk. 'Hey, is everything all on track for Saturday? Has Sam sent through the list of confirmed guests so we can send out the confidentiality agreements and start working on the photography brief?'

With only four days until Lulu and Jason's wedding, there was still a lot to be done. Given it was a major exclusive, Juice had to ensure all the details of the big day were kept under wraps as much as possible until the issue went on sale the following Friday. That meant getting the legal team to draw up a confidentiality agreement for every guest to sign, hiring security guards to confiscate people's phones on arrival to prevent any sneaky uploads to Facebook, Twitter or Instagram, and having large swathes of fabric on hand to shield Lulu and her rumoured $250,000 wedding dress from any lurking paparazzi who were determined to spoil Juice's monopoly on the photos. And that was just the start.

'I just got the guest list from Sam so I'll get Bella to start sending the confidentiality agreements out now,' Meg replied. Celebrity weddings were her forte – while some people could think of nothing worse than going to a stranger's wedding to hover in the background and report on every miniscule detail of the bouquets, the canapés, the cutting of the cake and the wedding dance while making small talk with people they didn't know from a stick of marzipan, Meg loved it. Through her job, she'd been to more celebrity weddings than Nina had shoes – and Nina had a lot of shoes.

'Great – once you've gone through the guest list to see which other celebs are attending, can you please send me the photography brief?' Nina asked, continuing to the kitchen. Grabbing a chilled can out of the vending machine, she was taking a swig on her way back to the office when she ran smack bang into Scarlett in the hallway and narrowly avoided showering both of them in sticky brown bubbles.

'Hey, it's my partner in marmalade mojito crime! I was just coming to find you – have you got a minute?' the TV producer asked.

'Sure, what's up?'

Scarlett had the grace to look embarrassed. 'You're not going to like it – you know that phone conversation you just had? With someone called Tony? Andy was just reviewing the footage from the camera in your office and is convinced we missed a juicy conversation that would have been great for adding a bit of drama to the TV show. But he could only hear your side of it, not what Tony was saying. He wants to know if you could call back, explain about the show and organise a time with him to recreate it.'

'What? To recreate it? How?'

'Once we get his permission, we'd send a crew over to his office at a pre-arranged time so we can mike him up and then film him recreating the conversation he just had with you. Obviously it would be great if you could amp up the drama a little, maybe get a little heated and finish the phone call with one of you slamming down the phone . . . or something,' Scarlett trailed off when she saw the look on Nina's face.

Nina shook her head. 'No way in hell. Not only do I have a problem with "recreating" something, especially given I'm a terrible actress, but I do not want that conversation being featured in the show. I don't care how much drama Andy thinks it needs – I am not going to ask Tony to recreate what was an uncomfortable conversation for both sides.'

'I knew you wouldn't like it, but I had to ask.' Looking decidedly uneasy, Scarlett added, 'That's not the worst of it – Andy wants to tap your phone so the sound guys can record both sides of your conversations from now on.'

'Are you kidding? That's a total violation of privacy! Has it occurred to him that a lot of my conversations are confidential? If some of those details were made public, especially the ones concerning payment for stories, *Juice* would never get an exclusive again! He can't do that!'

'Look, it was just an off-the-cuff comment, I don't know if he's actually planning to go ahead and do it,' Scarlett said, obviously in backtrack mode.

'You bet your marmalade mojito he's not going to go ahead and do it,' Nina stated. 'Sorry, Scarlett, I don't mean to shoot the messenger but Andy needs to pull his head in. Does Eric know about this phone-tapping idea?'

'I doubt it. As I said, it was just an off-the-cuff comment.'

'Well, he's going to know about it real quick. Jesus Christ, I thought the magazine industry was dodgy, but it's got nothing on the reality TV industry!' she fumed as she stormed off to Eric's office to give him a piece of her mind. This TV show was already a nightmare and it was only the first week of filming.

fifteen

Browsing the items in Baby Gap, Nina tried to dredge up some excitement about meeting Luna, aka the light of Jake and Lily's lives, for the first time. After putting it off for as long as possible, she'd eventually got in touch with a besotted-but-distracted Lily to arrange to see the new member of the family and was due at their house in just over an hour. Normally she would have roped Heidi in for some moral support and then they would debrief afterwards over a Sunday afternoon coffee or glass of wine, but given the two of them weren't on the best terms right now, she'd decided to go it alone. She didn't need Heidi getting on her high horse again; Nina was still smarting from their showdown at the baby shower a few weeks earlier.

'Oi, Ninja! Thought it was you! What the hell are you doing in a place like this? Got something to tell me?' a deep voice boomed through the quiet of the store.

Nina spun around, a tiny pair of pink and white striped leggings with ruffles on the butt clutched in her hand. She knew exactly who it was before she saw him – there was only one person in the world who called her Ninja and that was Max, the men's magazine editor who had gone on the New York junket with her the year before. She had to tilt her head all the way back to smile up at him – Max was a big, boofy Aussie bloke with hands the size of ham hocks and an appetite for beer that could not be sated. He was the anti-hipster who wouldn't be caught dead in skinny jeans or in a shirt buttoned all the way up to the neck sans tie, which made him the perfect editor for *Carnage*, the ocker men's magazine that was all about chicks, tits and flicks.

'I might ask you the same thing, mister! I wouldn't have picked Baby Gap as one of your usual haunts. And no, I'm not pregnant, thanks very much – a friend just had a baby. I'm going to see them this afternoon so figured I should take a present. Isn't that what you're supposed to do?'

'Dunno.' Max shrugged his man-mountain shoulders. 'I only came in here because I recognised that bird's nest on top of your head and thought I'd say hi. How've you been, mate?'

Nina patted her carefully deconstructed topknot self-consciously. Max had a knack for keeping things real, whether it was poking fun at her for copying the latest hairstyle worn by every other Sydney girl about town, or dragging her to a dingy dive bar in the middle of Manhattan when she could have been having a *Sex and the City* experience at a swanky Upper East Side establishment.

'Pretty good,' she replied. 'Hey, you'll never guess where I was a couple of weeks ago . . . your favourite place – the one and only Hogs and Heifers!'

'No way! How the hell did you end up there? That place was so awesome. Geez, some of those bar chicks . . .' He trailed off, clearly remembering the fit barmaids in bikinis.

'I was on a girls' trip and we stayed at the Standard again. Seeing the bar is just across the road, I figured it would have been rude not to pop in.'

'You got that right. So, how goes it with that reality TV show I read about?'

Nina rolled her eyes. 'How long have you got? It's a giant pain in the arse, if you must know.'

'Go on, tell Uncle Max. I could use something to cheer me up – hey, what are you doing now? Got time for a coffee?'

Nina checked her phone – she had some time to kill before she was due at Jake and Lily's place, and she hadn't seen Max for ages.

'Sure, why not? Let me just pay for these,' she said, gesturing to the leggings.

'I dunno, Ninja,' he said dubiously. 'I think they might be a bit small for you.'

Whacking him on the arm, she smiled as she headed for the cash register, wondering why she didn't make more of an effort to hang out with Max despite his bad jokes and out-of-date dress sense. They'd become instant friends during their New York trip and had caught up a couple of times when they were back in Sydney, mostly at the advertising functions they were both obliged to attend as editors. They'd stand around stuffing themselves with canapés and making fun of the boring speeches about the latest celebrity his'n'hers fragrances or whatever happened to be getting spruiked that day. But their catch-ups had been few and far between lately.

'So, enough about the fresh hell that is that goddamn TV show,' Nina said, after she'd finished entertaining him with stories about the production of *Freshly Squeezed Juice* while mainlining caffeine at Workshop Espresso on George Street. 'How's *Carnage?* Been on any more press trips? Have you made an honest woman out of Sally yet?' she asked, referring to Max's long-time girlfriend who she'd never met but had heard a lot about.

He shifted on his stool, staring over her head at the crowds that were battling their way across the road to the Queen Victoria Building. 'Uh, no. We broke up, actually,' he admitted.

'Oh . . . I . . . I'm sorry to hear that. Are you okay?' Nina mentally kicked herself for putting her foot in it.

'Yeah,' he said gruffly. 'It's still a bit fresh, it only happened the other week. But it's probably for the best.'

'Was it a mutual decision?' Nina gently probed, getting the impression he needed someone impartial to talk to.

'Kind of. The decision was made for us, you could say,' he replied. 'She wanted a kid; I said I wasn't ready and, if I was honest, I didn't know if I'd ever be ready. She said I wasn't willing to grow up and that she couldn't wait any longer while I fart-arsed around, so we decided it was best to go our separate ways.'

'That sucks,' Nina said, knowing she didn't need to elaborate any further.

'Yeah, it does,' Max sighed. 'But what sucks harder is that we're still shacked up together. We agreed I would move out, but I've been on print deadline with the magazine then down in Melbourne buttering up advertising clients, so I haven't had time to scratch my balls, let alone scratch the surface of the rental market. I'm worried that if I don't pull my finger out and make a break for it soon, we'll end up drunkenly shagging and then it'll be all too easy to slip back into old patterns. Before you know it, we'll be right back where we started and that wouldn't be fair on either of us,' he said glumly.

While patting Max's massive paw sympathetically, it dawned on Nina that somewhere, somehow, the property planets were aligning. Max needed somewhere to live as soon as possible. She needed a flatmate to help pay off her debt. They got on well but weren't so tight that they'd feel smothered by each other if they lived under the same roof. And it would be better than living with a complete stranger who she'd have to make awkward conversation with every night. She'd have to lay down some ground rules beforehand, but she could think of worse things than living with Max. The more she thought about it, the better the idea became. Something was actually going right for once – if he said yes.

'Actually, I might be able to help you out with your living situation,' Nina began.

Max visibly perked up. 'Yeah? Know someone who's looking for a housemate, do you?'

'Yep – you're looking at her. I've been living by myself ever since my cousin moved back to London, but after doing some serious damage to my credit card in New York, I've finally accepted I can't manage the rent and bills alone anymore. I'd just decided to get a flatmate earlier this week but haven't done anything about it yet, so the spare room is yours for the taking if you want it.'

He frowned. 'Where do you live again? Don't tell me it's bloody Bondi Beach – don't think I could cope with all the tourists,' he moaned.

'Nope, Potts Point. Two-bedroom, two-bathroom apartment. Which means I won't have to pick your pubes off the soap, thank God,' she grinned.

'That's what I like about you, Ninja – you're all class. Potts Point, eh? Well, it's a bit different to humble Marrickville, but a change of scenery might not be such a bad thing. What's the damage?'

Nina filled him in on the rent and asked if he wanted to think about it and get back to her.

'Nah, it's all good. Not like I've got any other offers on the table.' Max drained the last of his long black. 'If you're happy to live with a derelict like me, let's do it. When can I move in?'

As she walked towards Lily and Jake's leafy Paddington street, Nina spied an upmarket wine shop and spontaneously decided to grab a bottle of champagne to give to her friend as congratulations. 'Why should the baby get all the presents when Lily did all the hard work?' she thought, selecting a bottle of Moët & Chandon from the fridge and grabbing a Sunday paper from the pile on the counter to flick through after she'd got this visit out of the way. Not that she could really afford a pricey bottle of bubbles, but now that Max was moving in next weekend, her finances weren't looking quite so dire. And it would hopefully make up for the fact that her present for Luna wasn't gift-wrapped and she didn't have a card, making it rather obvious that she'd left it to the last minute. She'd meant to stop in at David Jones to get both card and wrapping paper, but coffee with Max had taken up more time than she'd anticipated, and then she was running so late she'd completely forgotten until she was practically standing outside their house.

'Hi, Nina, how are you?' a weary-looking Jake asked as he opened the front door and gave her a kiss. 'Come in – Lily's just feeding Luna in the back room.'

'Oh, do you want me to come back? Sorry I'm late, I ran into a friend on my way here,' Nina said, flustered. She wasn't sure if she was ready to see her friend with her giant boob flopped out and a baby guzzling away at the end of it.

'No, it's all good. One of the other girls is here too, so I'll make myself scarce while you guys catch up,' he said quickly, seemingly glad to have an excuse to get away from all the oestrogen that had invaded his house.

Nina plastered a smile onto her face as she made her way through the kitchen to where Lily was sitting in an armchair, gazing adoringly at the pink blob that was sucking furiously on her engorged nipple. 'Hi, Lily! Sorry I'm late! Congratulations! Here's a present for Luna and here's one for you!' she said brightly, kissing her friend quickly on the cheek before putting the shopping bag and the Moët on the coffee table next to her. Her smile faltered as she realised who else was there. Dammit, why couldn't it have been Steph or even Nat?

'Um, hi,' she said, nervously.

'Hi,' Heidi said coolly.

'Oh, Nina, thanks so much for the cute present, but Luna is only wearing clothes made from organic cotton,' Lily announced, oblivious to the frosty atmosphere as she stared at the leggings like they were radioactive. 'You just don't know what chemicals are used to treat fabrics these days and I don't want to take any chances. You should see what they say about non-organic baby clothes on the mummy forums; it's horrifying. But I could ask if anyone from my mother's group might like them?' she asked.

'Oh . . . um . . . sorry . . .' Nina stuttered, taken aback at Lily's directness. 'I can return them and get something else if you like?' she found herself offering.

'Could you? That would be great,' Lily said happily. 'Have a look online, there are plenty of places that sell eco-friendly clothes. Heidi, remind me where you got that adorable bamboo baby blanket you gave Luna when you visited us in the hospital? I know you already told me three times but my baby brain is seriously out of control.'

It took all of Nina's willpower not to roll her eyes – of course Lily just assumed she had the time and inclination to surf the internet looking for replacement baby clothes and of course Heidi had bought the perfect eco-friendly present that was probably so organic it would start automatically biodegrading when the baby grew too big for it.

'Look, Luna! It's Nina! Yes, she's the last one of the girls to finally come and meet you!' Lily crooned as she fastened her maternity bra and put the pink blob on her shoulder, patting her back gently to burp her.

Nina ignored the passive-aggressive comment – she probably deserved it after deliberately finding any excuse to put off visiting the new arrival. 'So, how's motherhood treating you?' she asked, for lack of anything else to say.

'It's indescribable,' Lily gushed. 'I knew as soon as we conceived that our child would be special, but when they laid her on my chest, she looked straight at me and we had an instant connection. I can just tell she's an old soul . . . aren't you, my precious?'

Some regurgitated milk bubbled out of Luna's mouth and onto the towel that was draped over her mother's shoulder.

'Nina, do you want to have a hold? Of course you do! Go on, she'll be asleep any minute now.'

'Uh . . . well . . .' Nina looked around for someone, anyone, to rescue her. She'd never held a baby in her life and she didn't intend to start now. And knowing her luck, Luna would be able to smell her fear and start screaming the house down and then Lily would probably call DOCS and have her arrested for child abuse. 'I'm not really down with how to hold a baby properly so it's probably better if I don't. I wouldn't want to break her,' she explained, backing away.

'For Christ's sake, Nina,' she heard Heidi mutter under her breath as she stepped forward. 'Here, give me a cuddle.' Heidi took the baby from Lily, snuggled her into the crook of her arm like a natural and started cooing at her, much to Nina's surprise. Surely Heidi wasn't getting clucky?

'You know, my arms feel so empty whenever she's not in them,' Lily began, then caught sight of the Moët. 'Oh, champagne!' she exclaimed, even though the bottle had been sitting there for a good ten minutes. 'Where did this come from?'

'I bought it for you as a congratulations present,' Nina said, trying not to show her impatience. Obviously Lily hadn't been exaggerating when she'd commented on her chronic case of baby brain. 'Although it's not eco-friendly either,' she was tempted to add.

'Lovely! Should we crack it open? I know it's naughty given I'm breastfeeding the little angel, but I'll just have a couple of sips. That's what pump and dump is for, right?'

Nina didn't need to be told twice. Collecting three champagne flutes from the kitchen cupboard, she popped the cork and started pouring. 'What the hell is pump and dump?' she asked, trying to sound vaguely interested.

'Rather than waiting for the alcohol to leave your breast milk, which can take a few hours, you use a breast pump to express all the milk after you've been drinking and throw it out,' Lily explained. 'That way, the baby won't get any alcohol when it has its next feed. Cheers!' she said, taking the tiniest sip.

'How are your episiotomy stitches?' Heidi asked sympathetically. 'Oh, no thanks, I won't have any,' she added as Nina went to hand her a glass of champagne. 'Are you still having to sit on the rubber ring?'

'Oh God yes, it's a war zone down there. I'm still too scared to poop. But the worst thing is how itchy they are. And it's not like the stitches are in a place when you can scratch them any time you want!'

As Lily regaled them with the gory details of her twenty-eight-hour labour, Nina stared into space while taking quick, angry sips of her drink. She couldn't believe Heidi had refused the bubbles she'd offered – probably because she was the one who had bought them. 'Maybe she thought I'd spat in it when she wasn't looking,' she thought miserably. Things between them were obviously much worse than she'd realised, although Nina thought Heidi was completely overreacting. 'Just call her tonight and say you're sorry,' she told herself, as Lily prattled on about her plans to consume Luna's placenta. 'It doesn't matter who's in the wrong; she's your only friend who isn't obsessed with babies, so you're going to need her more than ever once Daniela, Evie and Bec pop out their sprogs. Someone has to take the first step and it sure doesn't look like it's going to be her, so it's time to man up, Morey.'

Half an hour later, she'd managed to extricate herself from the endless talk of leaking boobs and baby monitors. Too mentally exhausted to walk home, Nina flagged down a taxi on Oxford Street and hopped in the back seat.

'Potts Point, please,' she instructed the driver as she opened the newspaper she'd bought at the bottle shop and started flicking through it.

'FUCK, FUCK, FUCK!' she yelled, causing the taxi driver to swerve dangerously into the other lane.

'Miss? Is everything alright?' he asked, nervously.

'No, everything is most definitely *not* alright,' she said tersely, staring at page three of the country's highest-circulating paper. There, as clear as day, was a giant colour photo of Lulu Hopkins, decked out in the biggest wedding dress Nina had ever seen, gazing lovingly into her new husband's eyes as they exited the church at their wedding the previous afternoon. *Juice*'s exclusive had just been totally and utterly ruined.

sixteen

Storming into her office on Monday morning, Nina slammed the door and threw the offending newspaper onto her desk where Meg was perched nervously. It landed with a thwack, the front page fluttering open as if on cue to reveal the photo of Lulu and Jason that had triggered what threatened to be World War III at *Juice* HQ.

'How . . . did . . . this . . . happen?' Nina demanded, drawing out her words menacingly while glaring at her news editor. 'This story is one of the biggest exclusives *Juice* has ever scored — all the other weekly magazines would kill to have it! Not to mention our circulation manager is counting on this issue to be a best-seller. You know that it's absolutely imperative to keep as many details as possible under wraps until our Friday on-sale date. Of course the Sunday papers were going to get wind of it and report that Lulu had got hitched, but they weren't supposed to know any of the specifics, except perhaps the location. They were definitely NOT supposed to get their hands on a big fat photo of her freaking dress so they could spoil our exclusive! Where the hell were the security guards to cover her up with the white sheets like we arranged?'

'They were there, I swear!' Meg squeaked. 'They swathed Lulu in sheets when she arrived so none of the paps could get a decent shot of her and they were instructed to do the same as soon as they emerged from the church. I don't know what went wrong, Nina. I'm sorry. I guess they were a split second too late or maybe the ceremony finished earlier than they were expecting and they weren't ready. I wasn't there when Lulu and Jason walked out; I was still inside taking notes about their vows and which celebrities sat where in the pews.'

'Well, you should have been there. Hashtag epic fail,' Nina said harshly. 'You've been to enough celebrity weddings to know that protecting the exclusive is one of the most important parts of the day, not the vows or who was sitting next to whom. Even if it meant throwing a sheet over Lulu's head and crash-tackling her to the ground yourself to prevent a pap getting a full-length shot of her dress, I would expect you to do it. Do you understand?'

'Yes, Nina,' Meg whispered, her face turning a deep shade of tomato.

'I want you to call the security company and demand a full explanation,' Nina raged. 'They can forget about any more business from us, needless to say, but I still want to know what the hell they were playing at.'

'Yes, Nina. I'll call them right now,' Meg said in a low voice.

'Good. When you've done that, I want the copy for the cover story on my desk by the end of the day. You are not to leave here until it's filed. Got it?' Nina turned away from her news editor and concentrated on her blank computer screen.

'Cut!' announced Scarlett. 'That was great, guys! Do you want to do it again or are you both happy?'

Nina felt drained; pretending to yell at a staff member for TV purposes was exhausting. 'I don't know if happy is the right word, but given that's the sixth take, I'm done,' she declared.

'Okay, now we just need to film some face-to-camera stuff with each of you separately, talking about the lead-up to this scene so the audience knows the background to the drama – who wants to go first?'

'Me,' Nina jumped in. 'Can we make it quick? I need to call Sam to tell him that, as per the contract, we won't be honouring the full payment seeing our exclusive has been spoiled. It was just as much their responsibility as ours to make sure the exclusive was protected. And no, you can't film me when I make the call,' she said firmly as she noticed Scarlett's face light up at the prospect of another juicy conversation to include in the story package. 'Meg, hang on a minute!' Nina grabbed the arm of her news editor as she was making a run for it and pulled her into a quiet corner of the main office. 'You know I didn't really mean any of what I said just then, don't you? During the filming? Obviously I'm pissed off at the security guards for not doing their job properly, but I know you can't be everywhere at once at big events like that. The situation isn't ideal, but it's not your fault.'

Meg glared at her. 'Then why did you just sell me out like that? I get that it makes good TV, but how do you think it will make me look? The people who watch the show are going to think I'm completely incompetent. Not to mention any prospective future employers – every time I go for an interview, they'll think, "Oh, it's the girl who didn't protect the Lulu wedding exclusive at *Juice*." I know I didn't do anything wrong, but no one else is going to know that, are they? This could be the end of my career! Did you ever stop to think about that when you decided to hand my arse to me on a platter on a national TV show?'

As Meg stalked off, Nina berated herself for allowing Scarlett to convince her to film the pretend confrontation. The *Freshly Squeezed Juice* production crew had been so stoked that something somewhat scandalous had finally happened that she'd felt she couldn't refuse when they'd suggested filming her blaming one of her staff for the stuff-up. Even though she'd tried to explain that it wasn't really Meg's fault and she didn't want to come across as a screaming banshee, they weren't interested. Once she'd capitulated, they'd lured Meg into her office for what Scarlett had taken to calling the 'showdown'. The first few takes, Nina had tried to go easy on Meg, skirting around the problem and trying to avoid obvious finger-pointing wherever possible. But she couldn't help notice Scarlett trying to hide her mounting frustration when Nina wouldn't deliver the drama goods, not to mention the rapid rate at which the clock was ticking as Scarlett insisted they did another take, then another and another. Finally, she'd capitulated and let loose at Meg on the sixth take, much to Scarlett's relief and Meg's obvious disgust. 'Kardashian sisters, eat your hearts out,' she thought, returning to her office and vowing to make it up to Meg just as soon as she'd worked out how.

'Princess got her frilly knickers in a knot?' Scarlett asked casually, while helping the camera crew to set up for the next part of the shoot.

'How did you guess?' Nina replied grimly.

'There's always one who gets on their high horse when they get told off on camera. Maybe I'll leave her solo segment for another day so she has a chance to calm down. Don't worry, when the show starts in two weeks and everyone is raving about it, she'll get over it. Now, are you going to get changed? This segment involves me asking you questions about the background of the Lulu story – how you scored the exclusive, if there was a bidding war involved, why Lulu is popular with your readers, how much organisation and stress were involved in the lead-up to the big day, what you hope to get out of it . . . things like that. But you can't wear the same thing as you did in the previous scene because it's supposed to be a different day. *Capisce?*'

Nina nodded. 'Let me go see what's in the fashion cupboard; there should be something I can borrow – I just hope it's not full of bikinis, for my sake as well as the audience's.'

An hour later, Nina had wrapped filming and was filling Scarlett in on the time their main competitor, *Bizarre*, had been a whole day late to the newsstand. No one could work out why until it had been revealed that their US-based CEO had been caught up in meetings and hadn't been able to approve the cover before they'd sent it to print. When he'd finally clapped eyes on it, he'd loathed the cover's colour scheme so much that he had ordered them to pulp the thousands of copies that had already come off the printing press and haul the editor and art director back into the office at one am to redesign the cover from scratch. It had cost *Bizarre* millions of dollars, not only in reprinting costs but also missed sales, which had resulted in some extremely irate supermarkets and newsagents.

'I can't believe he pulped all those magazines just because of a colour!' Scarlett exclaimed, removing her glasses to polish them with the hem of her coral Topshop dress. 'I mean, it's not like it's a monthly, where it'll be on stands for a few weeks. Seven days! That's it!'

'I know, but from all accounts, this CEO guy is a total prick – and not just when it comes to the colour green being used on the cover. He's been known to fire editors because he thinks they don't have enough "fuckability". Yeah, a real charmer,' Nina added when she saw Scarlett's raised eyebrows.

'Jesus . . . he sounds like he should work in TV! I love all these stories, I wish we could include them in the show – that would really blow people's socks off! So, when are we going out for another drink? I promise I won't force quite so many mojitos down your throat this time!'

'Now that you mention it, what are you up to this Thursday night? Don't suppose you want to come to the premiere of the new *Hunger Games* film with me? They're flying Jennifer Lawrence and Liam Hemsworth out for it, plus I have tickets to the VIP party afterwards.'

'Hell, yes! Team Gale all the way!' Scarlett said excitedly. 'Love me some *Hunger Games* — I can't believe who they cast as Finnick though, it's ridic! I don't think that Sam Whateverhisnameis is right at all; he's not even blond for starters.'

'Shit! Sam! I completely forgot I have to call him! Lulu's manager, not the actor playing Finnick,' Nina explained impatiently when she saw Scarlett's confused expression, annoyed at herself for letting it slip her mind. 'Time to scram, my friend. Shut the door on the way out, would you, please?'

After taking a moment to get her head back into the world of celebrity wedding contracts, Nina dialled Sam's number. Even if he hadn't seen it with his own eyes, she knew he would have heard about the spoiler photo being splashed all over the newspaper from one of his staff and would now be doing everything he could to avoid her call, so she almost dropped the phone when he picked up on the first ring.

'Nina! How are you this fine Monday afternoon?' he said smarmily.

'Sam! Uh . . . hi. To be honest, I was expecting to get your voicemail. I'm well – and you?'

'Great, just great. Saturday went down a treat. I'm so glad Lulu decided to go with *Juice* for her wedding exclusive, the day was just magical. Your readers are going to love it!'

Nina rolled her eyes – Sam seemed to have conveniently forgotten that *Juice* had scored the exclusive because she'd been smart enough to blackmail him when she'd had the chance, thanks to the idiocy of his client. She couldn't work out why he wasn't in defensive mode – after all, he must know she was calling to tell him that they wouldn't be paying the remaining fifty per cent of the story fee, thanks to the exclusive being ruined. And she was yet to meet a celebrity manager who would be happy about the prospect of having a rather large chunk of cash disappear from underneath their nose.

'Yes, I'm sure my readers will. But if I'm being honest, I would have loved it more if those security guards from the company you recommended had done their job properly. As I'm sure you're aware, they failed to prevent the paparazzi from getting a shot of Lulu in her dress. You did see page three of yesterday's paper, didn't you?' Nina asked, wondering why Sam wasn't throwing a fit.

'I sure did. Didn't she look stunning?'

Nina frowned. Was he acting dumb on purpose? 'Of course she did, but that's not the point, Sam. The point is that *Juice*'s exclusive has been ruined. You know that the dress is one of the most important elements in a wedding like this – it's the main thing my readers are gagging to see. You've been in this business long enough to know that when a full-length shot of the dress has already been printed in the country's highest-selling newspaper, it means our sales are going to suffer. Sam, I hate to do this, but as per the exclusivity clause in the contract that covers us in case any photos or major details leak before the publication of the magazine, I'm afraid we can't pay you the remaining fifty per cent of the agreed fee.' Nina held her breath, waiting for Sam to explode on the other end of the line.

But he didn't. Instead, he just chuckled. 'Oh, Nina, I think you can,' he said, sounding like he was enjoying himself.

'I'm sorry – I don't understand.'

'I think you *can* pay the rest of the money, and you will. I have a copy of the contract in front of me, and I can't see a clause anywhere that mentions a partial payment in the event of non-exclusivity.'

Nina froze. There had to be some mistake. 'Are you sure you're looking at the right contract, Sam?' she asked in what she hoped was a neutral tone, while frantically clicking her mouse to find the relevant folder on her computer where the final contract was saved. 'As you'd know, it's standard procedure for all of *Juice*'s contracts to have this clause. We have to protect our investment in case something goes wrong,' she explained, stalling for time as she sped-read through the contract on her screen. No exclusivity clause. She must have missed it. She forced herself to slow down as she started to read through the legalese again.

'Yes, I'm definitely looking at the correct contract, Nina. I remember being surprised that it wasn't included when your legal team sent it over, but I figured maybe you guys had decided to do things differently. And let's face it, who was I to argue?' he said smugly.

Nina had a sudden flashback – she was sitting at the same spot at her desk before she flew to New York reading over the contract multiple times, worried that it was missing something but not being able to put her finger on what exactly. 'Oh, just one of the most important clauses in any celebrity magazine deal,' she thought. 'Good one, you idiot. How on earth did you miss that? More importantly, how did the legal team omit the goddamn clause in the first place? Of course it would have been the first thing Sam noticed and of course he decided not to bring it to my attention. Not that anyone could blame him. If you make a mistake, you should pay for it. It's just that most people's mistakes don't cost tens of thousands of dollars. No wonder Sam sounds like all his Christmases have come at once. God, Eric is going to have kittens when he finds out.'

Nina cleared her throat, trying to decide how to best handle this nightmare situation. She knew she was backed into a corner but she didn't want to admit it until she'd had a chance to talk to the legal team to see if there was any chance of a loophole. She doubted it but sometimes straws were there to be clutched.

'Sam? So sorry about this hiccup, but I'm going to have to call you back.'

'Sure, Nina, no problem.' Sam's tone morphed from amiable to slightly threatening. 'But I think we both know *Juice* can't wriggle out of this one. Do me a favour and tell your accounts department that I want the outstanding money paid by the end of the week, would you? Pleasure doing business with you.' And on that triumphant note, he hung up.

seventeen

'Where's Miss TV Superstar off to, then? Dashing out to swan up and down Pitt Street Mall while mingling with her loyal fans? Or perhaps she's off to get a massage to relieve the stress of having the number-one TV show in the country? You'd better watch out for all the hangers-on that will emerge from the woodwork . . . owww!' Max yelled dramatically as Nina's expertly-thrown Havaiana hit him on the back of the head.

'Shut it,' she warned.

'Wait till I sell my story to your competitor – "*Freshly Squeezed Juice* star abused me with a thong". Wait, that sounds a bit kinky, doesn't it? Even better!' He grinned.

'Max, get back in your box.' Nina glared at him then resumed hunting for her house keys. 'How about I pour you a cold, frosty glass of shut-the-hell-up-about-the-goddamn-TV-show-already?

Yes, the first episode rated well and the show was trending on Twitter, but so it bloody well should, given the amount of publicity and advertising that went into hyping it up. I reckon a lot of people tuned in just to have a stickybeak, especially because of the way the production crew edited the promo reel to make the first episode look a lot more exciting than it actually was, in my opinion. So until we get audience numbers for the second episode, quit giving me shit. Between you and me, I'm fully expecting it to tank.'

'Wishful thinking, Ninja? Even if you lose half your audience for the second episode, which I seriously doubt, you know they'll keep filming till the bitter end, don't you?'

'Don't remind me. I can't believe there's still another three months of filming to go. The happiest day of my life will be when that bloody video camera is dismantled from the window of my office and things can go back to normal. Speaking of which, you look rougher than normal – were you on the sauce last night?'

'Was I ever,' Max groaned, stretching his massive frame out on the couch so he could marinate comfortably in his hangover. 'Me and the boys from work got stuck into the whisky at Baxter Inn until late o'clock. Don't suppose there's any bacon in the fridge?' he said hopefully. 'I'd kill for a fry-up.'

'Would you? That's nice, dear,' Nina replied. 'I'll leave you salivating over the thought of dead pig – I'm due to meet Heidi for lunch at North Bondi Italian, so I'll have to love you and leave you.'

'Of course you're going to North Bondi Italian – along with the rest of Sydney who wants to pretend they're someone when they're actually no one. Poncy bloody place, if you ask me,' Max muttered. 'Although they'll probably fall over themselves to give you the best seat in the house now that you're a prime-time TV celebrity,' he added, smirking.

'I'm sorry, did you say something?' Nina said airily as she snatched up her 'I heart New York' key ring from where it was hiding behind the coffee machine. 'And for your information, it was Heidi who suggested the venue, not me. So there.' Sticking her tongue out at her flatmate, Nina waltzed out the door before Max's hungover brain could think of a suitably scathing reply.

Since he'd moved in, they had settled into a comfortable routine of teasing each other mercilessly. She gave him crap about his love of cage-fighting and Coco Pops, while he never missed an opportunity to give her a serve about the TV show or her mammoth shoe collection. But that didn't mean they hadn't also bonded over the trials and tribulations of working in the magazine industry while hoovering up platefuls of Max's signature duck ragù with fresh homemade pasta – Nina had been pleasantly surprised to discover he knew his way around a kitchen, whereas her idea of cooking was to dial her local Thai for takeaway. It was also nice to be able to vent to someone who understood what was going on in the office – while Tess, Jeremy and Heidi had always listened to her and tried to help, it wasn't the same as having someone who also worked in the industry. Max had given her some good advice on how to get Meg's nose back into joint, although he hadn't been able to help her with the missing exclusivity clause in the Lulu Hopkins wedding contract. Luckily, Eric had heaped much of the blame on to the legal team, in particular the new junior lawyer who had drawn up the final contract and had somehow omitted the clause by mistake even though it was in previous versions – he had quietly left the building once Eric had finished with him, never to return.

Strolling up Victoria Street to the bus stop, Nina realised how much she was looking forward to meeting up with Heidi and getting their friendship back on track. After the wedding debacle at work, it had taken Nina a while to get around to swallowing her pride and making contact like she'd promised herself she would. Given the weird friction between them at Lily's house a few weeks ago, she had fully expected Heidi to make some lame excuse about not being able to meet up, but instead her friend sounded happy to hear from her, even suggesting they should catch up before Nina had had a chance to do it herself. Heidi had always had a soft spot for North Bondi Italian – she was obsessed with their spanner crab spaghetti cooked in a paper bag. And seeing it was forecast to be a sparkling Sydney day, Nina could think of worse places to be than overlooking the Bondi foreshore, sipping a Campari and soda while stuffing juicy green olives in her mouth. Maybe it would be a good time to start planning an Australia-based girls' trip like they'd talked about in New York? Plus she really wanted to ask Heidi about how Steph was coping with the baby influx and if she'd ever noticed her having random nosebleeds before. Seeing Nina had got nowhere when she'd tried to reach out to Steph after the baby shower, perhaps Heidi would have a better explanation.

Passing the cafe strip on the way to Oxford Street, Nina slowly became aware that she seemed to be a source of fascination. Some people stared outright, some did a double-take as she passed, while others pretended to ignore her then immediately elbowed their friends when they thought she wasn't looking.

'I must have something on my face,' she thought, surreptitiously checking if there was a gleaming ring of dried toothpaste around her mouth or a glob of unblended concealer under her eyes. 'Or maybe a bird pooped on me and I didn't realise?' She was about to duck into the nearest cafe so she could use their bathroom to check what was wrong when a group of girls in their late teens, who had been eyeballing her from the other side of the street, sidled up to her.

'Excuse me, are you Nina from *Juice?*' one of them asked hesitantly, as her friends giggled nervously in the background.

'Um, yes. That's me. What can I do for you?' Nina said, trying not to sound suspicious.

The gaggle erupted into excited squeals, all talking over the top of each other. The noise threatened to reach levels where only dogs could hear it.

'Oh my gawwwwwwd, we LOVE LOVE LOVE your new show!'

'It's totally awesomesauce! We can't wait for the second episode!'

'You are totally, like, my idol – we've just started studying journalism at university and I thought I wanted to become a foreign correspondent but now that I've seen *Freshly Squeezed Juice*, I think I'm going to concentrate on breaking into celebrity entertainment!'

'You guys look like you're having so much fun and it's all so glamorous; you're so my favourite character!'

'The show is totes amazeballs!'

'Can I get a photo with you for my Instagram?'

'Oh, me too, me too!'

'I have the latest issue of *Juice* here, can you autograph it for me? Please, please, please?'

Nina tried to act cool as she posed for multiple pictures and scrawled a message next to her editor's letter photo in the magazine that was thrust in front of her, but inside she was freaking out. It was one thing to be told that the first episode of *Freshly Squeezed Juice* had been a massive hit, with the kind of ratings *Home and Away* could only dream about, but it was another to experience the knock-on effects in real life. All of those nameless, faceless people who had tuned in two nights earlier were actual living, breathing human beings who obviously had no problem recognising her on the street. Call her naïve, but she hadn't bargained on this at all.

As Nina finished up with the group of girls, she realised there were now even more people waiting to talk to her, to ask for a photo, to compliment her on the show, or wanting to know if she'd ever met Lady Gaga or Justin Timberlake. Some of them hadn't even watched the show or heard of the magazine, but that didn't stop them from wandering over to see what all the fuss was about, then deciding to get a photo with her to show their friends in case *they* knew who the hell she was.

Finally extracting herself from the crowd after forty-five minutes, Nina realised she was seriously late for her lunch with Heidi. Shoving her massive Chanel sunglasses onto her face before anyone else recognised her, she hailed a taxi outside Bar Coluzzi and jumped in the back. 'Be thankful for small mercies,' she told herself, looking down at her white Zara mini-dress with the peplum hem. 'At least you got recognised while you were scrubbed up rather than when you were schlepping to the corner shop in your pyjamas and Uggs to get ice cream.'

'So sorry I'm late – did you get my text?' Nina asked, plopping herself opposite Heidi at the back corner table in the restaurant and putting her sunglasses away. Before Heidi could reply, an illegally handsome waiter appeared alongside them.

'Excuse me, *signorina*? The manager has advised me that another table has just become available if you two would like to follow me?'

'Oh . . . um . . . do you want to move or are you happy here?' Nina asked Heidi.

'Trust me, it is a much nicer table, is outside in the sun, overlooking the beach. The manager, he thinks you'll be much happier there,' the waiter insisted in his heavy Italian accent.

Heidi shrugged, looking confused. 'Sure, why not?'

As they settled into their new seats, drinking in the view of Bondi Beach that unfurled itself in front of them, Nina recalled Max's earlier comment about being given the best seat in the house and started to laugh.

'Heids, this is crazy. My life is officially crazy.'

'What do you mean?'

'You know how the first episode of the TV show aired the other night? Apparently it did really well. Like, *extremely* well. Didn't see that one coming, let me tell you – I totally expected it to bomb. Anyway, I'm convinced it was just a one-off and most people won't bother tuning into episode two, but in the meantime, I've got fans coming up to me on the street asking for photos and autographs! That's why I'm so late; I got caught up . . . sorry, can I help you with something?' she asked the glamorous middle-aged blonde who was hovering next to their table with a twenty-something replica hanging back behind her.

'Sorry to interrupt, sweetie, but you're Nina Morey, am I right? My daughter and I were just having lunch when she saw you walk in. She just loves your magazine and we both watched your new show the other night and thought it was fabulous! She wants to work in publishing but she's too shy to come over herself, so I took it upon myself to do her dirty work! Would you mind having a photo taken with her? If it's not too much trouble . . .'

'Of course not,' Nina smiled. 'What is your daughter's name?'

'Oh thank you – it's Madison. Come here, honey, Nina's happy to have a photo,' she urged her mini-me as she pulled a Swarovski-encrusted iPhone from her Coach tote.

'Hi, Madison, it's nice to meet you – I'm glad you like the show,' Nina said to the girl as they posed for her mother.

'Oh, it was so good! I'd love to work in magazines but I've heard it's really hard to get a foot in the door. Have you got any advice?' Madison asked breathlessly.

'Two words – work experience,' Nina advised. 'The majority of magazines have a work experience or intern program, so contact the editorial assistant of the titles you'd like to work for to see if they have any availability. You might have to go on a waiting list, but it's invaluable experience.'

'Great, thanks so much! And thanks for the photo – my friends will die when I tell them I ran into you! I can't wait to see the rest of the TV series!'

'No problem – enjoy your lunch,' Nina called out as Madison and her mother made their way back to their table. 'Sorry – but this is what I'm talking about,' she explained to a bemused-looking Heidi. 'Ever since I left the house this morning, people have been acting like I'm some kind of celebrity.'

'Well, I guess you kind of are. Simon and I watched the show and you came across really well – I'm not surprised everyone wants a piece of you. But how come the fans only started flocking today if the show was on Thursday night?'

'I guess because I wasn't out and about like I am today – I got into work early and left late yesterday so I had no idea what it would be like until now. Hopefully it will calm down a bit; I don't think I'm cut out for the fame game. Anyway, enough about me – how are things with you?' Nina asked, as another outrageously good-looking waiter placed a bowl of olives and some grissini sticks on the table.

'Compliments of the manager,' he smiled, ignoring Nina's embarrassment when she realised they were getting the VIP treatment again. 'Can I get you ladies something to drink?'

'Oh . . . I haven't decided yet . . .' Heidi said, sounding flustered. 'I'll just stick to sparkling water for the moment until I make up my mind.'

'Certainly. Anything for you?' he directed at Nina.

'A Campari and soda, please,' she requested. Switching her attention back to Heidi, she decided to get straight to the point. 'Listen, Heids, I know we've been through a bit of a rough time and I want to apologise. I know you think I've been acting like a selfish idiot, but I guess I didn't see this yummy mummy epidemic coming and I'm finding it a bit hard to get my head around. It's not that I mean to be a bitch about all the baby stuff, but it's like my friends have morphed into completely different people overnight and I feel like I don't know them anymore. But I admit I haven't dealt with it very well. I just wanted you to know that I'm going to try harder from now on – I haven't got to the hospital to see Daniela and Noah or Evie and Ruby yet, but I will, I promise . . .' Nina stopped when she realised the gay couple who had just sat down at the next table were staring at her. She threw them a quick smile and was about to continue her mea culpa when one of them leant over and said, 'Well, if it isn't Ms Nina Morey. Nathan and I just loved the show – didn't we, darls?' he said to his partner, who nodded vigorously. 'Of course, I work in PR so I have a vested interest and Nathan is obsessed with all things celebrity, so what's not to love? To be honest, when I heard about it, I thought it might end up being a dog, but you sure know how to give good TV! Cheers, honey – here's to the next episode!'

Nina smiled and thanked them – the interruptions were starting to get on her nerves but she didn't want to offend anyone. Despite her prediction that no one would bother tuning in for the rest of the series, she knew it was in Juice's best interest to keep as many people interested for as long as possible and if that meant posing for photos and being nice to strangers when she was trying to have a deep and meaningful with her best friend, she'd just have to suck it up.

'Sorry – again,' she sighed, putting her sunglasses back on in the hope that it would prevent her from getting recognised then turning back to Heidi. 'I told you it was crazy. What was I saying?'

Heidi smiled nervously. 'I know you've found the whole baby thing tough but I'm really glad you've come to realise that it's not a personal vendetta against you. Um, so . . . I guess there's no time like the present – I've got something to tell you.'

Popping an olive in her mouth, Nina leant back in her chair, enjoying the warmth of the sun on her face. She was so glad things were okay with her and Heidi again. 'Well, go on, spit it out,' she said when her best friend seemed hesitant.

'Let me guess – you and Simon have been together for three months now, so you're shacking up together?'

'Well, there's that,' Heidi confirmed. 'But that's not all. If I'm honest, I'm kind of scared to tell you given everything that's happened recently, but . . .' Heidi paused and took a deep breath. 'Nina, I'm pregnant.'

eighteen

Nina felt like she'd been clubbed over the head with a sterling silver Tiffany & Co baby rattle.

'You're what?' she choked out, expecting Heidi to crack up laughing and tell her she was kidding. Any minute now . . .

'I'm pregnant,' Heidi repeated. 'With twins.'

Nina smiled and mock-glared at her. Twins? Yeah, right. Of course she was kidding.

'Ha ha, very funny. And Mr Snuffleupagus is the father, I presume?'

Heidi leant forward with a deadly serious look on her face. 'Nina, I'm not joking. I'm twelve weeks pregnant. Simon is the father. We just found out we're having twins at the scan this week – I'm still trying to get my head around it! Apart from our families, you're the first to know. I thought you may have guessed actually, when I didn't drink any of the champagne you bought at Lily's place the other week. It obviously wasn't planned – I think I must have messed up when to take my pill due to the time difference in New York – but now that it's happening and we've got our heads around it, we figure it's meant to be. I really hope you can be happy for me.'

Nina stared at her silently, trying to absorb the news. Her best friend was pregnant. With twins, as the cherry on top. Her best friend who had always maintained she wasn't the maternal type, who used to scoff at the idea of swapping Prada for Play-Doh, who had sympathised with Nina whenever she rolled her eyes at all the never-ending Facebook debates among their friends about whether amber-bead teething necklaces really work or not. Her best friend who, it gradually dawned on her, had always hosed her down whenever she'd embarked on one of her rants about the mummy mafia takeover. The same friend who had happily volunteered to hold Luna when they'd visited Lily's baby the month before. The same friend who had gone from dating an endless string of cute no-hopers to moving in with a suited-and-booted business entrepreneur after a matter of months. Their supposedly shared attitude of carefree singledom had turned out to be bollocks. But she couldn't dump all the blame at her friend's feet – Nina realised too late that she'd been projecting her own views about children onto Heidi, not wanting to be the only one who didn't get what all the fuss was about. 'And now she's got two goddamn buns in the oven and is as happy as a clam about it. Didn't see that one coming, did you?' she thought bitterly.

'Aren't you going to say something?' Heidi asked quietly, looking at Nina's blank face with concern.

Nina hurriedly faked a wide smile, trying to act like it was the best news ever. Maybe if she pretended hard enough, she'd start to believe it herself.

'Um, wow! That's great!' she said. 'Twins, huh? Wow! Double trouble! You'll be one big happy family! Wow! So it happened around the time we were in New York? Wow!' Nina hoped she didn't come across as discombobulated as she felt, despite the fact her brain seemed to have hit repeat on the word 'wow'.

'I know it's a bit of a surprise, but I'm still me, even though I'm pregnant,' Heidi assured her. 'Don't worry, I'm not going to become one of those women who throws a gender-reveal party to announce the sex of their unborn child and who talks endlessly about the size of their haemorrhoids. Nothing's going to change, I promise.'

Despite her best intentions, Nina's vow to act more selflessly when it came to her friends evaporated – she couldn't help herself. 'Are you serious? How can you say that?' she demanded, scorching anger ripping through her. 'It's already changed! My best friend, who has never seemed interested in motherhood since I've known her, has just told me she's pregnant to a guy she's known for, like, a minute. I guess it's my fault for wanting to believe you were on the same page as me when it came to having babies. So you think nothing's going to change? You think you'll still be able to meet up for all-day shopping marathons, do you? Or bar-hop until two am every weekend? Or how about going on our girls' trips to Tasmania and Thailand or Byron and Barcelona – remember that deal we made in New York? You really think you'll be able to do all that after having twins? Colour me cynical, Heidi, but dream on. You'll be up to your neck in a literal shit storm, which is fine because dirty nappies will be the only thing you'll want to talk about anyway. You think you're the only person to swear you won't change once you have kids? Take a ticket and join the queue. You've already changed; I guess I just didn't want to see it. I think we're done here – I'll get the bill on the way out. It's my treat to say thanks for being such a great friend,' she declared, her words dripping with sarcasm as she scraped her chair back and stumbled inside, leaving a shaken Heidi at the table.

Floundering up Campbell Parade in a haze of tears, Nina kept her head down as she prayed for an available taxi to appear out of nowhere. There was no way she was taking the bus, not in the snivelling, shambolic state she was currently in. She needed someone to recognise her from *Freshly Squeezed Juice* like she needed a lesson on how to see only what she wanted to see, despite all the signs pointing to the contrary.

'Nina! Hey!'

She pretended not to hear and prayed harder for the taxi gods to smile on her.

'Nina! Nina! It's me! What's up, girl?'

Brushing away her tears, Nina tried to get her act together before having to deal with the person who had been chasing after her for the last few metres. She had never been more relieved to see Charlie's boyishly handsome face instead of the total stranger wanting to talk about the TV show that she'd been expecting. She'd completely forgotten she was in his 'hood.

'Charlie! Thank God it's you. I'm having a rough day and the thought of having to talk to more randoms is enough to push me over the edge.'

'Why would you have to talk to randoms?' her occasional shag asked, hopping on the skateboard he was carrying and cruising alongside her as they continued to battle the beachfront crowds.

'Because of the TV show,' she explained. 'Everyone wants a piece of me. I mean, it's great that it's so popular but I had no idea it would be like this and I just got some bad news so I don't really feel like being "Nina from *Juice*" right now. I just want to crawl into a hole.'

'Huh? What TV show?'

She almost melted into a puddle of relief when she remembered Charlie didn't own a TV – or much else – so wouldn't have the first clue about *Freshly Squeezed Juice*.

'Don't worry, I can't be bothered going into it right now. How are you, anyway?'

'Yeah, you know . . . everything's chill. Just hanging out, doing a bit of this and that. So what's the bad news? Are you okay?' he asked sweetly. 'Do you want to talk about it? We could go for a drink somewhere? My mate's working at Bondi Canteen, he'll probably give us free beer.'

Suddenly the idea of sinking a few cold amber ales with uncomplicated Charlie and his uncomplicated surfer mates seemed like the perfect antidote to what had turned into a hell of a day.

'Sure, sounds good.' She smiled at him gratefully.

They'd downed two longnecks and were halfway through their third before Nina wrapped up the sorry tale of Heidi's betrayal. It felt good to get it all off her chest, to unload onto someone who was a completely neutral third party. She'd never thought of Charlie as a good sounding board before, but that wasn't really surprising given their previous exploits hadn't exactly involved much talking.

'So now all my closest friends are either mothers or pregnant or desperately trying to get pregnant; my best friend who was supposed to be my partner in crime as we partied our way around the world has gone to the dark side and I have no one to play with. I know life doesn't always work out the way you want, but it just wasn't supposed to be like this, you know?' she finished miserably, wallowing in a huge vat of self-pity as she took another big swallow from her bottle of Coopers Green. She looked at Charlie's thoughtful face, hoping he was about to impart some pearls of wisdom that would help her to make sense of her massive friendship mess.

'Whoa, that's hectic,' Charlie declared with the gravity of a Jedi master. She waited for his analysis of the situation but he remained silent, looking off into the distance, eyes glazed over. Gradually Nina realised he wasn't milling through all the information so he could give her some brilliant advice – he was actually checking the surf conditions. 'That's hectic' was all the response she was going to get. Kicking herself for thinking she'd get anything more from a dopey-but-cute surfer dude, she started to giggle at her stupidity, feeling pleasantly light-headed as the alcohol seeped into her bloodstream. As Charlie looked at her enquiringly, she realised again how cute he was. Not to mention good in bed. It had been a while since they'd thrown each other around the bedroom . . . it might be just what the doctor ordered – and wasn't it universally accepted knowledge that there was no time like the present?

'Don't suppose you want to come back to my place?' she asked with a wink, charging straight towards the bush instead of beating half-heartedly around it as she slid her hand onto his knee.

Looking down at her hand, which was now crawling its way slowly up his inner thigh, he smiled.

'My place is closer,' he replied.

'Your place is a grotty tip that should be condemned. My place, end of story,' she said firmly, having made the mistake of going back to his house once before – it had taken days for the stench of his unwashed sheets to leave her nostrils.

'Your place it is then,' he capitulated, hurriedly downing the rest of his beer.

An hour later, Nina was having one of the best orgasms of her life thanks to Charlie's talented tongue. As she peeled herself off the ceiling, she hoped the pillow she'd used to muffle her moans had done the trick — she wasn't used to remembering to keep the volume down after living by herself for so long, but seeing she'd heard Max return from wherever he'd been halfway through their bedroom aerobics, she hadn't wanted to take any chances. Curling up contentedly next to Charlie's chest, she ran her hand over his tanned stomach. His body looked like it had been carved from caramel — slim, brown and lean from daily yoga and surfing sessions. As her hand continued its journey up along his shoulders and down his arms, she was reminded of his sister and how she had planned to ask Heidi about Steph's nosebleeds. Nina still couldn't shake the feeling that something was not quite right about that incident at the baby shower — there was no way someone as stylish as Steph wouldn't have noticed smeared blood all over her sleeves. And although Nina couldn't be one hundred per cent sure, she didn't remember seeing any stains when they'd first chatted outside the bathroom. Maybe the stress Steph was under had triggered some kind of skin condition that meant it bled easily when it was knocked or put under pressure? That would explain why she'd grimaced when Nina had grabbed her arm and why she'd taken to wearing long sleeves so much lately.

'Hey, Charlie, do you get nosebleeds all the time too, like Steph?' she asked. Maybe it was a hereditary condition.

'No idea what you're talking about,' he said, with a puzzled look. 'The last time I remember Steph getting a nosebleed was when she was a teenager, before our parents packed her off to the doctor to get her beak cauterised.'

'Her beak?! Okay, so does she have any skin conditions that you know of?' she enquired carefully.

'Huh? What do you mean? Like arthritis?'

'No . . . for starters, arthritis is a problem with your joints, it has nothing to do with skin,' Nina said patiently, remembering that Charlie wasn't the sharpest crayon in the box. 'I mean like eczema or maybe psoriasis . . . something that could aggravate her skin and perhaps make it bleed?'

Charlie shrugged. 'No idea. Don't think so. She's never mentioned anything to me and we talk all the time. Why?'

'No real reason; just wondering,' Nina replied, feeling even more certain that the various pieces of the Steph jigsaw didn't fit but coming no closer to finding out why. 'So what's the plan for the rest of the afternoon?'

Charlie checked the time and jumped out of bed. 'The plan is to catch a few waves – the surf report reckons there'll be a big swell coming in soon, so I gotta run.'

Nina didn't try to convince him otherwise – although she wouldn't have minded going for round two, she felt a bit awkward having Charlie in her bedroom now that Max was home. She certainly wasn't looking forward to the teasing she'd have to endure after he'd gone. Pulling on a pair of bleached denim cut-offs and an oversized grey marle t-shirt, she followed Charlie into the living room, where Max was prone in front of the TV, an empty bucket of what had been KFC grease beside him.

'Feeding the hangover beast, Max?' she asked to get his attention, hoping it wasn't screamingly obvious what she'd just been up to. 'This is my friend Charlie, by the way. Charlie, this is Max, my newish flatmate.'

As Max clambered off the couch to shake Charlie's hand, Nina noticed the guys sizing each other up. Next to Max's massive bulk, Charlie looked like a twelve-year-old who probably couldn't even spell puberty, let alone experience it anytime soon. While her flatmate tried his best to make small talk, Nina realised just how young Charlie was as he replied in monosyllabic grunts and ignored any opportunity to be polite and ask Max about himself. She couldn't help comparing the two – Max, who had a successful career and had travelled the world, and Charlie, who barely left Bondi and was happy to drift from one short-term job to another.

Suddenly she felt embarrassed – sure, Charlie was just someone to help scratch an itch, but she didn't want Max to think less of her because her choice of bed mate was barely out of nappies and could hardly string a sentence together. 'Don't be ridiculous,' she chastised herself. 'What does it matter what Max thinks? He's your flatmate, not your mother.'

Hurrying Charlie out the door, she dodged his mouth as he went in for a kiss and was deliberately non-committal when he suggested catching up again. Something told her it would be the last time she'd hook up with Steph's brother. 'Oh well, it was fun while it lasted,' she thought, closing the door behind him and steeling herself for the barrage of teasing that was sure to follow. To her surprise, Max stayed silent, only raising an eyebrow as she met his gaze defiantly. She could feel his eyes still on her as she attempted to saunter nonchalantly back to her room to strip the sheets. When she caught sight of herself in the mirrored doors of the built-in wardrobe, she realised her face was red – not with the afterglow of a satisfying bedroom session, but with the hot flush of shame.

nineteen

Nina pushed the thick wad of invitations across her desk and grinned as Scarlett looked at them with the glee of a six-year-old faced with a Mount Everest of presents on Christmas morning.

'There's more where that came from; that's just what's on tonight – Wednesday is always one of the most popular nights for parties because it's not too close to the start of the week, when everyone is recovering from their weekends. It also helps that the PR agencies pretty much count on coverage for their clients in the Sunday social pages – any later than Wednesday and they run the risk of missing out due to print deadlines and competition from better parties,' Nina explained while Scarlett started to thumb through the stack, deciding what was worth their time and what was too lame to bother with.

Thanks to *Freshly Squeezed Juice* continuing to attract a big audience halfway through its season, Nina had found herself filed under 'V' for VIP in the little black books of Sydney's numerous PR agencies. While she'd been invited to various functions as editor of *Juice* before the TV show had come to town, this was a whole new ballgame. What felt like an avalanche of invitations landed on her desk every day – from a swanky dinner at Otto to celebrate the launch of an Italian coffee machine to the opening of the new flagship store of the latest international designer to set up home on Castlereagh Street. Bella had PR assistants constantly on the phone, desperate to know if Nina would be gracing their client's function with her presence. Luckily, all of them were happy to accommodate Scarlett as her 'plus one' if it guaranteed she would turn up and get snapped by the newspapers' staff photographers for the social pages. A week or so ago, she'd been mortified when she realised she'd been featured in not just one, not just two, but four of the events covered in both of Sydney's Sunday papers. Luckily, they'd all been on different nights so she wasn't wearing the same outfit in any of the photos – she and Scarlett often function-hopped when there were multiple parties on the same night, flitting from one to another until they found the best vibe – and the best champagne. Her previous rule of not drinking during the week had taken a bit of a battering although she was still conscious of not overdoing it. In any case, with so many people wanting to talk to her at every event, Nina found that she didn't really get a chance to knock back a huge amount anyway. Of course, there were nights when she and Scarlett ended up a bit too squiffy, especially if magnums of Veuve were being poured as if they were tap water, like at the recent opening of a new bar in The Rocks, but she didn't have the constant craving to get obliterated like when she'd been the editor at *Candy*. She wasn't drinking due to stress this time; it was definitely more of a social thing. Plus with so many more eyes on her than ever before, the last thing she needed was for the gossip columnists to start sniping that she had a drinking problem – given her history, it was a little too close to home.

She'd also found that a small bump of Scarlett's 'snow', as her friend called it, helped to sober her up when she found herself feeling a bit too pissy. At first she'd been surprised when Scarlett had hustled her into a bathroom cubicle and produced a small bag of white powder, digging the end of her car key into the stash then snorting it before offering it to Nina, but it soon became a semi-regular occurrence although it was always Scarlett who instigated it. Usually it was at one of the high-end events when there were flocks of Sydney A-listers in attendance – Nina had a sneaking suspicion that Scarlett used it to give her confidence, especially when a lot of the big names wanted to talk to Nina about how much they loved the show, putting themselves forward for fashion shoots and 'at home' features in the mag. While she always made a point of introducing Scarlett and trying to include her in the conversation, there was only so much she could do when the celebs made it obvious that if Scarlett couldn't do anything for them, they weren't interested in making small talk. At least all the schmoozing was good for the magazine – thanks to the popularity of *Freshly Squeezed Juice*, her phone was ringing constantly with celebrity managers falling over themselves to lock away exclusives. Of course she knew full well that one of the reasons they wanted their talent to work with *Juice* was the potential of being included in an episode of the hugely popular TV show, but when it meant getting access to celebrities who had previously declined to do any work with celebrity weeklies, no matter how much money was thrown at them, Nina wasn't going to quibble. She knew *Bizarre*, their main rival, would be having hissy fits about the number of exclusives they were missing out on, but she was going to ride this gravy train until the very end.

'Thoughts on tonight's agenda?' Nina asked Scarlett. 'I like the look of the new Topshop store opening, the Marc Jacobs perfume launch and maybe the Samsung Galaxy event because it's just down the road. After that, we could check out the crowd at MTV's "Coachella Forever" bash? I got Bella to RSVP to all of them so we can go to as many or as few as we want. Speak of the devil . . .' she said, as *Juice*'s editorial assistant staggered into her office, doing her best packhorse impression thanks to the number of glossy carrier bags she had in one hand and the heap of garment bags draped over her other arm.

'Remind me not to leave it so long to do a courier dock pick-up next time,' she complained good-naturedly, hanging the clothes on the portable rail that now lived in Nina's office, then removing their plastic sheaths and placing the other bags next to Nina's chair.

The amount of freebies that had started to pour in as the TV show took off was another perk – clothing labels sent her cherry-picked edits of their new collections as well as coveted VIP discount cards to use in their stores whenever she wanted; beauty companies couriered over truckloads of perfume, cosmetics and skincare; lifestyle brands delivered their latest and greatest gadgets and she'd lost count of the number of cars that had been offered to her to zoom around in on a temporary basis while the show was on air. Nina did her best to share the love around with her staff, Scarlett and sometimes Max if he was lucky, but she had to admit she wasn't beyond snaffling the best bits and pieces for herself. She figured it was the pay-off for her lost anonymity – although she wasn't up there with the Lara Bingles of the world in terms of paparazzi, autograph-hunters and online trolls, there wasn't a day that went by without someone approaching her to ask if she was 'that bird from the magazine show my missus loves on the TV', as one forty-something guy had recently put it. She'd lost count of how many Instagram photos she'd posed for with fans and the size of her Twitter following was going gangbusters – she even had an official Verified account now, with the blue tick to prove it was really her.

'Thanks, Bella – hey, you like Chanel, don't you? Catch,' Nina said, fishing into the black and white carrier bag that had just been delivered and tossing her a lipstick from the iconic French brand's new season collection, which wouldn't be in store for another three months. 'I'm more of a lip gloss girl myself. Once I've had a chance to open everything, I'll put the rest on the meeting table for the staff to go through. Thanks for hauling everything up from the courier dock. What's wrong with you?' she asked a now-pouting Scarlett.

'I like Chanel too, you know,' she pointed out, somewhat petulantly.

'Don't we all, darling,' Nina drawled. 'But you didn't lug all those bags and parcels up from the bowels of the building, did you? And it's not like you haven't shared in the spoils before. Plus, you get to come to all these glittering soirées with me tonight. Which ones do you reckon?' she prodded.

'I'm good with the ones you like – as you say, if we get there and they're lame, then we can always move on to one of the others seeing your minion has RSVP'd to them all for you.'

'Don't call her that,' Nina said sharply. 'She's not my minion, she's the magazine's editorial assistant.'

Scarlett shrugged dismissively, obviously still miffed that Bella had scored Chanel loot and she hadn't. 'Whatever. Hey, do you think Ned will be at any of the parties tonight?' she said hopefully.

Nina smirked at her friend's eagerness. Scarlett had a mammoth crush on Ned Owens, the disgustingly charismatic singer from Sloth Robot, a B-list boy band that was on its way to becoming Australia's answer to a more mature One Direction. When *Juice* had done a recent photo shoot with him and the rest of the band, Scarlett had gone along as the producer of the behind-the-scenes TV segment and had fallen hook, line and sinker for Ned's copious charm. A big fan of the opening of any envelope, Ned was even more ubiquitous on the Sydney party scene than Nina, and the stories of his female conquests were legendary.

'I don't think, I know,' Nina confirmed. 'Sloth Robot are playing at MTV's party and knowing Ned, he'll probably be doing the rounds of all the other events tonight before he's due in East Sydney, depending on whether he can get away from the clutches of Sloth Robot's manager, who tries to keep him on a tight leash.'

'Oh my God, that means we *have* to go to the MTV party! The last time we saw him at that Bombay Sapphire launch, I lost my nerve, but this time I'm definitely going to talk to him. He would totally remember me from the photo shoot, right?'

Nina weighed up her options – on the one hand, she didn't want to burst her friend's bubble, but on the other, she suspected that Ned would have absolutely no memory of Scarlett. Given the number of photo shoots the band would do and the amount of people they would meet on all the different sets, she couldn't really blame him.

'There's only one way to find out!' Nina declared, neatly avoiding a definitive answer.

'What am I going to wear?' Scarlett wailed, while eyeing off the clothing rail that was now heaving with dresses, tops, skirts, jackets and trousers from high-end Australian labels like Rachel Gilbert and Ellery and high-street chains such as Sportsgirl and Witchery.

'You look just fine as you are,' Nina said distractedly, as she spied a new email from the magazine's circulation manager in her inbox. Opening it, she quickly skimmed the projected sales figures for that week's issue and did a mental fist pump. Thanks to the TV show and the increased number of celebrity exclusives they were scoring, the magazine was killing it at the cash register. She had to admit that, far from being the massive mistake she once thought it would be, *Freshly Squeezed Juice* was the magazine's new best friend. The only problem was figuring out how to milk it so the sales momentum continued after the show had wrapped.

'You cannot be serious,' Scarlett declared dramatically. 'This dress is, like, so last season and it makes me look like a heifer. Comfortable, yes. Flattering, no. I can't go out like this if I'm going to chat up Ned! There'll be loads of celebrities at the MTV party; I need to look shit-hot!'

Nina tried not to grimace. As much as she liked Scarlett and how much fun she was, not to mention how she was always up for a good time, the flip side was that sometimes she could be a little high-maintenance. But if it meant not having to deal with any of the fanatical baby mamas who were supposed to be her closest friends, she was prepared to put up with it. She hadn't seen Heidi since that day at North Bondi Italian several weeks ago – and quite frankly, she didn't particularly want to. She knew she was being unreasonable but the last thing she felt like doing was pasting on a fake smile and listening to stories about pregnancy cravings, antenatal classes and birth plans when the two of them should have been sinking margaritas at the El Loco pop-up restaurant at the Opera House while discussing a future girls' trip to Mexico. The incessant bleating about anything and everything baby-related had been bad enough with Lily, Daniela and Evie; she couldn't bear the thought of Heidi becoming a fully paid-up member of the mummy mafia as well. Bec had given birth the other week but Nina hadn't bothered to visit or even to write back to the blanket text she'd received announcing the arrival of Bec's son, Mason, and she still hadn't made an effort to meet Noah or Ruby, Daniela and Evie's kids. Heidi had actually tried to contact her a few times; Nina usually screened her calls, then sometimes texted back explaining she was busy with work and would call her later. But she never did. She knew she was pushing her friends away because of her own stubborn, selfish issues, but she told herself she just needed some time out to adjust to the new world order of her friendship group. It was easier to immerse herself in work, in going out, in having a good time. It was easier to forget and not have to deal with it. Ironically, the one person she had tried to keep in touch with seemed to be avoiding her – despite sending multiple texts, emails and Facebook messages, Steph remained elusive. Nina couldn't help wondering if it was because of the bloodstain incident or if Steph had shut herself off from everyone as she and Chris battled their fertility demons.

'Don't you think this would look good on me? It would be perfect for the MTV party!'

Nina snapped back to the present to find Scarlett stroking a mouth-watering matte silver leather mini-skirt with stud detailing that she'd plucked from the clothes rack, conveniently forgetting that it had been sent in for Nina, not her. But before she could reply, Layla rushed into the office, looking like she was about to self-combust with excitement.

'Nina! You won't believe this – I've just had a call from one of the photo agencies. The biggest celebrity scandal of the year, if not the decade, has just erupted! My contact is uploading the incriminating photo set to our file-sharing site as we speak. We need an emergency news conference, STAT!'

twenty

'What the hell is taking so long?' Nina demanded. 'We're wasting precious time here!'

Her key members of staff had been assembled around the meeting table for the past half hour, waiting to start the impromptu news conference that Nina had called, but they were under strict instructions from Andy, the TV show's executive producer, not to start until all the cameras were in place, everyone was miked up and the sound checks had been done. Given how big the scandal supposedly was, he was keen for this to be a major story arc in an upcoming episode and had instructed Scarlett to make sure it was filmed as the news conference happened, not as a mocked-up retake afterwards.

'Sorry for the delay, everyone, we now have lift-off,' Scarlett replied, looking at Nina apologetically. 'Please try not to talk over the top of each other and whatever you do, don't look directly into the cameras. Just pretend they're not there. Three, two, one, action!'

'Sorry to interrupt your afternoon so suddenly, people, but Layla just alerted me to the fact that something major is going down in Hollywood as we speak,' Nina began smoothly, knowing she had to set the scene for the TV audience. After multiple weeks of filming, she was so used to talking with a camera in her face, she barely even noticed it anymore. 'One of the photo agencies has got their hands on an exclusive set of pictures that will trigger the biggest celebrity scandal of the year. For a magazine like Juice, this is what we call the gift that keeps on giving – my guess is that the after-shocks of this story will reverberate for weeks to come. Of course you're all dying to know what it is – Layla, do you have the picture set?'

Her photo editor turned bright red as one of the cameras focused on her woodenly handing the sheaf of print-outs to Nina. Layla hated being part of the TV show and couldn't act naturally even if she'd wanted to, but as one of Nina's right-hand people, she had to be included in the filming whether she liked it or not. Showing the ins and outs of a weekly celebrity magazine without featuring the picture editor was like filming The Notebook without Ryan Gosling – unthinkable.

As Nina passed the print-outs around the table, Scarlett silently motioned for one of the cameras to zoom in on the photos while another panned over the stunned looks on the staff's faces. There had been no need for Scarlett to worry about them talking over the top of each other – they could barely finish a sentence as they stared at the scandalous images.

'Is that . . . ?'

'Is she . . . ?'

'Are they . . . ?'

'In the back of a . . . ?'

'Sweet baby Jesus,' Simone summed up as the photos finally reached her. 'Shit is going to hit the fan, big-time. I mean, I know the photos are pretty grainy, but this is EPIC.'

Nina smiled at the shocked silence that hung over the table and continued her monologue for the cameras. 'As you've all just seen, one of Hollywood's most famous starlets has been busted by a pap with a very long lens while getting busy with a guy who is not her long-term boyfriend. In the back of a pick-up truck. In broad daylight. What a muppet. And just to make things even more juicy, I think we all agree there is a particular photo sequence that shows him heading "downtown", shall we say. Given she's one half of the most adored off-screen couples in the world, both of whom have made millions playing a loved-up on-screen couple in a hugely successful movie franchise, there are no prizes for guessing how big this story is going to be.'

'What's the starting bid for this set? Surely it'll be beyond our budget?' Joe, the art director, asked Layla, completely forgetting that the conversation was being recorded.

'No need to worry about that; I've already spoken to our publisher and he's given me free rein to secure this set,' Nina quickly jumped in before Layla could answer. Much to the producers' disgust, one of her ground rules was that, while the cameras were rolling, there was no discussion of how much money changed hands when it came to buying exclusive picture sets and negotiating celebrity photo shoots. She realised people at home would be dying to know down to the very last cent, but she also knew that many of them would be outraged at the astronomical sums the magazine spent every week. While some of the general public might realise celebrities got paid to appear in weekly magazines, it only took one person to start a social media backlash, and of course it would be the magazines that got the blame, not the picture agencies or celebrity managers who cunningly played the titles off against each other in order to drive the prices up.

Scarlett had casually asked her about the financial side of things back when the Lulu Hopkins wedding exclusive had been ruined; she'd given her some off-the-record ballpark figures that she usually doled out to people she knew she could trust if they happened to ask, but there was no way in hell anything official was getting caught on film. Not only would the other magazines get their noses out of joint, she could kiss any more celebrity exclusives goodbye – the A-list managers would kill her if the punters found out that their clients only did photo shoots and interviews in return for cold hard cash. Unless they were contractually obliged to promote something, of course.

'But . . . I mean, I know this is a major story, especially seeing the guy looks a lot like the leading man from her most recent film, but does it matter that her relationship with her franchise star is a contract deal set up by their publicists? So really, she's not actually cheating on him and therefore she's not really doing anything wrong?' Gracie piped up, then immediately looked stricken as she remembered the cameras were rolling.

'CUT!' Nina yelled, as the TV crew's eyebrows collectively shot up to the ceiling. 'Sorry, Scarlett, but you absolutely have to scrap what Gracie just said. Guys, promise me you'll delete that bit of footage,' she pleaded with the camera crew.

They avoided her gaze and looked at Scarlett, out the window, at their non-existent watches – anywhere but at Nina.

'Seriously, that cannot go to air,' she stressed again.

'Stop rolling for a second,' Scarlett instructed her team. 'Did Gracie just say what I think she said?' she asked disbelievingly as *Juice's* entertainment editor tried to make herself as invisible as possible. 'Is this common knowledge?'

Nina tried her best to not sound irritated about Gracie letting the cat out of the bag, although she would have dearly loved to have ripped the girl's tongue out with her bare hands. 'Of course it isn't common knowledge; why do you think I said it absolutely cannot go to air? Do you know how much devastation you'd wreak on zillions of rabid fans around the globe if they knew their beloved couple was a sham, forced together by their publicists for the greater cause of the franchise?'

'I . . . I . . . wow . . . that blows my mind . . . and I don't even rate them as a couple,' Scarlett admitted. 'So you're saying that they're only together because of a contract? What about all the "are they together or aren't they?" speculation at the start of their relationship? And refusing to talk about each other in press interviews or walk the red carpet together at premieres? Hang on, weren't they just snapped at a concert holding hands?'

'Yep, but it's all bollocks,' Nina explained. 'Our sources tell us they're contracted to go on a certain number of public dates each month, where they'll always get photographed by a die-hard fan who can't resist uploading the pics to social media. Or a lurking pap will just happen to catch them leaving the back entrance of a dive bar together. Of course, they always look pissed off about it, but it's just pretend. Remember, they're actors – and good ones at that. The whole "relationship" has been based around the classic rule of "always leave them wanting more". If they had hooked up immediately after the first film was released when everyone and their guinea pig were desperate for them to be together in real life, it would have been just another on-set romance. But by refusing to confirm whether they were an item or not, it got people salivating. And they've never really come straight out and confirmed if they're officially an item or not, but by being photographed together on the sly now and then, they're giving their fans what they want – to believe in the fairytale.

'Plus it's also a business decision – they both know that at this point in time, they are more in demand together than they are separately. Although I've heard that not all is happy at home – apparently he now can't stand her and wants out, but he's locked into a watertight contract for another year or so, until the DVD of their last film is released. But now she's been busted getting her rocks off with Lover Boy, maybe he'll demand an early exit. I doubt their management teams would let that happen – they'd be too worried about alienating the franchise fans before the DVD hits the shelves. Isn't Hollywood romantic?' Nina said sarcastically.

'Anyway, that's why Gracie's comment has to get wiped. Seriously, we could have suicides on our hands if it gets out; their fan base is literally that obsessed. There's going to be global histrionics when these photos are made public, but at least their publicists can put a tortured "will he forgive her?" angle on it; rather that than the huge amount of damage control they'd have to do if it was revealed the relationship is purely a business arrangement. Anyway, keep that on the downlow, okay? Not that anyone would believe you anyway, given how many people they've duped into thinking it's eternal love.'

'Unbelievable,' muttered Scarlett, her eyes out on stalks. 'I'll do my best to explain why it can't make the final edit to Andy, but you might need to talk him through it if he doesn't buy it.'

'No problem,' Nina shrugged, knowing she could get Eric to personally oversee the final edit of the specific episode if Andy didn't play ball. Her publisher knew that for the greater good of the gossip smorgasbord, some industry secrets needed to stay exactly that – secret. 'Okay, let's try this again.'

At the packed MTV party later that night, Nina waved her glass under the nose of a passing waiter for another refill of champagne. She didn't recall finishing her previous glass of bubbles, but it was so hot inside the venue she could have drunk enough liquid to fill the Grand Canyon and still felt parched.

'Have you seen Ned since Sloth Robot's performance?' Scarlett shouted in her ear, as people pushed past her on the way to the dance floor. Nina shook her head, then frowned as she noticed the numerous champagne stains on the brand-new leather skirt Scarlett had begged Nina to let her wear, swearing on her grandmother's grave that she'd take extra-special care of it. 'Stop being so uptight, it's not like you paid for it,' she reminded herself. 'At least Scarlett is here with you having fun, unlike some other friends you could name.'

'Bugger. I wonder what time he'll come out from the green room. So, how much did those photos end up going for?' Scarlett asked, changing the subject, although her eyes were still darting around the room for any sign of Sloth Robot's lead singer.

'The cheating ones from this afternoon? Can't tell you, sorry,' Nina said apologetically.

'Oh go on, it's only me! Who am I going to tell?'

'I know, I know, but it's a seriously whopping amount – the most *Juice* has ever spent on a picture set. To be honest, it makes me feel a bit sick to think we just blew that kind of cash on photos of a couple getting down and dirty in a truck when it could have fed a family of six for a decade.'

Before Scarlett could reply, a large figure loomed over them.

'Evening, ladies. How many fans have you had to beat off with a stick tonight, Ninja?'

'Max! I didn't know you were coming tonight!' Nina exclaimed, wondering why a flock of butterflies had suddenly taken up residence in her stomach. She'd obviously put away too much champagne . . .

'Wasn't planning to but got my arm twisted, didn't I? Far too cool for my liking,' he grumbled, looking around at the crowd of twenty-something hipsters in their crop tops, skinny jeans and carefully styled hair – and that was just the guys.

'You just answered your own question – I've been pleasantly unbothered since I got here, as everyone is far too cool for school to admit they watch the TV show, let alone approach me for a chat about it,' Nina laughed. 'Max, this is my friend Scarlett – she's a producer on *Freshly Squeezed Juice*. Scarlett, this is my flatmate.'

'Nice to meet you,' Max said, looking surprised when Scarlett ignored his outstretched hand and instead kissed him flashily on both cheeks.

'What do you do for a crust, Max?' she wanted to know.

'I'm the editor of *Carnage*, the men's magazine.'

'Nice one! Look at you two, a proper media power couple! You could be like the Posh and Becks of magazines!' Scarlett gushed tipsily.

'Um, except we're not a couple,' Nina pointed out, hoping neither of them could see her blush.

'Minor details, minor details. Which celebrities have you met through your job, Max? Do you get as many perks as Nina? Does *Carnage* still feature that page where regular chicks with great racks pose in their underwear? Maybe that'll be my next career move! Either that or shag someone famous then sell the salacious details to a tabloid newspaper. Kidding!' she giggled. 'Oh my God, it's a sign – look who I spy with my little eye!'

Nina and Max were almost blinded by the light from the paparazzi's flashbulbs that ricocheted around the walls as Ned Owens made his grand entrance. Scarlett downed her full champagne glass in one go – 'Liquid courage,' she assured them – then undid another button of her shirt and winked at them. 'I don't know about you guys, but I'm off to throw myself at that fine piece of arse over there,' she announced, making a beeline for the singer.

'Well, I think I'm done here,' Max announced, finishing his beer.

Nina realised she didn't want him to go – with Scarlett off trying to impress Ned, she couldn't be bothered doing the rounds to find someone else to talk to. 'Stay for just one more,' she pleaded.

'Nah, this isn't my scene, Ninja. Plus I've got a big advertising presentation first thing tomorrow morning so I don't want to be dusty.'

She took a large slug from her glass to hide her disappointment. She liked hanging out with Max, even if it was at an industry event where the music was so loud it hurt her brain.

'I'll see you at home. By the way, I'd keep an eye on that one if I were you,' Max said, nodding towards Scarlett as he headed towards the exit.

twenty-one

An hour later, having being bailed up by one of the MTV publicists, Nina eventually found Scarlett in a back room doing a stellar job of fending off all the other Ned Owens groupies, sitting so close to him she looked like his Siamese twin. After five minutes of trying to catch her eye to let her know she was leaving, Nina sighed and waded into the sea of Scarlett lookalikes who were all desperate to have the dubious honour of being the next notch on Ned's bedpost.

'Scarlett? Sorry to interrupt, just wanted to let you know I'm off,' she said after finally getting her friend's attention.

'Nina! Meet my new buddy Ned! Isn't he pretty?' Scarlett squawked drunkenly.

'Uh, sure. Hi, Ned, I'm Nina.' She smiled at the singer, not wanting to be rude.

He looked her up and down, blatantly checking her out. 'Aren't you that chick from the TV?' he demanded. 'The one from that magazine?'

'Yes!' Scarlett jumped in. 'It's called *Juice*; it's the magazine you and the band did that photo shoot for the other week. The one with the TV crew there as well? The one where we met before, like I told you?' she asked hopefully, desperately trying to get him to remember her.

Ned ignored her, instead focusing all his attention on Nina. As if flicking a switch, he morphed from rude and arrogant to charming and attentive.

'Great to meet you, Nina. I love that dress you're wearing. Do you need something to drink? Here, let me pour you a vodka,' he offered, reaching for the bottle of Grey Goose in front of him.

'No thanks, I'm good. I'm about to head home,' she reminded him, fully aware that Scarlett was giving her the hairy eyeball.

'Home? Don't be ridiculous! I've decided it's absolutely imperative that you stay here and talk to me. Everyone else at this party is so utterly boring. Now, tell me all about your day at that magazine of yours. Come on, sit down here. Could you move over . . . uh . . . sorry, what did you say your name was again?' he asked Scarlett.

'It's Scarlett. Remember? We met at the photo shoot you did for *Juice*, Nina's magazine. I'm producing the TV show she's in,' Scarlett explained yet again. Nina had to give her credit for her stamina – she would have given up and been at home on the couch having a threesome with Ben & Jerry by now. 'Nina, take my place. I need to go to the bathroom anyway so you can save my seat for me – unless you want to come with me?'

'No, but thanks anyway,' Nina declined, knowing full well that Scarlett wasn't going to the bathroom to relieve any pressure on her bladder. 'I'll just wait till you get back.'

'So, where were we?' Ned leant in close to her – uncomfortably close. 'You know, I had a great time at the photo shoot for your magazine. Sometimes they're just so boring, but it was really fun. Although it would have been more fun if you had been there. Did I say how much I liked your dress? That colour really suits you.' He directed a dazzling smile her way, no doubt expecting her legs to magically open at the mega-wattage of it.

'Uh, thanks. Is the rest of the band still here?' she asked, trying to steer the conversation away from herself.

'Who knows? It's just me, myself and I at the moment. But I'm glad you're here, Nina. Don't tell any of the others, but you're the most interesting person I've talked to all night,' he said, looking deep into her eyes.

'Is that so?' Nina asked, knowing full well he was laying it on with a shovel only because she was the editor of a celebrity magazine. Ned might have been a charismatic sleazebag, but he wasn't stupid – he knew how to play the media game. Or thought he did, anyway.

'Tell me, Nina – are you a good kisser? You look like you'd be a good kisser,' he proclaimed in what she could only guess was his 'sexy' voice.

'Seeing I've never kissed myself, I really wouldn't know,' she shot back, wishing Scarlett would hurry up and get back from snorting illicit substances in the bathroom.

'In that case, let me tell you,' Ned declared. Before she realised what was happening, his hand snaked around the back of her head then he smooshed his face against hers and stuck his tongue into her mouth. It was so sudden, Nina was stunned into submission for a split second, before she managed to extricate herself from his saliva party.

'Are you quite right?' she demanded furiously, as Ned grinned lasciviously at her. Looking around to see who had witnessed his inappropriate behaviour, all she saw were the envious stares of Sloth Robot groupies wishing they could trade places with her. Then she saw a familiar figure standing in the doorway – from the distraught look on Scarlett's face, Nina immediately knew she'd seen everything.

'It's fine – he can kiss whoever he wants.'

'No, it's not fine,' Nina insisted, hurrying alongside Scarlett as she stalked towards the taxi rank.

'If he wants to kiss you and you want to kiss him, it has nothing to do with me,' Scarlett declared.

'But I didn't want to kiss him! He stuck his tongue in my mouth before I realised what he was doing!'

'That's not what it looked like to me, but it doesn't really matter. I mean, I was making good ground with Ned before you turned up, but he obviously prefers you over me so there isn't a lot I can do about it, is there?' The hurt in Scarlett's voice stung like a fresh paper cut.

Nina bit her lip in frustration. Given Ned hadn't even remembered Scarlett's name, let alone that they'd met before, she wouldn't exactly agree with her friend's view that she'd been making progress with Operation Get It On With Ned Owens, but now was probably not the time or place to point that out.

'Look, I'm really sorry. I swear, it was an accident. It wasn't like we had an instant connection – he only wanted to get into my pants in the hope I'd put him on the cover of the magazine or something!' she tried to joke.

'I don't want to talk about it anymore,' Scarlett announced. 'Really, Nina, it's fine. Don't worry, there are plenty more men out there; I might see if Jerome and Louie are out and about seeing I don't really feel like going home just yet. At least I know they're into me, not you,' she added snarkily.

Jerome and his mate Louie were two of Scarlett's more successful celebrity conquests, although they were decidedly more C-list than A-list. Jerome was the heart-throb of a top-rating reality cooking series, winning the devotion of women around Australia with his tarte Tatin and tear-jerk story of being brought up by a single mother doing it tough after his father ran off with her best friend. Since winning the show, he'd been taking full advantage of the stream of invitations and media opportunities that had come his way, which is how he'd met Louie, a male model who had also popped his reality TV show cherry with a brief stint in the *Big*

Brother house. With their good looks and unbridled enthusiasm for their newfound fame, the two guys had developed a full-blown bromance and were the life of whichever party they were at – and they went to a LOT of parties. Nina had introduced them to Scarlett at the opening of an edgy new gastro-pub in one of the seedier areas of Redfern; they'd hit it off immediately, with Scarlett entertaining them with tales of the other reality TV shows she'd worked on while the two guys dished the dirt on their fellow contestants. When Nina had to leave early to show her face at an advertising client's farewell drinks, the trio barely drew enough breath to say goodbye. The next day, Scarlett had looked exhausted – after a bit of cajoling from Nina, she'd confessed that after the gastro-pub, the three of them had hit up a string of bars in Surry Hills, spending more time in the bathroom doing lines than in the actual bar, until Louie had suggested going back to his place. Drunk and high, it had seemed like the most natural thing ever for Scarlett to shag him and Jerome – at the same time. Nina had decided it was best not to tell her that the two guys were renowned for their threesome conquests; Scarlett wasn't the first woman to fall for their combined charms and she definitely wouldn't be the last.

'Okay . . . if you're sure?' Nina double-checked, crossing her fingers that Jerome and Louie wouldn't be total arseholes and have absolutely no recollection of Scarlett when she called. If she was a better friend, she'd go out with her, but after the episode with Ned she just wanted to go straight home and gargle with Draino.

'I'm sure – sorry I overreacted. I'll see you tomorrow, okay? Thanks for tonight!' Scarlett climbed into the back of a cab, giving the taxi driver more than he bargained for with a quick flash of her knicker-less crotch as she did so, and blew Nina a kiss.

Nina winked at her, relieved that Scarlett seemed to have recovered from her earlier tantrum. 'Thank God that's blown over,' she thought as she started walking home, automatically smiling at a group of girls who were staring at her, nudging each other excitedly as she passed. 'Let's face it, I can't afford to lose any more friends right now.'

twenty-two

'They cannot be serious! What are they going on about? I mean, it's obviously referring to me, even though it's supposedly a blind item, but it's not even true!'

Nina stared at the 'Guess who, don't sue' column in the previous day's paper, shaking her head in disbelief before reading it again.

Which magazine maven, currently riding a wave of success thanks to a popular TV show, was looking the worse for wear at the MTV party last week? Sources say her increased level of fame has come hand in hand with an increased love of party drugs followed by an increased number of nasty comedowns while in the office. Tsk, tsk!

Scarlett looked at her sympathetically. 'Babe, we know it's not true. I mean, you didn't even do any blow that night. Don't worry about it; everyone knows what that particular gossip columnist writes is mostly bullshit anyway. People are always going to spread rumours; it's just what happens when you become a household name. And there were plenty of people at that party who may have decided to badmouth you just because they could. Trust me, I've seen it happen before. You have to take the bad with the good.'

'But this is defamation! Or slander! Or libel! Or all three! I can't remember what the differences are. Who the hell are these supposed sources? God, I wonder if Eric has seen it?' Nina stressed, worried that her publisher would actually believe it.

'Seeing it's been printed in Sydney's top-selling Sunday newspaper, I'd say probably,' Scarlett pointed out. 'But I'm sure he knows it's not true – if he had a problem with it, don't you think you would have been summonsed upstairs to explain yourself by now?'

'You're right . . . but what about everyone else? People are going to think I'm a pill-popping, coke-addicted fame whore!'

'I know it's frustrating, but you can't control what everyone thinks. If they want to believe it, they will, no matter how much you protest. Plus it's Sydney – do you really think a media identity with a rumoured fondness for drugs is that much of a surprise to anyone?'

Nina had to admit Scarlett was right – it just felt so unfair to be targeted like that. 'Ironic, huh?' she said with a small smile. 'Here I am, the editor of a celebrity magazine that trades on gossip and rumours – always backed up by legitimate sources, I might add – and I have a meltdown as soon as something gossipy is printed about me in a blind item. Onwards and upwards, I guess. God, I'm going to be glad when this bloody show is over and life can go back to normal.'

'You don't think you'll miss it? All the invites? All the free swag? All the adulation?' Scarlett asked curiously.

'Are you kidding? I can take it or leave it. Don't get me wrong: it's really nice to have people tell you how much they like the show and how they'd never realised how much work goes into making a magazine, plus the VIP treatment at parties and restaurants is a bonus, but I don't really like feeling so exposed. I wish I could just leave the house and not worry whether my nails are chipped or my jeans have stains from the guacamole I dropped on them the night before. Social media and camera phones are going to be the death of me. Now I know why A-listers upload so many selfies onto Instagram – at least that way they can control what they look like, rather than worrying whether their eyeliner has smeared or they have spinach in their teeth. Of course, the fact that they're all completely self-obsessed has something to do with it, too.

'And the freebies are great, but most of the time, I don't even like half the stuff that gets sent in – that's why I re-gift it to you and the others. It's not like I get to choose what people send me. Anyway, first world problems and all that. What's on the filming agenda this afternoon?' she asked, folding up the newspaper and throwing it in the recycling bin.

'I think we're doing some in-house stuff with Joe and the art department – he's pretending to design a cover and the designers will do some mock layouts. It's not particularly exciting, but we need to give the viewers a three-sixty-degree experience of the magazine and I guess some of them will be interested in how the pages come together visually. What are you doing for lunch? We've ordered a delivery from Miss Chu if you want to share?'

Nina's mouth watered at the thought of the Vietnamese deliciousness; the fresh spring rolls were to die for. But she still had a lingering bad taste about the blind item from the newspaper and wasn't really hungry. What she really wanted to do was get Max's take on it; he always seemed to have good advice. Then she remembered he was in Melbourne for the day for a *Carnage* reader event and cursed internally. Maybe some fresh air would help.

'Thanks, but I think I'm going to get out of the office and take a walk. I know, right? Who would have thought, given me and exercise aren't exactly the best of friends?!' she exclaimed, seeing Scarlett's surprise. 'I'll probably just stroll around the park or something; nothing that means breaking a sweat, God forbid. Actually, I should go now; I have to be back for a two o'clock meeting with the advertising manager. Enjoy your Miss Chu goodness!'

Deciding to pee before pretending to do some exercise, Nina nipped into the toilets near the *Juice* office, only to find both cubicles already taken by two girls who were gossiping furiously as they went about their business. Rummaging for her lip balm in the Marc by Marc Jacobs bag that was the newest addition to her freebie collection, she tuned in to their conversation and immediately felt like curling up in the foetal position as soon as she realised who they were talking about – herself.

'It *has* to be her! Who else could it be?' one of the girls demanded.

'I guess you're right – but it could be referring to someone else from the magazine who is also on the TV show? I've only met her briefly ages ago, but Nina never really struck me as someone who would get mixed up in all that,' the other replied.

As hard as Nina tried, she didn't recognise the voices at all, which was the clichéd silver lining, as it meant it wasn't any of her own team feasting on the blind item. It had to be staff from one of the other magazines that shared the same floor.

'Don't be so naïve – all the editors are into it,' the first girl said in an authoritative voice. 'Think about how much free blow she'd be getting offered at all the parties she goes to these days! Haven't you seen her in the social pages at all those events? She'd be snorting rails almost every night, I reckon. Half her luck! Plus at an MTV party, it's practically a given. But it's not exactly the kind of thing you want written about you in the Sunday paper – I'd love to know if she was hauled in front of her publisher to explain herself this morning.'

Nina knew if she had any sort of backbone, she'd make her presence known no matter how embarrassing it might be for herself and the gossip girls. But instead of waiting to confront them, she sprinted out the door as fast as her pointy studded snakeskin Valentino knock-offs could carry her before either of them finished up and busted her eavesdropping at the basins.

'That was super-mature of you, Nina – well done,' she chastised herself as she left the building. 'You had the perfect opportunity to confront them and explain that the blind item was absolute bollocks, but instead you ran away with your tail between your legs. Love your work, you pussy.'

Reaching the green lushness of Hyde Park, she found a sunny spot away from the garbage-munching flocks of ibises and checked her Facebook feed on her iPad. Ignoring all the friend requests from total randoms who thought she was their new best friend thanks to the show, her mood plummeted as she scrolled through the myriad photos of Lily, Evie, Daniela and Bec's babies. She couldn't help torturing herself even more by reading the gushing comments posted mostly by people Nina didn't know.

Noah is unbelievably gorgeous, my ovaries are weeping!

I can't wait to have another cuddle! Ruby is pure perfection.

Nothing more beautiful than a sleeping baby – enjoy every moment of this time with Mason, they grow up far too quickly.

It's all fun and games until your baby poos in someone else's paddling pool – this post was from Natalie, accompanying a graphic photo of Sasha's offending turd floating in the water. Nina almost threw up in her mouth at the sight of it, although she did have to cringe on Natalie's behalf, then rolled her eyes at Lily's status.

I've turned into one of those mummies who post way too many photos of my darling baby, but I just can't help it!!! She's just too cute!!!

'Newsflash – you can help it, Lily. It's called making a conscious decision not to upload photos and it's really not that hard,' Nina thought in exasperation.

Feeling excluded from a club she didn't even want to join, she logged in to her Skype app to start a video call. Seeing Max was unavailable and her friendship with Heidi wasn't exactly hunky dory right now, there was only one other person she wanted to talk to about this mess she'd found herself in with the blind item.

'Hello?' a sleepy voice eventually answered.

'Tess! What time is it there? Sorry, I think I got the time difference wrong. It's okay, go back to sleep, I'll call you another time.' Nina hadn't spoken to her cousin for ages – with the TV show filming and all the events she'd been attending with Scarlett, there never seemed to be a good time. They'd exchanged a few emails but it wasn't the same as a proper chat.

'S'okay, I worked a late shift tonight anyway so I only just got to bed.'

Nina smiled as her cousin's shadowy face suddenly appeared in the video stream once she'd switched on her bedside light on the other side of the world.

'You know how it can take a while to wind down after getting home,' she continued. Tess was still working in the hospitality industry in London and had recently scored a coveted managerial role at the Groucho Club, the private members club in Soho, overseeing every aspect of their relatively small offering of twenty bedrooms.

'You know what? Today I wouldn't mind going back to working in hotels,' Nina mused, remembering her days at the Bickford, the five-star hotel she'd worked at in London before getting her start in the magazine industry via an internship at British *Marie Claude*.

'That bad, huh? What's happened? Is the magazine getting sued again?'

'No, I wish – at least that could be properly managed. Remember the reality TV show I told you about? It's turned into kind of a big deal and one of the local gossip columnists decided to get their claws out – in yesterday's paper, there was a blind item saying I was getting stuck into a stash of drugs at an event last week, which is a total lie.'

'But if it was a blind item and it's not true, how do you know it's about you? Maybe it was referring to someone else?'

'Oh, believe me, it was clearly about me – it mentioned the person in question worked in magazines and was on a successful TV show. There's literally no other person it could be. In this case, one plus one definitely equals two.'

'Ouch. What are you going to do about it?'

'That's the problem – there's not much I can do. If I ask them to print a retraction, they'll use the excuse that it's a blind item. I've already overheard people in the office bathrooms dissecting it, saying it's obvious that all signs point directly to me. It's not a good look – for me, for the magazine or for the TV show.'

'Can you get some legal advice, just in case? Isn't Heidi's brother a lawyer? Why don't you get her to ask him on your behalf?' Tess suggested.

Nina was silent. She hadn't kept Tess up to date on her stagnated friendship status with Heidi and the other girls – she'd told herself it was because it was too involved, but after regaling Scarlett with the whole sorry story recently over a jug of sangria, it had dawned on Nina that none of it reflected particularly well on her, even though Scarlett had rolled her eyes and groaned in sympathy in all the right places. She was gradually beginning to realise how badly she'd handled the whole baby situation: the scathing outbursts, the tantrums, the refusal to apologise . . . The truth was, as much as they frustrated her with their one-track baby minds, she was starting to miss the girls even though she was the one who had pushed them away in the first place. She just wasn't sure if she was ready to admit it.

'Hello? Has the connection dropped out?' Tess asked.

'Sorry, I'm here. You're right, I guess I could ask Heidi,' Nina said. But it was no use – Tess knew her too well.

'What's up with you and Heidi?' her cousin asked, shooting a suspicious look at the webcam.

'Nothing – we just haven't seen each other for a while,' Nina fibbed.

'Did you have a fight?'

'Umm . . . sort of,' Nina admitted.

'What about? Come on, tell Aunty Tess — you know you want to.'

After Nina had finished explaining, the incredulous look on Tess's face confirmed her growing fears — she was acting like a petulant child.

'So let me get this straight — you're pissed off because all your friends are having babies and that's all they can talk about, and you're not interested?'

Nina nodded, avoiding Tess's accusing gaze.

'So even though you've been friends with them for some time, you've had loads of fun together and you still like them as people, you're letting this one temporary aspect affect your entire attitude towards them? You're whingeing because your Facebook feed is full of baby photos while you're being inundated with invites to the hottest bar openings and free handbags? Seriously, cry me a river of baby vomit. You know what my advice is? Get a grip, Nina. Get a grip, suck it up, and sort it out. Friendships can be tricky but that doesn't mean you throw them in the too-hard basket as soon as the going gets tough. You're not seven years old anymore; you can't just drop your friends because they prefer playing with their Cabbage Patch dolls instead of with you. You have to make amends with Heidi and the rest of them before it's too late — if it's not already,' Tess finished ominously.

Nina squirmed. Even though she was expecting to be read the riot act, hearing Tess's verdict wasn't exactly pleasant. But a lot of what she'd said herself wasn't exactly pleasant, either. 'What goes around comes around,' she told herself.

'You're right, you're right,' Nina sighed. 'I promise I'll make amends.'

And for the first time, she had every intention of doing so — just as soon as she'd figured out how.

twenty-three

A little birdie tells us that Nina Morey, star of reality TV smash *Freshly Squeezed Juice*, is taking full advantage of her single status while out on the town – which is often. From D-list male models, C-list cooking talent-show winners and B-list boy band members, it sounds like it's all happening between Nina's sheets. Lucky duck!

'1800 GOSSIP' column, *Sunday Star*

Here's a 'juicy' tidibit – given her current level of fame is only temporary, you'd think this magazine gal would be loving all the free swag that's currently being thrown her way. But that's not what we hear – instead, she bitches and moans that she doesn't even like the majority of the haul she receives and has no hesitation in re-gifting it. We're pretty sure all the brands who have generously contributed their products wouldn't be impressed if they knew. Oops!

BlindGossipAustralia.com.au

After last night's top-rating *End of the Day* segment revealed to its thousands of prime-time viewers that cold hard cash is the real reason so many showbiz types line up to do photo shoots for celebrity weekly magazines, the media industry is feverishly trying to discover just who leaked the mind-boggling sums that the current affairs program named. Of course, it's a well-known secret in media circles that celebrities only show off their homes, their weddings or their babies in return for a decent pay packet, but given the uproar from the public about the huge figures quoted, it's something magazines and celebrity managers would have preferred to be kept in the vault. We hear that a certain TV-friendly celebrity weekly editor was behind the salacious leak – maybe she collected her own pay packet in return to help pay for all those drugs we've been told she likes to indulge in? One thing's for certain – her magazine will be lucky to get any more of those freshly squeezed celebrity exclusives it has been dishing out recently if the collective fury of Australia's celebrity agents is anything to go by.

Media Mumblings daily e-newsletter

twenty-four

Nina had never felt more helpless as, over the next few weeks, the hits kept on coming. It was one of her worst nightmares coming true. Someone obviously had a vendetta against her but she was damned if she knew who it was. Her first thought had been Elizabeth, her nemesis from her disastrous days at *Candy*, but after making a few enquiries, she found out Elizabeth was now working in Dubai and would therefore have no idea what was happening in Sydney. She had wondered if perhaps the editors of *Bizarre* or *Fierce* were indulging in some corporate skulduggery to get back at *Juice* for the popularity of the TV show and its resulting increase in celebrity exclusives, but while discussing it with Max, they'd both come to the decision that it went beyond professional meddling — it was personal.

The problem was that Nina couldn't think of anyone who'd want to drag her down so much that they'd go to the trouble of contacting all the different media outlets to create this kind of smear campaign. It wasn't like she thought she was everyone's favourite person, but to go to that amount of effort meant someone really had it in for her. Max had tried to joke that she was a 'real' celebrity now that she had anonymous sources feeding salacious tidbits about her to the media and that a stalker would be next on the list, but Nina hadn't found it funny. It was alright for him; it wasn't his professional reputation getting flayed to within an inch of its life.

Glancing at the display on her office phone as it started to ring, she pulled a face as she read the name of Eric's PA. The summons she'd been expecting was finally happening.

'Hi, Christine,' she said dejectedly. 'I'm guessing Eric wants to see me?'

'Yes, hon,' the older woman replied sympathetically.

'Okay, I'm free in half an hour if that works for him?' Nina lied. She actually didn't have anything on right now; she just wanted some time to gather her thoughts before being confronted by her publisher.

'I'm afraid he wants to see you now.'

'Like, right now?'

'Right now,' the PA confirmed.

Nina tried to talk over the lump that had set up home in her throat. This was not looking good. 'Sure, tell him I'm on my way.' Glancing around her office, she wondered if the next time she saw it, she'd be accompanied by security guards watching over her as she cleared out her desk.

On the corporate floor, Christine gave her a small pat on the arm as she showed her into Eric's office then shut the door quickly behind her. There was no sign of anyone from HR, which Nina hoped was a good sign.

'I'm presuming you know why I want to see you,' her publisher began in a grim tone.

'Because of the item in today's Media Mumblings that points the finger directly at me as being the insider who told the current affairs program how much magazines pay celebrities in order to secure exclusives,' Nina said flatly. 'And let's not forget about all the other snippets that have been popping up online and in the newspaper gossip columns about my supposed drug problem and my fondness for sleeping with as many wannabes as possible.'

'Is any of it true? You know I have to ask. And don't even think of lying to me. I've had every celebrity manager and their pet ferret on the phone this morning threatening to blackball *Juice* from now on thanks to last night's TV segment. I don't need to tell you what kind of repercussions it will have for you and the magazine if no agent in town will talk to us.'

Nina tried to ignore the nausea that was slithering up the back of her throat. 'Of course it isn't true! Why would I sabotage my own magazine like that? Not to mention my own career! You know my history, Eric, and you also know how much I appreciate the fact that you gave me a second chance after my not-so-stellar exit from *Candy*. I live and breathe this job, so why would I purposely stuff it up?'

He looked at her evenly, giving nothing away. 'Maybe they're right – maybe the success of the TV series has gone to your head. Maybe you think you're the duck's nuts right now and that you're untouchable? Or maybe all the coke you're supposedly hoovering up has loosened your tongue and you told one of your supposed celebrity conquests confidential information about story fees while you were out partying? Maybe you don't even remember?'

'First of all, I am NOT hoovering up coke,' Nina argued, battling to stay calm. She knew Eric was testing her and she didn't blame him. And she wasn't really lying – a couple of small bumps here and there with Scarlett was completely different to racking up line after line and being so off her chops that she'd spill confidential information to virtual strangers and put her career in the firing line. 'Second, apart from one rather revolting kiss with a so-called celebrity who virtually jumped on me, I do not have any celebrity conquests. Third, the fees mentioned in the *End of the Day* segment were completely exaggerated – we've never paid anything near what they said, so their source might be someone without any real knowledge of the transactions who passed themselves off as an insider.'

'What you say may all be true – God knows, I want to believe that you had nothing to do with any of it, but when push comes to shove, if it wasn't you, then why are fingers being pointed at you from every direction?' Eric demanded.

'I don't know! I really do not know. I wish I did. All I can think of is that since the TV show took off, someone has it in for me and they've been planting all these strategic lies that will cause maximum damage in order to cut me down. I don't think it's a professional thing, I think it's personal. But I have no idea who it is or what I've ever done to them to make them want to do something like this. Seriously, Eric, you have to believe me! Do you think I wanted all this attention? You know I wasn't exactly frothing at the mouth about doing the TV show – I know it's been great for the magazine up until now, but I really wish things could go back to the way they were. I don't want to be Nina from *Freshly Squeezed Juice* anymore; I just want to be a magazine editor. I miss being no one, I really do.'

Her publisher sighed heavily as he doodled a rather fetching moustache and glasses on the face of Emma Stone, who was on the cover of that week's *Juice*. Finally, having successfully vandalised the Hollywood darling, he looked up.

'I believe you. But that doesn't mean others will,' he warned. 'You need to do some serious damage control with the major players in this business before they start refusing to accept your calls. Time isn't on our side – I want you to get on the phone ASAP and tell them briefly what you've just told me. Do whatever you have to do – offer to take them to Aria or whatever their favourite restaurant is so you can explain in depth. We just have to pray that the ones you have good relationships with will believe you and that will be enough to keep us going until this blows over. Oh, and Nina?' he called out as she was exiting his office at a rate of knots. 'Find out who is behind this smear campaign and shut it down. Fast.'

twenty-five

'How did you go with getting phone time with all the celebrity agents?' Scarlett asked sympathetically after Nina had finished debriefing her on her conversation with Eric over the phone. 'Did they agree to talk to you or did you get fobbed off by their assistants?'

'Imagine having all your teeth pulled out without any anaesthetic,' Nina explained as she struggled through the crowds mingling outside Westfield on Pitt Street Mall, Sydney's shrine to all things shopping. 'And then double the pain and suffering – it was pretty much like that.' After burning up the phone lines all morning, she'd decided to get out of the office and distract herself with a browse through the boutiques. Her sunglasses were firmly in place and she pulled the brim of her black leather baseball cap lower over her face – she felt like a fugitive, but she definitely wasn't in the mood for anyone to recognise her, even if they did happen to be genuine fans who had somehow missed the memo that she was a drug-addicted spoilt princess who couldn't wait to fall into bed with anyone who had a public profile. Or so some people said.

'Most of them pretended they were otherwise occupied and would call me back so I'll try them again this afternoon,' Nina continued. 'Others took my call but only to tell me in no uncertain terms what they thought of me and two of them eventually agreed to meet with me so I can attempt some damage control in person. Actually, I have to meet Sam, Lulu Hopkins' manager, tonight as he's in Melbourne for the rest of the week. Luckily I managed to get a last-minute early booking at Chiswick so he can chow down on their famous lamb while I throw myself at his mercy. There's just one thing I had to promise to make him agree to see me . . .'

'Why do I get the feeling I'm not going to like this?' Scarlett enquired.

'It's not that bad, I promise! He's desperate to be on the show, that's all. So I may have said that if he agreed to meet me tonight, we could film some of it – not the part where we discuss the rumour that I'm supposedly responsible for the End of the Day leak, obviously, but you could shoot some footage of us having a drink at the bar, general chit-chat, stuff like that. You know, to show people at home how much schmoozing is involved in the job . . .' Nina trailed off, crossing her fingers, eyes and toes that Scarlett would agree.

'Let me get this straight – you want me to organise a film crew to shoot you sucking up to a celebrity manager at a posh eastern suburbs restaurant, which will probably mean I have to organise a tricky last-minute film permit, plus convince Andy to include the footage in the final edit so it makes it to air?' Scarlett didn't sound particularly impressed.

'Uh, yep, that sounds about right. *Please*, Scarlett,' she begged as she entered Ksubi and started to browse through the range of denim, 'I really need your help on this. I would never normally promise something that's out of my jurisdiction, but Eric told me to do whatever it takes. I swear I'll make it up to you.'

Scarlett heaved a huge sigh. 'Let me see what I can do, okay?'

'Thank you, thank you, thank you! You're the bestest friend ever!' Nina exclaimed, relieved that something was finally going her way. Dropping her phone into her bag, she pulled a pair of heavily discounted distressed grey skinnies off the shelf and made a beeline for the change rooms. She may have been in the middle of a crisis, but a Ksubi sale didn't wait for anyone. 'Good to know you've got your priorities straight, Nina,' she scolded herself.

Just as she was about to enter the one free change room, she felt a tap on her shoulder.

'Excuse me, do you have these in any other sizes?' a familiar voice wanted to know.

Spinning around, Nina was about to explain she didn't actually work in the store when she realised who it was.

'Steph! It's me! Nina!' she announced, pulling off her sunglasses so her friend could see her better in the dim light.

'So sorry, lovely! I thought you were one of the shop assistants; it must have been that awesome cap you're rocking. Me likey! Me likey a lot,' Steph said admiringly. 'Fancy running into you here, of all places. Haven't seen you for ages, how have you been? The TV show is going gangbusters, from what I hear. Congratulations, that's major!' Standing in the entrance of the change room with the curtain pulled halfway across her body to hide her semi-nakedness, Steph was holding the same pair of jeans that Nina had picked up, which she'd obviously just tried on. As Nina was about to comment on what a bargain they were while wondering if she had the guts to ask Steph why she never returned her calls or replied to her messages, she noticed the strange pattern that seemed to be etched into Steph's inner forearm. Long, thin lines crisscrossed each other haphazardly with an angry mix of reddish fissures, broken micro-scabs and pale, puckered scar tissue.

'Steph, what happened to . . . ?' The words withered on her tongue as her friend hurriedly jerked her arm away and hid it behind the curtain, but not before Nina caught the reflection of her other arm in the mirror behind her – it too looked like a street map had been carved into it. 'Oh my God . . .' Nina didn't know what else to say. It all made sense now – why Steph had taken to always wearing long sleeves when the rest of them were in short sleeves or tank tops; the razors on the bathroom windowsill at the baby shower and the blood on the tissues under the cabinet; how she'd grimaced when Nina had grabbed her arm and the fresh blood that had seeped through the sleeves of her white shirt; why her explanation about having regular nosebleeds hadn't seemed quite right. Nina knew the cuts and scars on her arms weren't due to a horrible accident – Steph was self-harming.

'Honey, why don't you get dressed?' she suggested gently, making a concerted effort to look her friend straight in the eye rather than at the gruesome sight in the mirror. 'We need to talk.'

Placing two coffees on the table of the deserted cafe, Nina sat down and handed Steph a napkin to soak up the tears that were threatening to spill at any second.

'You weren't supposed to see that,' she whispered, avoiding Nina's gaze.

'I know. But now that I have, what are we going to do about it?'

Steph looked at her defiantly. 'Who says I want to do anything about it? You have no idea what I'm going through! You don't know how hard it is! This is my way of coping with it, so who are you to judge?' she snapped.

'You're right, I don't know what you're going through and I'm in no way an expert on this kind of thing, but I do know cutting yourself isn't going to help,' Nina pointed out.

'How would you know? You don't know how good it feels when you cut; it's like all the pressure that's been building up is released as soon as the razor slices into your skin. When the blood comes, there's a wave of relief and everything you've been bottling up seems to dissipate — it's just you and the pain and the blood,' Steph said in an empty voice. All the fight had gone out of her, leaving only suffering in its place. 'And then, just for a minute, I can forget about all the fertility tests, the invasive ultrasounds, the hormone injections, the egg harvests, the crushing disappointment when yet another pregnancy test shows up negative. It helps take my mind off the constant questions from everyone about why Chris and I haven't started a family yet. Why? Because we bloody well can't!' Her voice broke as the tears cascaded down her face. 'Knowing I can get relief from cutting helps me get through the torture of being surrounded by pregnant women and newborn babies. Do you have any idea what it's like? To want something so badly and be told you have zero chance of it happening naturally and then all your friends start falling pregnant like it's the easiest thing in the world? And I have to sit there and pretend to be happy for them when all I want is what they've got. I hate myself for hating them but it's not fair, Nina. It's just not fair,' she sobbed.

Nina held her friend's hands, letting her cry it out. She hadn't realised Steph and Chris had already started IVF without any success. While Nina had been freaking out about her friends becoming parents, Steph was going through her own private pain, punishing her body for not doing what she so desperately wanted it to do.

'Steph . . . I'm so sorry . . . I should have cottoned on to what was happening earlier — I didn't really believe it when you told me the stains on your sleeves were from a nosebleed but I didn't want to push it any further . . .' Nina murmured, hating herself for taking the easy road and letting it slide when her gut feeling had been right all along.

'Oh God, that was an awful day. I'd been told earlier that yet another IVF round hadn't worked and I just couldn't bear it anymore. You know, I try not to take it out on the girls because it's not their fault I can't get pregnant, but the thought of having to play baby-related games and watch them opening all the presents was too much that day. I felt like I was going to hurt someone so instead I went to the bathroom and hurt myself. It's the only time I've ever done it at someone else's house and I was so ashamed but I couldn't help myself; I needed to do it. And then when you called me afterwards, I was so angry at myself for coming so close to getting caught. You kept trying to get in touch with me so I assumed you'd guessed I was self-harming but I didn't want to admit it. I mean, you hear of tortured teenagers cutting themselves, but grown women with successful careers? It's so stupid.'

'It's not stupid, Steph,' Nina said firmly. 'You're going through a hell of a lot right now but you can't keep doing this to yourself. Does Chris know?'

Steph's shrug couldn't have contained more misery if she'd tried. 'I don't know. I try to hide the evidence but it's hard to keep my arms covered up all the time at home, like when I'm in the shower and he's brushing his teeth or something. But you know what guys are like – they're not the most observant species. Plus he's going through just as much pain as I am, but he deals with it in a different way. He might suspect what I'm doing, but he probably can't face the idea of confronting me about it – I haven't been the easiest person to be with recently,' she admitted.

'That's perfectly understandable,' Nina reassured her. 'I know it's probably the last thing you want to do, but I really think you need to talk to someone – does the IVF clinic have any psychologists?'

'I don't know,' Steph sighed. 'I don't know if I want to talk about it. I mean, what is there to say? I can't get pregnant so I cut myself – the end. What are they going to do about it? It's their job to get me pregnant, not deal with the side-effects of me not being able to cope with my infertility,' she said bitterly.

'But you never know, it could be linked – I'm obviously not a fertility expert, but being in a constant state of toxic stress and anger isn't going to help. If you're finding it hard to process your emotions, maybe it could be affecting the chances of the treatment being successful? I know you say the cutting helps and gives you relief, but what you need is a healthier alternative. Maybe a psychologist can teach you different methods to deal with the stress so you have other ways to cope instead of everything festering inside?'

Steph wiped her eyes and gave her a wobbly smile. 'I guess . . .' she said uncertainly. 'I mean, if it improves my chances of getting pregnant, then it'd be stupid not to look into it. I don't know how many more unsuccessful IVF cycles I can go through; Chris and I are already near breaking point.'

'Why don't you call them this afternoon and ask if there's someone who you can talk to? If not, I can give you details of a psychology clinic that I used to go to when I had my drinking problem – I'm sure they'd be able to help,' Nina said encouragingly.

'Maybe I will. I'll think about it. Thanks, Nina,' Steph said, giving her a hug. 'At first I was angry that you saw my scars, but now I'm starting to think maybe it's a good thing. Sorry to bolt but I'm due at the Dion Lee showroom in ten minutes to pull clothes for a shoot next week. Thanks for listening – I really mean it. I know this baby epidemic hasn't been easy on you either.' Tugging unconsciously at the sleeves of her embellished Fleur Wood jacket to make sure her wounds were covered, Steph gave her a quick wave as she left the cafe.

'I'll call you tomorrow,' Nina mouthed as she waved back. Finishing her drink, she paid the bill and headed back to the office, trying to make sense of it all. As much as she could understand the reasons behind Steph's self-harm, she was still shocked that one of her friends would do that to herself. 'I can't even begin to understand how much she must be going through,' Nina thought. Then she remembered Steph's last words – 'I know this baby epidemic hasn't been easy on you either' – and cringed. She knew she didn't deserve any sympathy. While Steph had bottled everything up inside, refusing to take it out on the girls despite being reminded of her inability to fall pregnant every time she saw them, Nina had acted like a three-year-old with anger-management issues, throwing tantrums left, right and centre because her friends were moving on to a different life stage and she wanted things to stay exactly the same. She'd been openly rude to their faces, she'd complained about them at any chance she got and then acted like they were the ones in the wrong, just because they had chosen an alternative path to her. The mask of delusion she'd been wearing for the past few months finally slipped; she felt utterly ashamed of herself and her behaviour. If anyone had a right to behave as atrociously as she had, it was Steph, not her. There were a million other people with bigger problems who had acted a million times better than she had.

In the middle of chastising herself for turning into the friend nightmares are made of, she barely heard her phone ringing. Expecting it to be Scarlett with an update on that night's filming at Chiswick, Nina came to a standstill in the middle of Pitt Street when she saw Heidi's name on the display. 'I'm not ready for this,' she thought, panicked. 'I need to make the biggest apology in the history of the world and I don't know what I'm going to say.' Telling herself to man up, she resisted the urge to let it go to voicemail and answered the call.

'Hi –'

Heidi's hysterical voice cut her off before she could get any further. 'Nina, I need your help! I don't care what your problem with me is right now, I just need you to help me! Simon's in New York again and I'm bleeding! Like, seriously bleeding.' Her panic streamed through the phone line, making Nina's heart beat faster.

'What do you mean you're bleeding?' Nina asked, swiping her security card in the lobby and waiting for the lift, ignoring the strange looks being thrown her way by a group of suits. 'Like, is that normal?'

'No! No, it's not normal! I've been bleeding all day but my obstetrician has been busy with other patients and only just called me back. He says I have to go to the hospital straight away to be monitored, because I might . . .' She faltered, her voice strangled with fear. 'Nina, he says I might be miscarrying the twins.'

twenty-six

'Oh my God,' Nina breathed. This was too much bad news for one day – first Steph, now Heidi. Nina had a sickening thought – maybe it was her fault? Maybe her constant moaning and wanting everyone to shut up about babies already had something to do with Heidi's problems? Maybe it was the Friendship God's way of punishing her? Immediately she told her brain to shut up. Her best friend was going through a major crisis; it was time to stop thinking about herself for a change and pull up her friendship socks, stat. She'd been selfishly thinking the world revolved around her for too long.

'Will you come to the hospital with me? I'm freaking out,' Heidi pleaded tearfully. 'Mum and Dad are holidaying on some remote island in Indonesia with no phone reception, Simon's on his way to JFK now to try to get on the first plane back to Sydney, but I don't want to go to the hospital by myself. Please, Nina, you're the only person I can ask.'

Barrelling down the hallway to the *Juice* office, Nina was opening her mouth to tell Heidi she'd be there straight away, then stopped short as she remembered she already had plans. Plans that involved schmoozing one of the most important celebrity managers in the business in a desperate effort to convince him she hadn't betrayed confidential information to a salacious current affairs program. Plans that also involved filming for the TV show, filming that she'd made Scarlett pull multiple strings to organise at the last minute, even though it wasn't important to the show's content. There was no way she could bail out on her plans – not only was Sam expecting her to turn up to Chiswick with a camera crew in tow in just a couple of hours, there was also the small matter of the future of the magazine depending on it. Eric had specifically told her to deal with this fiasco as soon as possible; they couldn't afford to wait around while the rumours and finger-pointing snowballed. If she could get Sam on her side, it would be a big 'eff you' to her detractors – as one of the most powerful managers in the industry, a lot of the smaller players would think twice about blackballing the magazine if they knew the magazine had his support. There was no way she could cancel tonight's dinner. Just no way.

But Heidi needed her. She was all alone, she was terrified of losing the twins and, even after the horrible way Nina had treated her, by some miracle she still wanted Nina by her side at the hospital. Dropping everything to be with her now was a chance to prove to Heidi that she'd turned a corner, to try to make good on all the crappy things she'd said and done over the past few months. Maybe she could go to the hospital for an hour or so, then once Heidi was out of the danger zone, she would be able to make the dinner with Sam? She'd just have to make it work, no matter what.

'Of course, Heids – which hospital are you going to? Are you already on your way or should I swing past in a taxi? Don't worry, everything's going to be fine,' Nina reassured her, mentally crossing her fingers and hoping for the best – not only for Heidi's twins but also for her plans for later that evening.

'I'm already on my way to the Royal – give the nurses my name at the maternity ward, I'll let them know you're coming. Thanks, Nina, you don't know how much this means to me. I know it's the last thing you probably want to do right now, but I can't go through this by myself. I'm so scared,' Heidi whimpered.

'It's okay, it's okay,' Nina soothed, striding into Juice HQ and beckoning to Scarlett when she saw her chatting to Gracie at the photocopier. 'Try not to panic, I'm sure they'll get everything under control. I'll be there as soon as I can.'

Nina pulled an apologetic face as Scarlett followed her into her office.

'I know you're going to hate me, but I'm not sure if I'm going to make this dinner at Chiswick tonight. There's an emergency –'

'WHAT? Didn't you get my voicemail? It's all confirmed! I've been running around like a pork chop trying to get everything organised in time – I had to sweet-talk Chiswick's PR company to get them to waive the seventy-two hours' advance notice they usually require for filming, I've been on the phone non-stop trying to find a crew who are free tonight because our guys have already worked the maximum number of hours today, and I had to promise my firstborn to Andy to get him to agree to include the footage in an upcoming episode! Why did I do all this? Oh, that's right – because you begged me to in order to save your own arse and now you're telling me you might not be able to make it?' Scarlett stared at her incredulously.

'I know, I know, I'm sorry! I know it's not the most convenient timing. Trust me, I'd much rather be dining at Chiswick,' she lied in the hope it would placate Scarlett, 'but Heidi just called and she needs me at the hospital – her doctor thinks she might be losing the twins. Her partner is in New York and her parents are overseas, so what am I supposed to do? It's not exactly ideal but I just have to suck it up. I'm hoping I won't have to be there for too long so I can meet Sam at the arranged time but I just don't know. Believe me, I'm praying it all works out because otherwise the magazine is going to be up shit creek without a paddle. I'll keep you in the loop, okay? I really, really appreciate you pulling everything together for me, but I've got to run.' She grabbed her bag and gave Scarlett a quick hug before dashing out the door.

In Heidi's hospital room, Nina held her friend's hand as she tried to comprehend the news she'd just been delivered.

'You mean you need to do it now?' Heidi whispered, her face white.

'I'm afraid so, Ms Chambers,' the doctor confirmed. 'In order for either of your babies to survive, we need to perform an emergency caesarean as soon as possible.'

'But I'm only twenty-eight weeks! It's too soon! Can't you just monitor me? My partner isn't even here, he's trying to get back from the States . . .'

'I'm sorry, but if your twins are to have the best chance, we need to get them out now. One of the twins isn't getting enough blood supply and has stopped growing. Remember how one of your earlier ultrasounds showed that they shared a placenta? This is one of the complications of monochorionic twins – it's not your fault, it's just one of those things that can happen. The important thing is that the lack of growth has been detected so we can act on it. If the babies are removed and placed into the neo-natal intensive care unit, they'll both be able to get the care they need.'

'Can you guarantee they'll both make it if I have the C-section and they go into ICU?' Heidi wanted to know.

'Unfortunately we can never make guarantees. As you say, twenty-eight weeks is very premature, even for identical twins. They'll have to stay in hospital for quite some time and there may be some developmental problems later down the track due to being born so early. But I can tell you that it's their best chance of pulling through. And the sooner we do it, the better,' the doctor said gravely.

Heidi unconsciously rubbed her bump as the doctor continued to fill her in on the procedure, the risks, the possible outcomes. After he'd left the room, Nina offered to wait outside while Heidi called Simon to update him on the situation, but she refused. 'I don't want to be alone right now,' she explained.

Nina tried not to listen in as Heidi recounted the doctor's verdict through racking sobs, but found herself almost in tears too as the gravity of the situation became clear. Even if both of the twins survived the caesarean, they'd be facing months and months in hospital. Heidi and Simon wouldn't even be allowed to hold their babies until their immune systems had improved dramatically; they would have to be fed via an eye dropper until their mouths developed to normal size. Whether Heidi and Simon would ever get to take them home wasn't even a certainty right now. And to make matters worse, Heidi would have to go through the birth all by herself because Simon's flight wasn't due to land for another twenty-four hours unless . . . unless Nina offered to go into the operating theatre with her. Given she wasn't family, Nina wasn't even sure if she'd be allowed. What she did know was that it meant she would definitely miss the crucial dinner with Sam – by the time the hospital staff booked a free slot in the theatre, prepped Heidi for the operation and performed the procedure, there was no way she would get to the restaurant in time. And it wasn't as if she'd be able to leave Heidi as soon as the twins were born – after seeing how tiny and fragile they were and not being able to hold them, Heidi would probably be even more distressed than she was now.

'Excuse me,' Nina said quietly to the nurse who was checking Heidi's blood pressure while she spoke to Simon. 'I know I'm not family, but if Heidi wants me there, would it be possible for me to be in the operating theatre with her if she goes ahead with the caesarean?'

'I don't see why not,' the nurse said briskly. 'It's just the same as having an unrelated birth partner – not everyone has a family member or significant other with them when they're in labour. As long as Ms Chambers gives her okay and you promise to behave in the theatre, then the doctor shouldn't have a problem with it.'

Nina smiled her thanks and turned to Heidi as she held out the phone. 'Simon wants to talk to you,' she said, her voice clogged with misery. Nina hesitated – she hadn't spoken to Simon since New York and she didn't want to know what Heidi had told him about her behaviour since then.

'Hi, Simon, it's Nina. I'm so sorry,' she said, hoping he realised she was apologising for more than just Heidi's current situation.

'Thank you so much for being there for her, I can't tell you how much it means to me and Heidi,' he said gruffly. 'We've made the decision to go ahead with the caesarean. It's an absolute nightmare being on the other side of the world when something like this happens, but it helps to know that Heidi has her best friend with her so she doesn't have to go through it alone. Especially if . . .' He stopped, clearly reluctant to verbalise what they both knew was a very real possibility – that one or both of the twins might not survive the first few hours out of the womb.

'It'll be okay,' Nina promised him, not knowing what else to say. 'If Heidi wants me there, I'll be with her during the operation, too. When does your flight leave?'

'The next flight to LA isn't for another couple of hours, then I have to stay overnight there before getting the next available flight to Australia. I'm at JFK airport already so I just have to sit tight and wait,' he said, his frustration apparent in his voice.

'At least that means you won't be in the air when the twins are born – we can call you with an update as soon as the doctor gives us the go-ahead,' Nina pointed out.

'That would be great. Thanks, Nina. I'm really glad you're there. Can I talk to Heidi again?'

'Of course. Speak to you soon.' Giving the phone back to Heidi, she nipped into the bathroom to give them some privacy. When she came out, Heidi had both hands on her stomach, whispering to her babies as tears ran down her cheeks.

'Heids?' Nina said gently when her friend fell silent. 'It's totally up to you, but the nurse said that if you want, I can be with you in the operating theatre so you're not alone for the birth. I know it won't be the same as having Simon there, but it might help to have someone to hold your hand?'

'I would love that,' Heidi said simply. 'Thank you for being here, it really means a lot.'

'Hey, that's what friends are for,' Nina replied with a smile. She still had a lot of ground to make up, but she would be there when Heidi needed her the most, which was a start. Whether Sam or Scarlett would understand was another matter, but she knew she was doing the right thing. 'I just need to make a few calls; I'll be right back.'

twenty-seven

'Please tell me that's a skim flat white with my name on it,' Nina begged Max as he walked through the door carrying coffees, the Sunday papers and what looked like a bulging Bourke Street Bakery bag.

'Your wish is my command,' he replied, handing her the caffeine injection and dumping the papers on the coffee table before removing a selection of croissants and pains au chocolat from the bag. Nina almost went cross-eyed with food lust as he arranged them on a tray and slotted it into the oven to warm up.

'You are too good to me,' she sighed as the heavenly smell of butter-laden pastry filled the room.

After spending the previous two nights at the hospital with Heidi, she was physically and emotionally exhausted. When

Nina had called Eric and told him it was a matter of life or death for her best friend, he'd offered to step in and go to the dinner with Sam on her behalf. It wasn't the best-case scenario but at least it meant Eric could do some damage control before Sam flew to Melbourne. The twins had survived the birth and were doing okay so far – two tiny little girls, one a lot bigger than the other but both as fragile as glass. After the twins had been taken straight to the neo-natal intensive care unit, Nina had stayed with Heidi, trying to comfort her distraught friend as she realised how helpless she was when it came to her children's survival. There was literally nothing Heidi could do except wait – wait for Simon to arrive, wait to recover from her caesarean, wait for her milk to come in, wait for the specialists to deliver their verdict on her daughters' future. But she didn't have to wait alone. Nina had refused to leave Heidi's side until Simon got there, so she'd called Max and asked him to grab a few things from her wardrobe so at least she had her pyjamas, a change of clothes and her toothbrush. The thought of him pawing through her underwear drawer had made her giggle, but he hadn't looked the least bit embarrassed when she met him outside the hospital so he could drop it all off – just full of concern for Heidi, bless him. It had seemed the most natural thing to give him a kiss on the cheek by way of thanks, but she hadn't been prepared for the streak of lightning that seemed to bounce off his skin onto her lips when she'd made contact. Or for the hothouse of butterflies that once again made themselves known in the pit of her stomach, before she realised it was starting to happen quite regularly whenever Max was around. It was something she didn't want to think about too carefully – there was too much other stuff going on right now. Her first priority was her friend, not her love-life or her career.

Simon had finally arrived that morning after his original LAX flight had been cancelled so Nina was taking the opportunity to recharge while he was reunited with his new family. Heidi and Simon had agreed not to name the girls just yet, as neither of them were out of the woods – they didn't want to tempt fate. It was going to be a case of taking one small step at a time, but the prognosis was looking as positive as it could be for such premature births. It had been a rollercoaster thirty-six hours.

'You look knackered.' Max started to give her a shoulder rub after carrying the plate of warm pastries to the coffee table.

'I am – trying to sleep on a miniscule fold-out bed in a hospital room full of beeping machines and nurses coming in at all hours to check on Heidi is not my idea of a good night's kip, let alone two, but I'm glad I did it,' Nina said, while tearing into a gooey pain au chocolat. 'I've realised true friendship means being there for each other no matter what, even when you have different priorities. God, listen to me getting all Hallmark Occasion on you,' she said disparagingly, trying to ignore the lump in her throat. 'Sorry, it's been quite emotionally draining, trying to encourage Heidi to think positive and believe that everything will be alright.'

'Of course it has,' Max said, as if it was the most obvious thing in the world. 'While it's been hell for Heidi and Simon, it's also not easy to be the cheerleader, the one who tries to keep everyone's spirits up in a time of crisis. I'm sure they really appreciate your efforts – when you're in that kind of dire situation, it would be hard not to wallow in all the worst-case scenarios, so having someone there to remind them that things may turn out to be not as bad as they could be is invaluable. George Michael wasn't wrong when he said, "You gotta have faith." Whatever works, you know?'

'Yeah, I know.' Nina looked at her flatmate, thinking there was a lot going on in that big boofy brain of his. 'Can we talk about how you just quoted George Michael?' she couldn't resist adding with a smirk.

'Hey, knock him all you want, Ninja, but tell me I'm not right,' he said, reaching for his own dose of pastry goodness.

They flicked through the papers in companionable silence. As Nina finished her coffee and checked out the clouds rolling in over the harbour, she decided it was Ugg boot o'clock. In her bedroom, she sent a quick text to Steph to check if she'd thought any more about her suggestion of seeing a psychologist to help with her self-harming and if she'd worked up the courage to tell Chris. Nina knew that it would be very easy for Steph to slip back into old habits, to deny she had a problem or that she needed help to deal with her situation, but Nina was determined not to let her fall through the cracks. She'd been a crap friend for too long – it was time for her to step up and focus on her friends who had way bigger problems than she did.

When Nina schlepped her way back into the living room, she found Max hurriedly trying to cover up the segment he'd been reading in the *Sunday Star's* 1800 GOSSIP section, but he wasn't nearly quick enough. Alongside a large photo of herself at the Ray-Ban party she'd been to earlier that week screamed the headline 'That's what friends AREN'T for'.

'Give it to me,' Nina demanded.

'Trust me, you don't want to read it,' Max told her.

'Of course I don't want to; I already know it's going to be another bunch of filthy lies just like all the others, but I need to read it. I need to know what they're saying about me this time,' she insisted, snatching the paper from his hands. Skimming the segment, she felt like she was going to throw up all over her sheepskin-encased feet.

It's no secret that Nina Morey has been enjoying the trappings of success lately, such as the saucy romps with D-list celebrities and the endless amount of freebies falling into her lap thanks to her hit show *Freshly Squeezed Juice*, but has all that success gone to her head, making her lose sight of what's really important? Rumoured to be responsible for the leak behind *End of the Day's* scandalous exposé on just how much weekly magazines pay celebrities to be on their pages, it's understandable that Ms Morey would be feeling somewhat vulnerable in her position as editor of *Juice* and desperate to convince the all-powerful celebrity agents that her hands are clean. However, when her pregnant best friend called to tell her she was at the point of miscarrying twins and begged her to come to the hospital, did Ms Morey drop everything to be with her friend in need? Eventually, yes. But not before having a lengthy bitch and moan about the inconvenient timing, as it meant cancelling a dinner with a VIP agent who she really needs to get back on side. That's right – instead of immediately putting her friend first, this power-hungry editor made it clear that it wasn't ideal and that she'd much rather be wining and dining with the agent. Selfish, much?

Collapsing onto the couch, Nina clamped her eyes shut, hoping that when she opened them again the offending article would have magically disappeared. After a few seconds, she took another look at the page. No such luck.

'I don't believe it,' she whispered, barely aware of the tangy taste of panic on her tongue. 'I don't freaking believe it.'

'Don't worry, no one else will believe it either,' Max tried to reassure her.

'What if Heidi or Simon sees it? You don't understand – I've only just started to repair my friendship with Heidi and if she sees this . . .'

'Nina, you're forgetting that Heidi and Simon have got a lot more on their plate right now than reading a Sunday newspaper gossip column. I seriously doubt they even remember what day it is, let alone that the *Sunday Star* exists. And if by some miracle they do read it, just tell them it's bullshit. It is bullshit, right? Just like all the others?'

She couldn't bring herself to look at him. 'I . . . I . . . kind of,' she eventually managed.

'Define "kind of",' Max said abruptly.

'It's not what you think! It was bad timing, even you have to agree with that! It would have been fine if I'd had nothing on when I got the call, but I had Eric breathing down my neck, insisting I set up meetings with all the major agents to convince them I wasn't behind the *End of the Day* leak. I managed to book in dinner with Sam, Lulu Hopkins' manager, before he went to Melbourne the next day but he would only meet me if we agreed to film it for the show. When Heidi asked me to go to the hospital, the reason I hesitated was because I knew I'd be putting other people out – Sam, the film crew, the restaurant . . . It wasn't because I didn't want to be there for my friend or because I preferred to schmooze Sam over a bottle of cabernet sauvignon like the *Sunday Star* makes out! I was caught between a rock and a hard place!' She hated herself for the disappointed look on Max's face as she admitted the truth.

'Look, what matters is that you did the right thing in the end, and I'm sure people will realise that – but what's more important is who did you supposedly bitch and moan about it to?' Max asked.

'I didn't bitch and moan about it to anyone! I literally got the phone call from Heidi, went straight to the office to shut down my computer and I told Scarlett that I might not be able to make it to the dinner but I'd let her know once I got to the hospital and knew what was happening.'

Max raised his eyebrows. 'Scarlett? The TV producer you've been hanging out with a lot?'

'Yes, but she would never . . .' Nina began, then trailed off when she saw the look on Max's face.

Scarlett? Could it be? Surely not . . . she was her friend! She would never do that to her! 'How do you know?' a voice in her head demanded. 'After all, how well do you really know her? You've only been friends for what – a couple of months? What do you know about her besides the fact she's a TV producer who likes to go out and have a good time? Look at you, getting all high and mighty about how a friend would never do that – you're a fine one to talk! You acted like an immature brat with your friends just because they all decided to have babies, so why couldn't she do something like this to you? After all, she was pretty pissed off when you told her you weren't sure if you'd be able to make it to Chiswick. Who's to say she didn't have a rant about it to someone else and it found its way back to the gossip columnist? You know how people love to talk; you work at a celebrity gossip magazine, for Christ's sake! Don't be so naïve!'

Nina felt like the world was spinning too fast as all the other blind items and scathing rumours about her popped up in her head. If Scarlett really had told someone what she'd said about Heidi's phone call, then what else had she told people?

'I think you'd better give Miss Scarlett a call and see what she's got to say for herself, don't you?' Max said, passing Nina her phone.

twenty-eight

When she got to the Tilbury in Woolloomooloo that afternoon, Nina was relieved to find the small balcony upstairs was free. At least they'd have some degree of privacy in the event Scarlett didn't take too kindly to Nina wanting to know who she'd told about her dilemma with Heidi, and hopefully it meant they wouldn't get interrupted by any fans of the TV show wanting a chat or a photo. 'Thank God there are only a couple more episodes to go and then people will move on to something else,' she thought.

By now, Nina had convinced herself that the whole debacle was just an unfortunate mistake – Scarlett must have divulged some stories to someone she knew in confidence, which had then made their way to various media outlets, Chinese whispers-style, so that the end result was a skewed version that painted Nina in the worst light possible. After all, no one was interested in hearing good things about people in the public eye – they preferred to gnaw on the carcasses of rumoured infidelity, drug use, eating disorders and diva antics simply because it made them feel better about their own lives.

'Hey, babe, how's tricks? Almost didn't see you hiding there!' Scarlett plonked herself down on the chair opposite amid a cloud of overpowering perfume and helped herself to the vodka tonic Nina had bought her without bothering to say thanks. 'So, where's the fire?'

'There's no fire . . .' Now that she was here, Nina wasn't quite sure how to start. 'It's just that there's another gossip item about me in today's paper which I'm really upset about and I wondered if you knew who had told them?' She pulled the offending page out of her bag and pushed it across the table.

'Me? Why would I know?' Scarlett asked uninterestedly, busy checking out the group of guys playing pool inside the pub.

'Because you were the only one I told,' Nina pointed out.

'Told what?'

'What was happening with Heidi on Friday. You know, how she was in danger of miscarrying the twins?' Nina realised Scarlett hadn't even asked how Heidi was, although she couldn't really blame her given Nina hadn't painted Heidi in exactly the most flattering light during her various bitch sessions about her baby-obsessed friends. 'I just wondered if you'd told anyone who would have shared the information with the 1800 GOSSIP columnist.'

'Nope, didn't tell anyone. I mean, I don't want to be rude but it's not really that interesting, is it? Must have been a slow gossip week,' Scarlett laughed.

'Apparently it's interesting enough, seeing they've dedicated almost half a page to it,' Nina said, her hackles rising. 'I'm not saying it's not true, but they've twisted my words to make it sound a lot worse than it was. Are you sure you didn't tell anyone? One of the other producers or another friend, perhaps? Please, Scarlett, this is really important.'

'Jesus, Nina! I told you I didn't tell anyone! Maybe it was Eric? You told him about it, didn't you? Maybe he's trying to push you out and is using this as an excuse to get rid of you — did you stop to think about that before you accused me of snitching on you?'

'I'm sorry, but I just want to get to the bottom of this. It couldn't have been Eric because I didn't go into detail with him, I just told him a friend was in dire trouble. And that doesn't explain who planted all the other items — me supposedly doing drugs at the MTV party, allegedly getting into bed with all those guys, complaining about the freebies and revealing how much celebs get paid to do photo shoots for the weekly mags . . .'

As Nina ran through all the accusations that had been thrown at her, her brain suddenly joined the dots . . . and they all happened to be Scarlett-shaped dots. Suddenly she knew what Max had been trying to suggest. She'd been so close but had got it so wrong — it wasn't that Scarlett had told other people who had then twisted the tales and dobbed on her to the media. It was Scarlett herself.

'Scarlett, cut the crap,' Nina said sharply. 'It's you, isn't it? You're the one who's been feeding these lies to the media about me, trying to wreck my reputation. Why? Why would you do this to me?'

'I don't know what you're talking about!' Scarlett insisted a bit too quickly, but it was too late – Nina had already seen a flicker of alarm cross her face.

'Yes, you damn well do. You're the only person I told about Heidi's situation in detail and you're the only person I've recently told about the kind of money that changes hands with celebrities in this industry. You were there at the MTV party, although it was you who was dabbling in drugs that night, not me. That's when it all started – after the MTV party when you saw Ned kissing me,' Nina realised out loud. 'Is that what this is all about? Is this your way of paying me back because you wanted Ned and he kissed me?'

'It wasn't just that!' Scarlett snapped, goaded into forgetting her proclamation of innocence. 'That was enough to tip me over the edge but when you kept giving me ammunition, I couldn't help myself. The mountains of freebies, the endless invitations, all the celebrities wanting to talk to you, the hot guys throwing themselves at you . . . do you have any idea what it's like to stand by and watch someone else rake in all the good stuff while you're stuck behind the scenes, slaving away on the show that makes them a star? Do you know how invisible you feel when no one wants to talk to you at a party because you're not famous? Or what it's like to open up the social pages to see a photo of the two of us captioned as "*Freshly Squeezed Juice* star Nina Morey and friend" for the fifth week in a row, like I'm a nobody who doesn't even have a name? No one cared about me, they only cared about you! And the most infuriating thing is that you don't even want to be famous! You get it handed to you on a silver platter and you don't even like it! It's not fair!'

If she didn't know better, Nina could have sworn her mouth was full of superglue. Her mind raced to catch up with Scarlett's outburst. As much as it was a shock to hear the truth, she knew she only had herself to blame. She'd been so caught up in feeling sorry for herself because her friends were leaving her behind that she'd rushed to fill the gap left by Heidi, Lily, Daniela and the others with a girl who didn't want to hang with her because she actually liked her, but because she wanted to *be* her. Scarlett had told her what she wanted to hear, reassuring her that the way she was acting about her friends' baby boom was completely justified and had never said no to taking advantage of Nina's many perks, yet all along she was plotting to sabotage her.

Eventually Nina managed to croak, 'But I shared all those freebies with you . . . I asked publicists if you could be my "plus one" at all the events . . . I did my best to introduce you to the celebrities who came up to talk to me . . . I spelt your name out to the photographers who snapped us together . . . what more could I have done?'

'I don't want to be your charity case! I want to be the one who's famous! I want people to know my name, to rush up to me on the street to tell me how much they love me, to courier bags full of clothes to my house in the hope I'll get papped wearing them while going to yet another fancy event, to send me the latest must-have phone so all my Instagram and Twitter followers will buy the same one when I upload a photo of it! I don't want to be jealous of you anymore, Nina – I want you to be jealous of me when I'm more famous than you!'

Nina looked at the stranger opposite her; all she felt was pity. If that's what Scarlett really wanted, then she wanted fame for all the wrong reasons. The TV show may have done wonders for the magazine but Nina couldn't help thinking that if she'd left the fame game to the real celebrities and stayed behind the scenes where she belonged, she wouldn't have been in this mess.

'Scarlett, I will never, ever be jealous of you. I thought you were my friend, but friends don't try to destroy their friend's career just because they have something you don't. I know I have a lot of ground to make up when it comes to my friendships, but you take the cake. If you think being famous is the be all and end all, then good luck to you. But after all the parties are over, all the fans have moved on and all the freebies have dried up, you'll realise that your real friends are the ones who matter the most. I'm telling Andy tomorrow that I want another producer to work on the remaining segments for the TV show that I need to film. If you're lucky, I won't tell him why. If I never see you again, it will be too soon.'

Nina got up and walked out, trying to control her shaking as she made her way down the stairs. Sucking in a lungful of air outside, she belatedly realised what perfume Scarlett had doused herself in — it was the distinctive smell of Gucci's Envy.

twenty-nine

Five months later

'Bella, I'm just going out to run some errands; I should be back in half an hour or so,' Nina told her assistant on her way out of the office. Looking at her to-do list while zooming down in the lift, she decided to tackle the most fun thing first and started walking towards Martin Place in her new five-inch Alexander McQueen heels.

Volunteering to throw a surprise 'welcome home' party for Maggie and Mila, Heidi and Simon's twins, had seemed like the best idea ever when she'd first thought of it, especially seeing Heidi didn't get a chance to have a baby shower, but it was fast becoming bigger than the Oscars, only with way more children. Thankfully Simon was in on the surprise and had offered to pay for a babysitter to be on hand to keep Luna, Ruby, Mason, Sasha and Noah occupied while their parents celebrated with fresh fruit daiquiris, pulled pork sliders, pistachio and rosewater macarons, and salted caramel popcorn. Oh, and French champagne, of course. She'd ordered plenty of it, knowing she would need it to get through the afternoon of cooing and clucking – but as she constantly reminded herself whenever she was around the girls and their babies, it wasn't about her: this time it was all about celebrating the fact that Heidi, Simon, Maggie and Mila were finally able to begin their family life at home. Although she suspected that Lily, who was already pregnant again having not realised that breastfeeding wasn't a fail-safe contraceptive, would find a way to make it all about her, for at least some of the time. The only downside was that Steph and Chris wouldn't be able to make it – after acting on a suggestion from their infertility counsellor, they were having their first interview to be considered for foster parenting and understandably didn't want to cancel after being on the waitlist for months.

Nina still enjoyed the novelty of being able to cruise around the city without hastily slipping on a pair of sunglasses to avoid getting recognised. After the final episode of *Freshly Squeezed Juice* had aired, she'd been relieved when all the attention switched to the women who bitch-slapped their way through the inaugural series of *The Real Housewives of Australia*, which had finally aired after being delayed by multiple defamation suits from some of the talent. Some people would have been peeved at how quickly the fans forgot about her, but Nina couldn't have cared less. She still got sent a healthy amount of freebies and invitations, but nothing like before – and that was fine with her. These days, she preferred to concentrate on editing the magazine then going home to curl up on the couch with Max rather than getting her photo taken in front of the media wall at yet another red-carpet event.

'Speak of the devil,' she thought, seeing Max's name flash up on her ringing phone. 'Hey, mister, what's up?' she asked, trying not to blush as she remembered what they'd got up to the previous night. They'd been an item for a couple of months now – after Heidi had met Max, she'd promptly called Nina to demand why they hadn't hooked up yet seeing it was obvious that they were both into each other. At first Nina had denied it, not really believing that Max would be interested given all her recent dramas, but eventually she'd allowed the idea to germinate, culminating in her presenting him with a home-cooked meal one night, pouring red wine down his throat then summoning up all her courage to put her emotional cards on the table. Luckily, Heidi had been right – Max was well and truly into her but hadn't wanted to make a move until her life had calmed down a bit.

'Just checking in – I've been losing the will to live in a budget meeting for the past few hours so I just want to talk to someone who doesn't think analysing a profit-and-loss spreadsheet is the most scintillating thing you can do with your time. How goes the party planning?'

'It's pretty much under control, I think. You know I don't expect you to come. I mean, it's fine if you want to but I don't expect you to. They're my friends and it's going to be baby central, so if you prefer to give it a miss, I'll completely understand . . .'

'Ninja, shut up. I said I'm happy to go, so I'm going. You'd better have ordered a triple portion of those pulled pork things, though. And I can't be held responsible if I happen to smuggle a six-pack of Coopers Green in with me.'

'I'll pretend you didn't say that,' she said, smiling. As hard as she tried, she couldn't conjure up an image of Max sipping delicately from a flute of French champagne or polishing off a fruit daiquiri. 'Gotta go, I've got another call. See you tonight, babe.'

Switching into editor mode, she answered the waiting call immediately when she saw who it was. 'Sam! How's tricks?'

'Great, Nina, thanks for asking. Sorry to call you on your mobile but your assistant said you wouldn't mind. Have you got a second? I want to run something by you.'

'Of course – hit me,' Nina said, ducking into a quiet alleyway.

'I'm sitting on an exclusive that your readers are going to love!' He began the usual spiel, dodging around the subject of what the exclusive was about and who it pertained to, talking it up in the hope that Nina would be foaming at the mouth by the time he revealed all the juicy details. After letting him waffle on for five minutes, Nina interrupted: 'It all sounds great, Sam, but what's the actual story and who is it about?'

'Obviously this is completely confidential, but it's Lulu,' he admitted. 'She's pregnant! She and Jason want to do a story with *Juice* to announce it to the public! Isn't it wonderful?!'

'Amazing,' Nina agreed, trying to guess how many dollar signs Sam had in his eyes. Not that it really mattered – she already knew she'd cough it up. Celebrity babies were big business in the world of magazines – she might not be into them, but as she'd finally accepted, there were plenty of people who were and, more importantly, there was nothing wrong with that. She wondered if he'd be willing to stitch up a package deal so *Juice* got the exclusive on the pregnancy announcement as well as the first baby pictures, with a 'How I got my body back!' follow-up story a couple of months after Lulu gave birth.

'Sam, thanks so much for coming to us with this opportunity – you're right, *Juice's* readers are going to love it. Please pass on my congratulations to Lulu and Jason. I'll be back in the office in less than half an hour, so how about you shoot over an email with the figure you have in mind and we can get the ball rolling when I get back?'

'Sounds great, Nina. She's beginning to show already so I don't want to wait around on this; the photo shoot needs to happen ASAP before the gossip columnists start to speculate. Give me a call when you've looked at your budget.'

'Will do,' Nina promised, rounding the corner of the alleyway and pushing open the door of the swanky store she'd trekked to Martin Place for. Ten minutes later, she emerged carrying two of the store's famous duck-egg blue carry bags tied with thick white ribbon. Inside each bag was a box containing a Tiffany & Co sterling silver baby rattle – one for Maggie and one for Mila.

Acknowledgements

If someone had told me a couple of years ago that I would be the author of not one but two novels, I would have thought they were coco bananas. But here I am, although I couldn't have got here by myself.

First of all, thank you to everyone who read *Be Careful What You Wish For* and took the time to tell me how much they enjoyed it. And for those who begged for a sequel on Twitter, your wish is my command!

The Allen & Unwin crew have been a dream to work with once again – thank you Christa Munns, Ali Lavau, Marie Slocombe, Louise Cornege and the sales team. Extra-special thanks to my publisher, Claire Kingston, who is always there for me (even while on maternity leave – hi, Coco!); and Acacia Stichter, my graphic design go-to girl who mocked up millions of cover options without a word of complaint until we hit the nail on the head.

As always, big love goes to Mickey, Tina, Dan, Benny and Bree. Especially to Bree, who gets lumped with reading my first drafts and is always brutally honest, even if I don't want to hear it at the time.

Even bigger love to Gareth, who had to deal with the not always pleasant side-effects of me being house-bound for three months while writing this book.

Finally, to all my friends with kids – remember, I never let the truth get in the way of a good story!

ALSO FROM ALLEN & UNWIN

Be Careful What You Wish For

Gemma Crisp

Strap on your highest heels for a fast-paced peek inside the glossy world of magazines.

When Nina Morey gets her perfectly pedicured toe on the first rung of the highly competitive magazine publishing ladder, she can't believe her luck.

Then she lands the hottest man in town *and* her best friend relocates from the other side of the world to help her paint the town neon pink. Nina's life has suddenly turned from dull to dream come true.

Soon she's scaling the magazine ladder faster than you can say 'Anna Wintour', securing dream job after dream job, while schmoozing her way around Sydney's hottest spots.

Life is good. What could possibly go wrong?

ISBN 978 1 74331 740 2